## *ABDUCTED!*

Mimi's eyes glared with fright, the strength slipping from her body as she fearfully studied the huge mountain of muscle who appeared to be the savages' leader. In his native sounds he ordered a leather thong tied around Paul's neck and lashed to the mast. Mimi's body slumped in her captor's arms as she watched the Indian dip the leather in the salt water on the deck and pull it unmercifully tight around Paul's neck. Paul moved his head in an attempt to prevent it and was struck violently by the infuriated savage; his unconscious body fell against the mast.

Mimi's screams never left her lips, still clamped with the muscular hand. Bewildered and wide-eyed she viewed her lover's body hanging there as the native leader moved toward her. Everything inside her went limp as she watched him approach. Her heart pounded wildly.

The warrior grinned as he pointed at her breasts protruding in her tight sailor shirt. "This is squaw," he said moving closer. . . .

We will send you a free catalog on request. Any titles not in your local book store can be purchased by mail. Send the price of the book plus 50¢ shipping charge to Tower Books, P.O. Box 270, Norwalk, Connecticut 06852.

Titles currently in print are available for industrial and sales promotion at reduced rates. Address inquiries to Tower Publications, Inc., Two Park Avenue, New York, New York 10016, Attention: Premium Sales Department.

# *IN PASSION'S TEMPEST*

Cassandra Dorth

TOWER BOOKS　　NEW YORK CITY

A TOWER BOOK

Published by

Tower Publications, Inc.
Two Park Avenue
New York, N.Y. 10016

Copyright © 1981 by Cassandra Dorth

All rights reserved
Printed in the United States

*To librarians and historians everywhere*
*Long may they guide*

In the early 1700's the area in and around the north eastern part of the United States (New York State) was known to the explorers as Niagara Country, taken from the Indian word Onguiaahra.

Likewise, Canada, the north shore of the Onguiaahra River was still occupied by many Indian tribes and still to be settled by the white man, except for seaports along the St. Lawrence River, the largest being Mont Real, or Montreal as it is now known.

## Chapter One

"A toast to my lady." Phillip raised his glass high as he stood wavering in the carriage. The lurch of the horses as they began down the circular drive threw him into the seat, his wine splattering his waistcoat. Phillip's uproarious laugh diminished as the speeding carriage moved on.

Mimi stood at the steps laughing at his antics. "Oh! That man!" She waved her hand after him. "I thought he'd never leave, but he is such a good one to keep a party alive. I'm glad you invited him, Uncle Nathane."

In the lovely warm July night horse-drawn carriages clattered down the drive, away from the mansion, as the collection of youthful men and women left the ball at the Marchamp estate. The loud laughter and sometimes tearful goodbyes, provoked by the heady wines, rang across the lavish grounds. Young maidens clung to Mimi Pean, while young blades planted prolonged kisses on her cheeks until she brushed them off playfully. It was their last adieu to their childhood friend. Mimi Pean was leaving Uncle Nathane and his lovely home to sail across the seas.

The ball ended in the morning's early hours, and though Mimi loved parties, especially dancing, she had seen how different it was without Francois Laloque as her partner. She felt strange having other young men whirl her across the floor. Of course, she was glad it was many—not just one or two; she wanted no talk that she had forgotten Francois, nor any hint that another had taken his place in her heart since he'd left. Mimi remembered that August day in 1754 well, and had never ceased to miss her fiance.

Nathane Marchamp felt the party was the least he could do, and not nearly as much as he wanted to do. Privately, he knew it prolonged Mimi's stay in France and he was never happier than when his home was filled with her young, vigorous friends. What appeared to be unnecessary work to Mimi was far more important to her aged uncle than the young girl could ever suspect. He was sure that it had never occurred to Mimi, but Nathane knew it would be the last time he would see his beloved niece.

The young Mimi Pean came to Nathane's home and into his life when she was five years old, filling the void. Now, as she prepared to leave to marry Francois, he harbored no hope that he'd still be there for her return. He found it difficult to maintain his attitude; he lacked the courage to let her go easily.

The party over, he listened to the lilt of her young voice as she bade farewell to the last of the guests and he shivered with the thought of her departure.

As the servants closed the large doors upon the last of the guests Mimi returned to the ballroom where Nathane waited. The musicians were packing their instruments and slowly filing out. Mimi placed her arms around Nathane's neck and smiled up at him. "It was a lovely party, Uncle. I enjoyed it much more than I had ever hoped, but you shouldn't have gone to the trouble. You know how those sickly young men in their powdered wigs irritate me."

"*Oui*, you never could see anyone but Francois. But,

my dear, it would hardly have been proper for me to invite my old cronies; this was your party. I'm quite glad I went against your wishes. I thoroughly enjoyed the banter and play among the guests. And I think secretly you enjoyed it too." He touched her on her tiny nose with the tip of a finger.

Mimi looked at him with loving, glinting eyes. She was used to Uncle Nathane's mischievousness and had known all along that, regardless of her wishes, there would be a party. "My darling Uncle Nathane, you know I have stopped going to parties since Francois left, and I know you enjoy these people almost more than I." She kissed him lightly on the cheek.

"I'll tell you frankly, dear Niece, I had hoped you'd find an interest in someone else, however much I approve of your present choice for a husband. America is much too far away. I simply hoped you'd realize this when you became aware that all your friends would not be there with you. You must forgive an old fool and his dreams."

"I can see that you are still against my going." Mimi knew he was beginning another of the tirades she'd grown weary of these past months.

"I shall always be against it. I should think you would be too. Savages! What can Francois be thinking to ask you into that kind of life? The man must be demented from life in the wilderness." Nathane waved a hand through the air as he did when his temper was beginning to rise. "It was all I could do to be civil tonight, just thinking of you going there."

"Please, Uncle. Do we have to get into this again and at this hour? I took the party to mean you'd relented somewhat." Mimi flicked open her fan and nervously waved it before her. Her patience was wearing thin with these arguments and she found herself wanting to leave as much to be out from under his suffocating ways as to be with her fiance.

"Never! But, you leave me no choice with your strong will. I guess I have no one but myself to thank for that; always letting you have your way with everything. I shall just have to make up my mind that you intend to take this voyage regardless of my feelings." Then in a burst of temper he waved his arm still holding the head of his cane. "Never think for a moment that my approval goes with it," he said vehemently as he stormed over to the fireplace.

Nathane's calculated bid for sympathy failed. Mimi sidled up beside him and in her most beguiling manner took his arm. "Dear Uncle, please don't think I'm ungrateful for everything you've done for me. It's just that I miss Francois so much, and if his life is going to be as an explorer then that's where I belong too. Besides, I fear my friends are laughing behind my back, still unmarried as I am, and they married and several with children already."

Nathane broke from her grip. "That's nonsense! You're a child yourself." He walked to the window and, as if his eyes could see beyond the night, he stared out. "You don't know what you're talking about." His voice rose with irritation.

"It won't be forever." Mimi had tried every argument before. She hoped this one last time she could make Nathane understand. "Francois doesn't intend to be in Niagara forever. We will be back to make our home here with you. You'll see, we will be home within the year."

Nathane dejectedly slumped into a nearby chair. "No, my dear, I shall never see you again." He closed his eyes a moment, then standing he wavered slightly as he leaned on his cane. "Ah! But you are going and that's that." He tried to sound lighthearted. "Now, I must find passage and that, my dear child, is going to be the most difficult part."

"I know you can do it." Mimi smiled her most loving smile and stood on tiptoes to kiss his cheek. "Now, Uncle, if you don't mind I'd like to retire. It has been a long day for both of us."

Mimi swirled from the large room, the mirrored walls reflecting her over and over, on and on, to infinity. Her full paniered skirt swept the floor as she ascended the winding staircase to her chambers.

Nathane sat, leaning back wearily against the highbacked chair, letting his thoughts wander. He had never married and though there had been many beautiful women who'd have been overjoyed to be Madame Marchamp he had been too fired by the family business to give thought to marriage. Even his mother complained of his neglect of her and through the years Nathane himself had wondered if he had shunned marriage to spare himself from the same sort of suffocation his mother created about him—always questioning, kissing, holding and pretending illnesses to keep him nearby.

After her death, and when he finally arrived at the stage where he felt he could leave business, all the beautiful women had given up hope and succumbed to other proposals. Nathane now felt that he had purposely put off marrying until he was much too old to consider it, preferring to remain alone with his freedom which he so cherished since his mother's death.

Then Mimi Pean came into his life quite unexpectedly after the death of her parents. To Nathane's surprise he found real joy in lavishing his affection and wealth on his new daughter. She filled his life and time and need, so taken was he with the duties of being a proper father.

For the past fifteen years she had been his reason for living, and he never knew that he raised his young niece under the same selfish, suffocating atmosphere he had fought so hard to be rid of. His large estate rang with joy and laughter after she arrived, and Mimi had a truly large group of friends, Francois Laloque among them, who filled his halls and his heart. He was desolate at her leaving.

Even excited as she was with her departure for Niagara, Mimi had little difficulty falling asleep. Though she was very fond of her friends she had found the ball boring without Francois and felt no reluctance leaving any of them. It was only since Francois had gone that she realized her entire youth had revolved around him, and now her desire to join him was total, strong and unrelenting. She hoped that Uncle Nathane had said his last about her leaving, it being a source of tenseness between the two for these months since Francois's letter.

When Mimi awoke the following morning Elaine served her breakfast in bed as usual. After she rose her maid began to clean the clutter of pantaloons and petticoats strewn on the chairs and chaise, where Mimi had carelessly tossed them the night before. The thought never occurred to Mimi that Francois could never provide the same kind of services to which she was so accustomed. Although his family was one of the wealthiest in France, Francois was, after all, in the military—a truth which Mimi had not quite faced in her planning.

Taking her time in selecting a costume for her trip to the seaport, she leisurely dressed, shouting orders to Elaine to bring her this and that. It took several ensembles before Mimi was satisfied with her appearance and Elaine collapsed on the chaise as quickly as her mistress was out of sight.

Uncle Nathane had his breakfast in the morning room as usual and was nervously pacing the large foyer at the foot of the staircase. His carriage and footmen also waited at the entrance and the former had been shined to a fair-thee-well in their efforts to find occupation while they waited. Now, completely beside himself with impatience, Nathane ordered a servant to see what was delaying his niece.

At that moment Mimi swung through the door, her usual cheerful self, totally oblivious to the inconvenience she had caused, for indeed she had always been less than thoughtful about such things.

Looking like a vision to Nathane's sad eyes, he watched her gracefully glide down the long staircase to the waiting carriage. "Come, Mimi, we don't have all day, you know. My land, girl, stop to consider others for a change." So gentle were Nathane's rebuffs Mimi scarcely heard them.

"I'm sorry, Uncle," Mimi said as she straightened her skirts, spreading them across the carriage seat. "I didn't realize you were ready."

"You really are a test, Mimi," Nathane said with some irritation. "One would think it was I taking this trip—up so early, pacing and waiting."

Mimi could see it was going to be one of those days. She had thought Nathane was resigned, but now it appeared he was far from accepting her decision. She thought better of saying anything lest their arguments begin again making Nathane testy enough to rescind the permission she had extracted from him in a moment of weakness. She knew he could forbid her leaving since she had no money of her own.

"Let's move along. Lord knows where we are going

to find passage for you. In all these months I have yet to talk to a captain who is interested in a woman aboard his ship. It is considered bad luck they say." Nathane escorted his niece into the carriage.

"Fiddlesticks! Uncle, you don't really believe that do you?"

"I'm not a ship's captain. I would have no way of knowing, but I can say this, my dear, if ever there were going to be any truth to the problem of a woman aboard ship, the likes of you would be the perfect one to set it off."

"Oh, Uncle, you are funny." Mimi laughed at what she considered Nathane's attempt to jest. She never placed credence in his remarks. She knew he felt nothing but love for her and much of his blustering was because he would rather hide his feelings.

Hours later, Nathane pulled his watch from his waistcoat. "Mimi, it's near lunch time." He glanced around. "There's certainly no place I'd care to dine here. We've spent the morning trudging up and down this dingy port, getting nowhere. We'd better give up and head home immediately."

The captains they had talked to had vehemently refused her passage, leaving no doubt in Mimi's mind that a woman would never set foot aboard their ships. The others were unapproachable; the whiskey on their breath almost "stunting the growth of our hair," as Nathane had put it. Mimi had begun to fear it was all hopeless, and now with Uncle Nathane wanting to leave she had to think fast. "Uncle, let's ask someone. There might be a very nice place for lunch. How do we know, we've never been here before?"

"Nonsense! These people *drink*, they don't eat. Besides, I must send for my footmen. Should never have discharged them. I certainly regret that; can't imagine whom I could trust to deliver the message for their return. What was I thinking of?" Nathane glanced around looking for someone he would judge respectable for such an errand.

It was a distant walk to the tearoom and back. While Mimi had found it quite interesting, it didn't satisfy Nathane, and he picked at his food muttering something about it being poisoned. Now, by evening, they had made no headway at all in securing Mimi's passage. The dark had fallen and Nathane's exasperation had reached fever pitch, absolutely uncontrollable. He fumed at Mimi and everything in general since returning to the seaport. "We shall make this one last try. I have been in and out of saloons I shunned even in my wildest days of youth, talking to captains who could barely understand me through their drunken stupor." He stopped to pull a note from his vest pocket. "This is our last attempt, the *Premier*, and I don't hold out much hope here. The drunk who gave me this hasn't breathed a sober breath since the middle of last year." Nathane impatiently tapped the piece of paper with a jittery finger. "Let's get this over with, Mimi. I've had a full day." He took her by the arm and pulled her along the dock.

Mimi drew her cape hood over her head as the fog and mist swirled in from the endless black abyss just beyond the wet, slippery cobblestone road. The ramshackled saloons were now overflowing with boisterous seamen stumbling in and out, carrying bottles of rum with their arms slung around the waists of painted, giggly women. Laughter and obscenities rose from the doorsteps where men huddled around their women and others slept off their rum and wine in the ditch where the sewers ran. If Nathane had thought it a den of iniquity during the daylight he was at a loss for words to describe the nightlife and his temper was reaching a point of no return. Mimi had uttered placating words, trying to keep him going until some arrangements could be found, concerned that time was running out and Nathane would tire and drag her home forevermore.

They chose their steps carefully along the crowded, decaying dock where they were obliged to duck flying bottles cast by disgruntled sailors. Nathane could not help but remark on the acceleration of activity as the sun went down. He was thoroughly disgusted with everything, including the fact that Mimi was along to see such wild behavior. While it had Nathane extremely upset, Mimi was taking great delight in observing the seamier side of life, something she had only heard of. She took it as an adventure which added to Nathane's annoyance, particularly when she insisted they stop and watch. Nathane Marchamp would have none of that and swiftly moved Mimi along.

In the distance a dull clanging of a buoybell was smothered by the burden of the dense fog, and somewhere beyond a monotonous foghorn droaned desolately, making Mimi shiver at the eerie sound. She clung to her uncle's arm as leering men grinned and uttered obscene remarks. She decided the adventure had vanished from the whole scene and wanted to get out of there as quickly as possible.

The raucous seamen jostled Mimi and her guardian, impeding their progress and causing Nathane to wield his cane sword-fashion to fend them off. Mimi pressed closer to her uncle, side-stepping advances from the inebriated men.

"This is repulsive, Mimi. These are the kind of misfits you shall have to share your ship with. I become more incensed with each step I take. Why are you so ssessed with this hapless voyage? I fear I've spent these past months contracting your demise."

"Now, Uncle, we have been over this again and again." It was now Mimi's turn to become upset and irritated. She, too, was exhausted and in no mood to argue again with Nathane about her trip to America.

"Indeed, we have and I am no more excited at the prospects now than I was at the beginning. And, I tell you . . ." He waved his arms angrily. "This is your last hope. If we fail this time I shall give up this charade once and for all."

"We can't fail, Uncle." Mimi said determinedly.

Nathane squinted, trying to read the names on ships along the dock. Shaking the young girl from his arm he walked toward the edge of the pier where the tall masted ships could barely be seen through the fog.

"Help me find it, Mimi." Nathane ordered with impatience. "It's called the *Premier*. If I don't find it, I cease, do you hear me?" His voice was on the edge of shouting.

"Yes, Uncle." Mimi said moving to his side. "Is that it?" She pointed into the darkness.

"Ah, these young eyes, what do you see? Where?" His eyes followed along her finger leading into the blackness, then he walked to the pier where a dim lantern hung on a post. He could faintly detect the vague outline of the ascending gangplank. "Is there anyone there?" he shouted.

"*Oui*." A deep voice penetrated the night.

"Ah!" Nathane said with satisfaction as he tapped a jittery hand on Mimi's arm. "Maybe we have succeeded." He edged closer, selecting his steps carefully. "I seek Captain Paul Regis, of the ship *Premier*." He was shouting into the pitch black and a feeling of ridiculousness spread over him.

"I am the captain, monsieur. What can I do for you?"

Nathane could see nothing, but he went on. "May we come aboard, Captain? We have a matter of some importance to discuss with you?"

"Come aboard." A dim lantern moved from the mysterious depth below the ship's rail and descended the gangplank. Holding it high Paul Regis surveyed their faces. "Come aboard," he repeated.

Mimi preceded her uncle up the gangplank while the captain held the lantern aloft to light the way. Placing it on the rail Regis lit his pipe. "What can I do for you, monsieur?"

"I am Nathane Marchamp. I understand that you plan to sail to the New World soon."

"That is correct, monsieur, but not until five, six days hence. I await my crew. When they get their fill of drink and women they will sail."

"*Mon Dieu*! This is awful. Do I understand you will then take drunken men aboard to sail this ship?" Marchamp was totally disbelieving. In his entire life he had never seen such an abysmal scene as that seaport and its milling, drunken seamen.

"I can't sail without them, I can tell you that," the captain replied.

"Indeed, I should think you could not sail *with* them." Nathane was close to leaving the ship and dragging Mimi by the hair, if need be. But, he knew his niece would never permit it. "I want you to know that it is against my wishes entirely, monsieur, that I make this transaction with you, but my niece and ward . . ." Nathane then remembered his manners. "Allow me to present my niece, Mimi Pean. Mademoiselle Pean is bent on reaching the New World and I have failed miserably to disuade her. She seeks a rendezvous with her fiance, Captain Laloque, who is presently with the French explorers. Tell me, Captain, may we book her passage with you?"

Regis lifted the lantern from the rail, holding it above their heads. He thoughtfully studied the man and woman. Even in the dim light he could see Mimi's delicate porcelain skin and jet black eyes shining beneath the hood of her pale blue cape. Marchamp wore a silken coat with white satin lining which swung over a heavily brocaded vest. His silk hat shimmered in the glow and lace cuffs hung below his sleeves, falling over a hand which grasped the gold carved handle of an ebony cane.

"Monsieur, you can't be serious! Why would a gallant gentleman like yourself wish to put his young niece aboard my ship—any ship? We are just a rough crew transporting cargo." He swept his hand through the air directing their eyes to the barrels and crates on deck, still to be placed in the cargo hold.

"Monsieur Captain, may I make it quite clear? As I have stated, this is not what I wish for my niece. In fact, were she a year younger, I would forbid it. We understand completely what your ship is. There seems to be very little choice on this miserable port." Marchamp was again figiting, waving a loose hand aimlessly in the air. "Now, sir, if you would be so kind as to give me some sort of answer. I have spent many days running from pillar to post, seeking her passage. It seems there are few captains willing to undertake a voyage to this unsettled land. My niece . . ." He gestured toward Mimi who was quietly standing at his side. "My niece has given me no rest these many months, so I must succeed. I shall make it worth your while, Captain. You are her last hope." Nathane found that he was now anxious to have the affair settled and done with, being fully aware that Mimi had ceased to listen to his pleas. He was only succeeding in making himself more excited, upset and ill-mannered by not concluding the business quickly. And his deep fatigue was catching up with him.

"But, Monsieur Marchamp, we do not have passenger accommodations on the *Premier*. As I have said, we carry cargo to and from the New World. Surely you can find a passenger ship?"

"No I cannot, Captain. If I could do you think I would be here ready to subject this young woman to the likes of what we see here on this filthy dock? I am a man of taste. This, you must know, is the last resort."

"This is nonsense! What am I to do with a woman on my ship?" Paul Regis's mind had already run the gamut of situations that would present themselves if he were to take a woman aboard. "I do not have accommodations for such things. I can understand your plight, but please do not ask me to do this. Speak to your niece again. She must be convinced this is all wrong."

"Monsieur Captain." Mimi impulsively stepped into the conversation. It was becoming clear to her that she would have more than her uncle to convince and was risking the possibility that Captain Regis would cause Nathane to force her to stay home. "I can adjust to whatever accommodations you can offer. I beg you to reconsider."

Paul Regis detected her urgency. "Mademoiselle, I have explained the conditions of my ship. I expect I can place the mate in the seaman's quarters but . . . it will cost you. My mate will not take kindly to the arrangement."

"*Oui*, Captain, we understand." Marchamp fumbled excitedly in the pocket of his waistcoat and withdrew a packet of money. "What is the fare?" he asked giving Regis no further choice.

"You are aware of the dangers?" Paul Regis looked directly at Mimi.

"Yes, yes," Marchamp answered for her. "She will not be happy otherwise."

"It will cost you a thousand francs for her passage, monsieur." Regis answered, resigned to their insistence.

Nathane looked at Mimi in surprise. "One thousand francs? Do you take me for a fool, sir?" Immediately Nathane realized his ill-considered remark concerning it being Mimi's last hope.

"One thousand francs," Regis repeated. "And, for the assured safety of your niece, I am forced to request another hundred francs for my trouble. And I assure you, sir, there will be trouble. Take my advice, persuade this young woman to reconsider the voyage."

Mimi took but a moment to contemplate his last remark. The thought of Francois erased any qualms she might have had, and Captain Regis could no more influence her decision than Uncle Nathane.

"But, this is robbery!" Marchamp nervously protested with a wave of his hand clamped to the gold-headed cane.

"Perhaps, monsieur," replied Regis. "But those are my terms." He hoped the exorbitant figure would abort the trip for the young woman, as he was no more willing to have her aboard than any other captain. But, Paul had detected the intenseness of Mimi's plea for help, and her exquisite beauty had not gone unnoticed.

"You deal a hard bargain, Captain." Nathane was aggravated by the high price and made a move to replace the money in his pocket.

"Uncle!" Mimi grasped his arm gazing at him with pleading eyes.

"Mimi, this is an outrage! I will not be swindled so easily." He shrugged her hand from his arm.

"Consider it my dowry, Uncle, I beg you."

Marchamp waved his hands. "Mimi, you can be most

exasperating at times. Very well, but I shall hold you entirely responsible for my niece's safety." Marchamp looked sternly at Regis as he counted out the money.

"Monsieur Marchamp, you have cajoled me into this business; it's not the other way around. I don't like to be threatened under any circumstances—least of all those in which I would as soon not be involved. I shall, as promised, take care of your niece as much as my duties will allow. Beyond that I can promise nothing." Paul Regis tapped his pipe on the rail in an annoyed gesture. "My word! She is sailing to a savage land of which she knows nothing. Who is to protect her there? She must be made aware of the danger which could befall her."

Mimi was beginning to feel as though she were not present as the two men discussed her fate.

"I must be insane to entertain the idea of a woman aboard my ship. If you don't think it's worth a hundred francs, monsieur, take her home and spare me your threats."

Mimi could hear the anger rising in Regis's voice. She was becoming increasingly alarmed that the whole business would collapse if Uncle Nathane continued with his threatening attitude.

"Captain Regis, allow me to assure you that I am not frightened of the New World. It is my decision to join my intended husband. My uncle is upset at my going, so please do not take it too seriously. I am grateful to you for your help."

"But your uncle is right, it will be difficult for everyone."

"Please, monsieur."

"Very well, mademoiselle, I've said all I can say."

Nathane counted out the money and turning toward the gangplank he addressed the captain. "You said five days hence?"

"That's right."

"Very well, then." Nathane took Mimi's arm and together they uneasily felt their way down the gangplank.

"I don't like this," Nathane insisted as they made their way through the seaport. "I don't like it at all."

"Don't worry, Uncle. I shall be safe. We have the captain's word."

"The word of a thief is worth nothing," he stormed. "but, I have done what you asked, I can do no more. You are twenty and a full-grown woman but, you are naive to the ways of the world. I can't say I am happy about any of this." Nathane could not overcome his anger as he walked along flailing his arms in aggitation.

"I shall be fine." Mimi spoke calmly, although inwardly, this final step overwhelmed her as she thought of joining Francois. None of the dangers of the voyage nor any of the warnings by Regis had registered with her at all, so intent was she upon reaching Niagara Country.

## Chapter Two

The next few days were a frenzy of activity. Mimi kept her maid in a state of near hysteria, selecting gowns, then discarding them, only to change her mind again. Although Francois had alluded to Niagara's lack of luxury Mimi completely disregarded his words, thinking only that she must be as beautiful to her intended husband as she was three years ago when he left. Her chamber was scattered with gowns, shoes, and velvet and fur capes. One trunk was jammed so full it required three of the footmen to close it and another stood half full while she pawed through her wardrobe for other selections.

"My word, Mimi!" Nathane exclaimed as he entered the cluttered room. "You will take all the cargo space if you intend to pack all this. You have enough here for twenty years abroad. Cease all this and think of what you're doing—where you're going. Do you have delusions that you will be entertained every evening in that wild land?" His impatience was breaking all bounds. "My dear Mimi, you haven't the vaguest idea of what this place is like."

Mimi paused and gave it some thought. "Perhaps you are right, Uncle. I shall take only my largest trunk. You can always send the other later, when I am settled."

"Settled, indeed!" stormed Nathane fidgeting

nervously, shifting from one foot to the other as he leaned upon his cane. "They aren't even civilized in Niagara. Mimi you are stretching my patience. You will take only one trunk and that will have to be sufficient."

Mimi acceded to this one small order. Leaving, as she was, under Nathane's protest, she knew it would be more prudent to please him on this. "Very well then, I have enough. That will have to do me. Elaine, you may hang the others until I send for them."

Nathane slumped in the tiny boudoir chair, the exhaustion showing on his lined face. "Mimi, my child," he said quietly, "you shall be leaving very early in the morning." He turned to Elaine who was still replacing the clothes in the wardrobe. "Please leave us alone." Elaine gave a curtsy and quietly left. "My dear, come over here and sit beside me." He beckoned her to his side. "You can spare me these few moments."

"Oh, Uncle Nathane." Mimi threw herself at his feet hugging his waist. "Don't look so sad."

"I fear you don't realize the importance of all this." His eyes held a concerned expression as he looked down at her. "I am an old man. I may not live to see you return."

"Please, don't talk like that." She hugged him tighter, pressing her face close to his chest.

"It's true you know. I am not going to try to stop you, don't worry about that. I have said everything I can say on the matter. I just want to spend these few moments with you." He wearily sat back in the small chair, hands resting on his cane. "You have been my whole life these past years. You've given me joy I never would have known but for you. And, I am grateful for every minute of it. I love you as my own, Mimi."

"Uncle Nathane, please. You're talking as if I won't be back. I will and Francois will be with me, I promise."

Nathane stopped. He was trying to say what he knew would be his last goodbye to his ward, but she was too filled with excitement to appreciate the gravity of it. He knew he would not be alive when she returned. "Very well, my dear, get your sleep," he said resignedly. "I'll see you early in the morning." He kissed her forehead holding his lips tightly to her for a long moment then wearily stood and left the room.

When Mimi Pean took her first look at the tiny cabin she drew in her breath. It was far worse than she had imagined. Again, Nathane made feeble attempts to prevail upon her to remain in spite of his promise, but she waved him off with a determined hand. The small musty cell contained a wooden bunk; there was no resemblance to the soft, luxurious mattress that her own chamber provided. A single, thin coverlet lay at the foot of the bunk. A small commode stood nearby, atop of which was a cracked porcelain bowl and pitcher. The wooden floor planks creaked as she walked to the wardrobe to hang her gowns. Finding barely enough room for her night dresses Mimi carefully refolded her satins and silks replacing them in her sea trunk.

Although she could stand erect in the cabin, she could easily touch the planked ceiling and wondered how a man could possibly be comfortable in the small cubicle. There were none of the amenities, such as gold and marble fixtures, Mimi was so used to at her uncle's estate. This she was sure of as she surveyed the convenience mug beneath the commode. But further pleadings by her uncle were to no avail. Kissing her on the cheek he reluctantly bade his niece adieu. He heavyheartedly left her cabin, turning and blowing kisses as he walked from the ship and out of sight.

Some time later, after she was as settled in the cabin

as she could possibly be, Mimi decided to go on deck. She had taken little notice of the ship when she boarded, being primarily concerned with her trunk as Uncle Nathane's servant toted it aboard. She had been only slightly cognizant of the sailors in striped breeches, moving on deck busy with something or other. Mimi ascended three steps and looked at the sea and was immediately aware they were already moving; feeling their way slowly past the anchored ships at the port. The crew hurriedly adjusted ropes, winding them into coils along the deck while others, high above, hung confidently from rope ladders suspended from the yardarms.

Captain Regis stood at the helm shouting orders, all of which were completely foreign to Mimi's ears. She had never been farther from home than a shopping trip to Paris, much less aboard a masted ship. She watched the pier and anchored ships become more distant as the haze rose between the *Premier* and land. For a brief moment her heart sank as she looked into the mist and let herself think of the gigantic step she had undertaken. She thought of the strong arguments she and Uncle Nathane had when first she proposed the voyage and of his utter shock when he learned she would be unescorted.

Standing by the rail, watching the sea slap the side, becoming more rough as they progressed, Mimi became mindful of the sensation that she was being watched. The crew, still tending to duties, were staring at her. Becoming self-conscious, she retreated immediately toward her cabin.

"Mademoiselle must become used to this." Captain Regis stood before her blocking her retreat.

"They will become used to me as I will to them," she replied defiantly and much in the manner she would address one of the Marchamp servants.

"Perhaps," replied the captain sardonically. "But in the meantime, if I were you, I should make myself as scarce as possible, mademoiselle. I do not wish my added duties of seeing to your safety begin too soon. Fighting the sea is sufficient in itself." He stepped aside to let her pass.

It was then Mimi realized that Regis was much younger than she had first thought that dark night she and Uncle Nathane made her passage arrangements. He wore a neatly trimmed beard which masked his youth. Mimi judged him to be in his early thirties. He was strong looking with piercing blue eyes and beneath his tricorn she detected dark, curly hair. His virile handsomeness was quite different from the insipid, pale-faced young men she had been obliged to entertain at her uncle's fancy balls these past years. His rugged countenance would be a welcome relief from the haze of powdered wigs and overwhelming scents of perfumes which could make one faint.

Now the tiny hole in which she found herself began to close in on her. In her youthful exuberance for adventure she had overlooked the fact, among others, that it would be difficult to keep occupied in the confines of such a small cabin. The dim lantern hanging in the cell hardly provided sufficient light for the needlework she had brought and there wasn't nearly enough room to twirl her many skirts. Hardly out of port, she began to fear that her strong desire to be with Francois had blinded her to the reality of the situation; already she was beginning to feel the confinement of the pressing quarters. Just then, Uncle Nathane's words began to have meaning, and for that brief moment she realized that Nathane was right. But she waved off these thoughts and tried to concentrate on Francois and the new land she was soon to call her home. Reaching into her trunk she withdrew a small packet of letters she had so carefully packed along with her clothing, and began to read:

October 6, 1756

My beloved Mimi:
The time between us has stretched into years and I fear I will never see you again. This savage wilderness has kept us busy enough, but I long to hold you in my arms once more. Mon chere, I think often of our planned nuptials, but they may well be in the distant future, as I see no immediate hope of my return. I hesitate to ask, but, mon chere, unless you come to Niagara, I shall be an old man before our wedding day. Please seek the permission of your uncle to join me here. I shall pen a letter to him this very day, again requesting your hand in marriage. But, Mimi I must also warn you of the hard life we live in Niagara Country. It is far different from our beloved France and I fear living here will never rise to the luxury you are presently enjoying. Still, I beg of you, please persuade your uncle to seek your passage so that you may join me soon.

Your loving<br>Francois

Mimi leaned back against the planks beside her bunk and thought of the years she and Francois had known each other. He was the first young gentleman caller, along with his mother, right after she had joined her uncle. Both families took it for granted from that first moment, that Francois Laloque and Mimi Pean would marry. She remembered they had pledged themselves to each other when he was fifteen and Mimi twelve, and she had never broken her word. She had never swayed from her promise to Francois, in spite of many hopeful suitors.

The young woman was abruptly shaken back to reality by the clanging of a bell above her head and a simultaneous pounding on her cabin door. Rising to her feet with a start, she cracked open her ddoor and peeked out.

"Mademoiselle." Paul Regis touched the tip of is tricorn. "Did you not hear the bells?"

"Why I . . ." Mimi was perplexed. "I don't know, I'm not sure. Why?"

"The bells, mademoiselle, mean mess."

"Mess?"

"I beg your pardon." Regis bowed low, mockingly. "Perhaps you call it dining."

"I see." The smile left her face. "And, where am I to dine, Captain?" she said haughtily.

The captain eyed her for a moment. "That is something I had not thought out too well. Perhaps it would serve better purpose if I had your meals delivered here, to your cabin. A woman aboard this ship does give one pause for thought."

Mimi was struck by the captain's genteel way of speaking. Having left most of the arrangements and the talking to Uncle Nathane on their first encounter, and somewhat upset when Nathane and Captain Regis argued about the money, Mimi hadn't noticed this before. It was ludicrous in view of his profession and rough exterior, together with his mercenary dickering methods. Now she was truly puzzled by this man and, to her surprise, somewhat intrigued.

Mimi wasn't looking forward to meals in her cabin, but she could see no alternative. In spite of Regis's attitude—his knack of making light of her proper upbringing and a general attitude of unpleasantness—she found that she had to agree with his suggestion. "Taking my meals in my cabin will do nicely, Captain," she said.

Regis backed off, lightly touching his hat, and disappeared into the thick blackness while Mimi stood looking after him. Even the black wall of nothingness outside gave a slight feeling of expansiveness to the tight little room she occupied, but she was unable to see a thing. The creaking and moaning of the ship as it rose and fell and the light mist on her face seemed to be all there was.

As she stood there a crude-looking sailor appeared, balancing a covered tray in one hand and a lantern in the other. He descended the narrow stairs; saying nothing, he brushed past her placing the tray on the bunk. Mimi leaned against the open door watching the sailor as he swiftly replaced the bowl and pitcher on the commode with the tray of food.

"Thank you—" Mimi had no idea how one addressed a member of a cargo crew and, indeed, having been raised among servants doing her bidding, she didn't feel much more of a reply was needed.

On seeing her hestiation the mate grinned, revealing missing front teeth. "Mate!" he said filling in the word for her. "I am the captain's mate," he reiterated firmly. "And this here be my cabin you've took over."

The man's entire countenance was abhorrent and the menace in his voice made Mimi recoil with fear.

"I hopes ya like it," he grinned. "I had to scrub it all nice and clean fer ya."

"Ah yes, mate." She was trying to act proper, but knowing well the situation didn't warrant undo friendliness.

The snearing sailor threw back his head and laughed at her propriety. Then, with a fling of his arm he slammed the cabin door. His eyes and threatening grin widened as he moved closer. Seizing Mimi roughly he pinned her against the bunk post, and pressed his face close to her. "Is the bitch going to show proper gratitude for the takin' of the mate's cabin?" he hissed.

His leering eyes wandered over her bare, white shoulders and down to the cleavage, where the bodice of her gown barely covered her white breasts. She became embarrassed as he ogled her with piercing eyes and a salivating grin. Mimi was shaking from fear at what was becoming increasingly clear—the man was about to assault her. She was so filled with the threat she was unable to find her voice to scream and somewhere in the back of her mind she recalled the captain's warning about his crew. Even in such fear, the thought of Paul Regis's anger kept her from shouting out as the leering sailor pressed closer and closer.

"Don't worry, whore, I ain't gonna hurt ya." He eyed her vasciviously. "Now, be nice and show proper gratitude fer this cabin I give ya." He pressed his body against hers, smothering her neck and shoulders with kisses.

With a repugnance she had never before experienced her stomach churned and Mimi pulled herself from his grasp and charged for the door. He hauled her by the skirts, whirling her onto the bunk, then throwing himself on top he tore at her clothing. Ripping away the bodice, he exposed her naked breasts and waist, and pinned her to the hard bunk with his full weight. She could smell the pungent odor of his filthy body and holding her face with a calloused hand, he kissed her mouth hard, while his other hand began to move over her body. Mimi's free hand swayed in the air, seeking something, anything, as a weapon. It fell upon the tray of food, sending it crashing to the floor.

"Avast you bastard!" The muscular figure of the captain stood over them. His huge hands hauled the mate from the bunk slamming him into the planked door so forcefully the sailor slumped to the floor unconscious. Mimi recoiled into the corner of the bunk, crying uncontrollably.

"It begins!" Regis roared as she dabbed her eyes with the tattered pieces of her clothing. "Now I earn my fee! Perhaps, mademoiselle, you are beginning to understand my meaning?" He was fiercely agitated. "Tomorrow at three bells present yourself on deck for the lashing of this man." In one move he heaved the unconscious seaman over his broad shoulders and stalked from the cabin.

It was a long time before Mimi's tears subsided. Even in her mortification she found herself wondering what Paul Regis must think of her. Mimi's quiet and tender upbringing had not prepared her for such atrocities. Her world had always been one of gentility. There, no man would so much as hold her hand without permission. Finally regaining control, she sat on the edge of the bunk and wiping away the tears she viewed the shattered dishes and food. Like a small child she slipped slowly to her knees; still sobbing, she began to gather up the pieces.

## Chapter Three

Mimi slept very little that night. The creaking ship and an empty stomach added to her nervous reaction to the episode with the mate. She succumbed to little catnaps which were intermittently broken by thoughts of what had happened to her. It was a whole new experience for the young French girl and she spent a good deal of her waking moments recalling Uncle Nathane's warnings about misadventures which could occur on such a voyage.

Lying in her sheer nightdress, shining dark hair flowing about her shoulders, Mimi began to slowly rouse. As she opened her eyes a shaft of light lit the cabin; she turned toward the door with a start. Imagining the worst, she clasped her hand to her mouth. The large figure of the captain stood over her. He was dressed differently; the frockcoat was replaced by a white shirt with a jabot flounce at the neck and lace cuffs falling over his hands. His dark blue pantaloons fit tightly against his well-structured body, white gaiters extended from his knees to black boots with large gold buckles, and in his hand he held a coiled bullwhip.

"Did you not hear the bells, mademoiselle" He asked in an uncharacteristically quiet voice.

Mimi clutched the coverlet to her, aware of her lowcut sleeping gown. If she hadn't been so startled she would have been annoyed with Paul Regis and his everlasting bells. "I'm afraid not, Captain. I must have overslept," she apologized.

"You must become used to the ways of a sailing ship, mademoiselle," he replied quietly. "Aboard my ship my orders are to be heeded by all. As a passenger you also are to comply." His voice was becoming more firm. "The punishment proceedings, mademoiselle. Must this poor wretch suffer all the longer, awaiting your pleasure?"

Captain Regis's voice, now approaching a crescendo, stirred Mimi to move to the floor. She had never been addressed so strongly before. As she stood, still clinging to the inadequate coverlet, which did little to hide her lithe figure, she began to stutter nervously. "I . . . I prefer n-not to at-tend . . . if you don't m-mind, Captain."

"But, I do mind," he said firmly. "If it were not for you this would not be taking place. I hardly think it proper for you to *not* seek proper satisfaction. There should be no need for me to be telling this to someone of your breeding."

"But, Captain, I prefer to have this affair dropped. I don't wish—"

"Enough," he roared as he whirled out the door. "Dress! We shall await your presence atop deck."

Mimi knew it was not a matter of choice. It was evident that the childish pleadings she worked on Uncle Nathane to get her wishes would be of no use to her here. She rose and after ablutions, powdered her body in a fragrance which filled the entire cabin. She donned several petticoats over sheer pantaloons and stepped into a pink satin gown from her sea chest. Deftly brushing her hair she twisted it into her accustomed chignon. One would think she had nothing but time with such leisurely pace. Opening the door Mimi grasped her skirts and ascended the stairs to the upper deck. As she reached the last step she became painfully aware that the captain's mate was hanging by ropes tied to his thumbs, amidship. The remainder of the crew stood around at attention, while Captain Regis stood rigidly, whip in hand. Throwing a meaningful glare in Mimi's direction the captain watched her smooth her dress in an embarrassed gesture. Mimi meekly and self-consciously stood there as the first crack of the whip split the air.

Minutes later, the mate's unconscious and bleeding body hung loosely, his feet dragging like a puppet with slackened strings.

"Cut him down and take him below," Regis ordered. As he twirled the whip into loops Mimi stood silently, wondering if she had permission to leave or if she was to stay until given the command. Although the young woman had no sympathy for the man under the whip she had not watched the torture on deck. Never in her young life had she been forcefully subjected to such brutality. Now her mind was numbed by the thought of the long voyage she had embarked upon. The folly of her impetuousness—traveling alone with no protector—had finally struck home.

The captain walked slowly toward her. "Mademoiselle, that was only thirty lashes; ordinarily such an offence would warrant fifty."

Although still shaken, Mimi found herself furious with him. "One can only assume from your remark that you don't feel I am worth much more. Or is it, perhaps, that you feel I am guilty of some complicity?" Without waiting for an answer she went on. "At any rate, Captain, I am grateful for small favors." She didn't feel now that Captain Regis stood many steps above the mate, having put her through all this. "In the future, I shall do my best to see I am never, again, the cause of such an occurrence."

"I'm sincerely glad you realize you were the cause, mademoiselle," he said rather harshly.

Mimi's temper rose and her breasts heaved with anger. "Monsieur Captain, despite my last remark I fail to see how I was the cause. I did nothing to warrant his advances. If you hadn't ordered him to deliver my dinner it would never have happened." She became more irate with each word she spoke.

"My dear Mademoiselle Pean, we do not have servants aboard this ship, merely rugged seamen. Whomever delivers your meals will be of a kind. From now on you shall dine with me in my cabin. But for that, henceforth you will confine yourself to your cabin."

"Captain, do you mean I am never to leave my cabin at all?" Her dark eyes snapped as she spoke and she could feel her blood heat. She shuddered with the thought of such total confinement.

"I have been paid by your doting uncle to see you safely to the new country. You'll just have to understand that I shall take whatever measures are necessary to carry that out. You will accede to my wishes."

"But I might as well be your prisoner. My uncle has paid you well. He hardly meant that I should be restricted unmercifully. Is this what I am to expect during the entire voyage?"

"We will have to see," he retorted matter-of-factly. "In the meantime dinner in my cabin at six bells, sharp. And, mademoiselle," he continued as he walked away, "I trust you will not wear such provocative costumes before my men again."

The thought of her confinement, his attitude, everything, sent Mimi's anger soaring. "I trust it is fine enough for the likes of you," she snapped.

Picking up her bulky skirts she ran to her quarters

slamming the door with all her might. Frustrated at finding nothing to heave in anger she threw herself on the bunk and sobbed.

Moments later she raised her head; her hand went to her stomach, then to her mouth. Flinging the cabin door wide, she struggled through the lurching passageway to the rail where she wretched uncontrollably. The ship's motion had finally seized her and made her ill.

In the heat of July 1757, Mimi's illness and the weight of her abundant skirts forced her to strip to her pantaloons for relief. The tiny room was sweltering as the heat beat down and there were no portholes for fresh air. The room was certainly not made for comfort, she thought. Probably as a deterrent to relaxation and to keep the mate on the job. But Mimi refused to allow herself to feel any compassion for a ship's mate after the recent attack. As far as she was concerned they deserved it, all of them, but that thought was of no help to her as relief from the heat. She removed the long bone pines from her chignon; her hair fell about her shoulders in tiny damp ringlets.

Lying idly on the hard bunk she fanned herself with the parchment letters from Francois. With little else to do, she began to think about the voyage and questioned the advisibility of such an arduous trip across the vast sea, realizing how little thought she had given the idea before. Listlessly she lay back against the cabin wall. Her head and stomach again began to spin, but she had no time to head for the rail. She dove, instead, beneath the commode and clutched the porcelain convenience jug, just in time.

"Mademoiselle!"

Mimi was aroused by the rapping on the door. She hadn't realized she had fallen asleep. The sudden awakening disoriented her and there was a drumming in her head. She was much too ill to rise. "*Oui*," she said weakly. "Who is it?"

"Captain Regis. May I enter?"

Mimi was too spent to don a dressing gown. "Monsieur, I beg of you, I cannot receive you."

Again Regis smiled to himself, at her properness. He swung the door open slowly. "*Mon Dieu*! This cabin is like an oven." Leaning toward Mimi he felt her forehead. His hand felt cool against her burning temples; her beautiful bare shoulders looked even more frail and beads of perspiration covered her brow. He gently swept her into his arms, carrying her into his cabin, where strong breezes blew through the open ports. Lying her upon his bunk, he stroked her soft hair, his heart throbbing wildly as he looked at her delicate loveliness. Lifting her head gently he looked deep into her eyes.

In spite of her sickness, Mimi felt a strange longing sweep through her body as she felt his nearness. She was terrified that the feeling was so strong. He bent slowly over her and their mouths met in a soft, sensuous kiss. Mimi felt strangely fearless and natural about the act. She was not at all surprised that she relented to him, but she summoned all her reserve strength to stop the inevitable. She was utterly confused by her feelings toward this man.

"Captain," she whispered as her heart pounded in her chest, "I beg of you . . . I am too ill."

"Oh, Mimi," Paul panted as he lay his head upon her breast. "Have no fear of me, I have thought of nothing but you from the first moment I saw you."

His head rose with her heavy breathing as she realized she had used frustration and anger to hide her more tender feelings for Paul Regis. Suddenly, completely caught up in a burst of passion, she ran her fingers through his hair and with a strength almost beyond her delicate frame, she forced his lips to hers.

## Chapter Four

The August heat fell upon the *Premier* with all its fury. Mimi, by now used to the raging sea, was no longer besieged by sickness. Still the glaring heat was almost unbearable. Captain Regis had insisted upon her occupying his cabin, while he slept in the mate's, and they had dined each evening together. Mimi rarely walked on deck unless late at night and Paul accompanied her, never taking his longing eyes from her beautiful body and face. But he never again held her in his arms.

His strong exercise of restraint amazed Mimi for she had left herself open to his advances when impulsively and passionately she had drawn his lips to hers that night. Now her body ached for him, but she tried to continue the pretense that it was only an impulsive moment and nothing more. She knew, in her heart that he too longed for her, but his gentleness resembled more of a fatherly concern than that of a man steaming with want. More than once Mimi had read Francois's letters, trying to regain the emotions she had felt for him, but each time Paul looked at her she wanted to melt into his body.

Her confinement to his cabin was less unpleasant and the breezes through the portholes cooled the dense summer air, though never enough for any real comfort.

There were times when Mimi picked up her needlework to try to forget the unbearable heat, and for hours she embroidered linens with the crest of her intended husband. Each time she did she felt a tug of remorse, for as time went on she knew that what she had felt for Francois could never compare to her feelings for Paul who filled a need Mimi had never known existed. He had a strength she had longed for, a strength she thought she had seen in Francois. Even more, Mimi began to realize that she had concocted love from the feeling she had felt for Francois Laloque because he, of all the young men she had known as suitors, was more virile in appearance and attitude. Mimi was ready to admit to herself that Francois's position in the military, and the fact he was in the wild country across the sea, seemed to make him even more interesting than any of the others.

With nothing better to do, and tired of merely pacing the cabin, Mimi continued to embroider the crest. And there were times when even Paul remarked on her ability, admiring her work as she laid aside finished pieces. This silently infuriated her, and, at times, she thought she must be imagining the burning desire she felt was within him.

One late afternoon, sitting in the cabin enjoying the unusual surge of cool air, she heard the ship's bell clang loudly and a sudden scurry on the upper deck caused an uneasiness to rise within her. Dropping her work on the small table she ran to the door, but was unable to see anything from where she was. Lifting her skirts, and breaking all of Paul's rules, she ascended the steps to the deck.

A belaying pin barely missed her head as she rose above the stair encasement. Throwing herself against the rail she watched a pitched battle between two crew members. She could see Paul standing steadfastly in his place by the helm, the bullwhip clutched in his hand. Sailors danced about the outskirts of the two fighters, goading them on, shouting vulgarities. The bawdy men lustily shouted for blood from those engaged in the fight. And they waited impatiently for an excuse to burn off their own fire in the contest.

"Kill 'im, Jacque!" shouted the men. One of the sailors grinned, waiting for his chance. As one opponent heaved the other to the deck he slid to the feet of the jeering onlooker. This was a definite invitation for him to enter the melee and he did so willingly. He picked up the stunned seaman and with a series of blows and shouted obscenities he pressed him against the rail, forcing his head over, choking off his breath.

Mimi, who stood near the stairs, watched as the sailor's body went limp, blood running from his mouth. She was aghast at the horror of it all.

"Avast!" Captain Regis's whip cracked the air. As it wrapped around the body of the attacker, Regis whipped his arm sending the sailor rolling across the deck. "Enough!" he shouted. "Get back to your posts at once. Time enough for your raucous behavior when we reach port in a few days."

As Paul, still unaware of Mimi's presence, turned to his helmsman he caught a glimpse of her standing there. "Mademoiselle, I have repeatedly asked you to stay below. Please do as I ask."

After these many weeks of knowing his gentle nature Mimi was hurt by his command, but she said nothing as she ran for the cabin. It was several hours later when she heard the door of the cabin next to hers close; she knew Paul was making ready to join her as he did every evening for dinner. Shortly, he tapped lightly on her door. Mimi had tended to her midday ablutions, having selected one of her most elegant gowns. She had never been used to anything but dressing for dinner in their estate back in France. Indeed, she had little else to wear, having been raised to be a lady. She now belatedly realized that it would have been prudent to bring along more suitable clothing than she had. Uncle Nathane was right again, she thought. And now she was glad she had listened to him when he chided her about too many trunks. Even so, she had too many gowns and not enough useful clothing.

"Enter," Mimi said as Paul again tapped on the door. Sometime after she had fully occupied Paul's cabin, Mimi noticed that he no longer barged into her quarters. Now he waited to be invited and as he entered Mimi turned away from him, afraid that her displeasure with him could be seen on her face.

"Mimi, I must apologize for my behavior earlier. It was no place for you to be." His voice was tender and solicitous.

Since Paul had mentioned it, Mimi was full of questions about the incident. "Paul, how could you stand there and watch those horrid men commit murder?"

"It was not murder, Mimi. You don't understand. A lady, such as yourself, couldn't understand the feelings of men at sea for so many months. They have pent-up feelings of all kinds that must be released. A good fight to them is what making love is to your gentlemen of the gentry."

Mimi blushed at the comparison. "You are quite outspoken, Paul." She turned her eyes away. Then, turning to face him again, she said, "You could have stopped it sooner."

"Indeed, I could have, only to have it rekindle another day. Now, they have cleansed their systems for a while."

The whole thing was almost too much. She was appalled that he would openly discuss such matters with her. No man had ever spoken so frankly in her presence. Such talk was only for the libraries, along with brandy and cigars after dinner. Yet, she knew he was right and a sudden admiration for his eloquent explanation and deep understanding of his men overwhelmed her. She wanted to rush to him to feel his strong body against hers, his lips upon hers, but she didn't dare. In an effort to restrain herself she changed the subject. "I heard you say we'd be in port in a few days. Is that so, Paul?"

"Yes, one or two days more." He pulled a chair up to the small table and sat down. "If we continue with our luck, as we have, and aren't pulled off course by storms, we will be in Niagara very soon. That should make you very happy." A slight, but insincere smile crossed his face.

He wishes to see me gone, she thought. Visibly shaken by the idea, she walked to the porthole where she studied the undulating sea in an effort to hold back her tears. Why was she on this ship? Certainly her original plan to meet and marry Francois was forever gone. Her feelings had changed since meeting Paul Regis. Now she wondered if he felt the same for her as she did for him. Yet she could not bring herself to take the first step and openly declare her love. No lady would ever do such a thing.

Paul left his chair and stood close behind her. "I have offended you?" he asked after long moments of her silence.

She turned to meet his eyes. "Oh, Paul, do you wish to be rid of me?" she said with trembling lips.

"Is that not why you took this treacherous voyage?"

"Of course it is." She leaped from his side toward the bunk, placing her hand on the rail tapping it in annoyance. "Of course it is," she repeated with quavering voice, wanting more to scream than to be so civil. Sobbing she slumped to the edge of the bunk.

Paul rushed to her and knelt beside her. "Mimi, what is it? Why are you crying?" He tipped her face toward his with a gentle finger and looked deeply into her misty eyes.

Tears rolled down Mimi's cheeks. Slowly he drew his hands down over her bare shoulders causing her to gasp as he lightly touched her breast. As she placed her arms gently around his neck they fell back on the bunk. He could feel his heart pounding as he fondled her body and she lightly moaned under his gentle touch. Pulling the bone pins from her chignon he watched her dark hair fall about her white shoulders. Then, slipping her bodice from her he exposed her breasts completely, smothering her with kisses. Mimi writhed with the passion welling up in her, a passion she had never before known.

"Mimi, my Mimi. I can't let you go. I love you so." He pressed his lips to her eager mouth as he fumbled with the buttons on her dress. Soon it fell away and he tore it from her, exposing her beautifully sleek body and kissed her from her neck to the perfect dark triangle.

Mimi moaned. "Paul, my dearest, take me please."

As she pressed her face into his muscular chest, she could feel his manhood hard against her body. Wrapping her long limbs about him, she forced him inside her, moaning as his body heaved and lowered slowly.

"My virgin," he whispered. "I shall take your maidenhead from you."

"Take me, Paul." She pressed her lips tightly against his as he administered the final thrust. Her body rose and dropped with passion. Her strong response further ignited his desire locking them together in the final fiery embrace as the tide of their feelings washed over them and was spent—together.

Lying side by side, they gently caressed each other and regained their strength.

"Paul, I won't leave you. I love you with all my heart. I have never felt this way before." She gently stroked his face with her finger. "What shall I do?" She looked into his smiling face as he twirled her dark hair about his finger.

"Stay with me, darling. Stay with me." His meaning was definite, his voice firm.

"But this voyage has been so difficult for me. I can't think of the return."

"I know, my sweet, but now there will be more happiness for both of us as we share our love together."

Mimi had never thought of the rigors of sea life before. As she lay beside him, touching his face, she saw her lover in a new and different light. How difficult it has been for Paul, she thought. He could watch his crew release their pent-up emotions by rallying against each other, but his duty was to see that no harm came to them. Only then must he command them to stop and he, as captain, must store his own needs and frustrations all within his body. She loved him completely, but only now did she realize why. He was both gentle and strong, stern but understanding, dependable and just—the captain of the *Premier*.

"Paul," she whispered as she lay beside him, "I do love you so."

## Chapter Five

Paul had spent the night with Mimi, the two curled together side by side on the small bunk. Now as Mimi awoke it was still dark and he was gone. The raging sea slapped heavily against the ship and water poured through the portholes as the vessel dipped into huge swells. Clutching the robe from the foot of the bunk she threw it over her shoulders. When Mimi stood the cold ocean water rushed over her bare feet. This would be the first storm they had encountered and her apprehension rose as she swung open the door. A gigantic wave hovered above like a green wall, before crashing over the deck.

Terrified, she called Paul, but her voice was lost in the thunderous impact of the water and driving rain. Forced back, Mimi closed the portholes and, wading through the cold water, she searched for dry clothing. Everything in her sea chest was drenched from the seeping water. There was nothing but nightdresses in the wardrobe and Mimi knew it would be futile to try to find anything she could wear so she pushed her way through the lurching passageway to the deck above. Her drenched night clothes clung to her, her long wet hair dripped and rivulets of water ran down her face.

On deck the crew were trying to secure the sails, while Paul fought the wheel at the helm, each gust of wind and fall of the ship forcing it from his grip.

As Mimi pulled herself to the upper deck, seamen jostled her in their efforts to control the slackened lines. She was pushed against the mast and, clinging with all her strength, she screamed into the night, "Paul!"

He turned to see her pressed against the mast in an effort to steady herself in the heavy wind and pelting water, her thin gown totally revealing her body beneath. Quickly he lashed the wheel, jumping to the deck below where he forced her under the partial overhang of the hatch. "Stay here until I return," he shouted to her as the rain drenched his face.

She clung to a coil of rope where she had been pushed, only slightly sheltered from the elements. Shivering and consumed with an anxiety she had never experienced in her life, she waited for Paul to return, when a heavy hand fell upon her. She brushed the wet, matted hair from her eyes and looked into the face of Jacque, the sailor who had been in the fight. A scream escaped her lips but was lost in the din.

Almost hysterical now, Mimi began to fight him. But his strength forced her down on the deck planks, his face moving closer, again revealing his hideous grin. He pressed his full weight against her and wrestled her arms over her head, when suddenly he was raised from behind and thrown to the other side of the ship. Paul's eyes blazed with anger. He charged wildly at the mate who was trying to stand. Paul dove and, dragging the sailor to his feet, he crashed his fist into the man's face again and again. Jacque fell against the rail where he clutched a belaying pin and stormed toward Paul. Regis reached with his muscular arm, stemming the force of his swing, then twisting Jacque's arm the pin fell from his grip. Bleeding and hotly intent upon putting Paul away, the fierce sailor threw the captain to the deck pouncing on top. They rolled over and over across the slippery planks. As the ship rolled and heaved out of control, the wheel broke from its mooring. Waves slammed over the fighting men, sliding them from one side to the other.

The helpless woman could do nothing but watch as their scuffling inched them closer to where she lay. The sailor bellowed like some wild animal as he fell upon Paul again. Mimi screamed in terror, clutching both fists to her mouth. She was overcome by helplessness, but her terror was swiftly replaced with anger as she watched Jacque pummel Paul to the deck. Her head swiveled in search of a weapon, something with which to help him, when her eyes fell upon a gaff hook piercing the hatch above her head. She reached above and tugged at it, tearing it from its place, splinters of wood flying. Then, turning and watching the men grapple, she wrapped both hands around the handle and waited.

With a sudden thrust Jacque was thrown to the deck, sliding to where Mimi coiled, waiting. She raised the hook high above her head and with a swift lunge she buried it in the back of the captain's mate. His head rose, his eyes rolled back, and death streaked across his face. Again Mimi screamed in a deafening pitch with the knowledge of what she had done.

Her body began to shake uncontrollably and her mind seemed to float above the events happening around her. She felt as though she had left the world and entered a space where she'd never been. In her imagined state, her mind reeled as she thought of her quiet life in France. Mimi could never imagine life being so rugged and hard. Hysterically she bit her hand, almost drawing blood. Pressing herself against the hatch she stared at the dead man's still-grinning face.

She had killed him! Her thoughts spun in her head. Murdered! Mimi Pean slumped into a heap as the horror of it all settled upon her bewildered brain.

Ordering the crew to man the sails, Paul ran to help her back to the cabin where he had laid out sailor's togs and boots. "Put these on quickly," he said. "I'm going on deck. I'm sure we are way off course and land should be sighted very soon. We stand the danger of being beached before we reach our port."

Mimi dressed, the death-face of Jacque imprinted on her brain. Then a shout of "Land ho!" snapped her back to the present. Dressed in her uniform, Mimi hauled herself to the helm as Paul shouted to the crew to lower all sails.

This would be her first sight of the New World and now, an utterly changed woman, she set herself for the trials that lay ahead; her reasons for coming to Niagara and the memory of Francois had almost faded completely.

Within the sight of land the ship dropped anchor in the quiet sea. The storm had spent itself, leaving havoc on deck, and only a cool breeze now remained. As Paul scanned the shoreline with his glass he called to his second in command to secure the ship then turned to Mimi. "We've been thrown off course. We're nowhere near the St. Lawrence River. My maps indicate we'll have to try to reach the Hudson River instead."

"Is this near Niagara Country?" Mimi asked innocently.

"We're farther south than that. I think it would be wise to port somewhere on the Hudson. We'll remain anchored while the crew rows to shore to look around. In the meantime we'll be safe here."

The following morning, the ship shifted languidly on the calm waters within view of the thin line of shore.

The winds had died and the sails were lowered. Ocean water seeped through the cracks of the deck planks, dripping incessantly into the cabins below where Mimi had tried to salvage her possessions. Most everything was ruined by the salt water and the few she thought could be used were hung on the rails and ropes of the ship.

The shore was clear in the captain's glass and he could see the beached crafts from the *Premier*, but no movement on shore.

Mimi opened the ports of the cabin, allowing the slight but warm breeze to blow through. Only she, Paul and two remaining seamen were aboard. Satisfied that nothing more could be done in the cabin, Mimi went to where Paul stood searching the shoreline.

Sitting quietly, Mimi began to think of the events of the previous day. Until now she had been too alarmed, too busy, to allow her mind to dwell on Jacque's death. She shuddered each time she thought of it and of the look on his face. The full impact of what she had done hadn't hit her until she saw Paul lift the body and heave it into the ocean. Then a sick feeling engulfed her.

Mimi's thoughts wandered to Uncle Nathane, how far she had already come, and what had befallen her in those few months. She relived the arguments she had when Nathane attempted to convince her to remain in France. Only now did she fully realize the meaning of what he tried to say, all too late.

The murder of Jacque would forever be imbedded in her mind, but the only thing that really mattered to her was that Paul was alive because of her actions.

The sun had risen brightly that morning, but now dusk began to settle over the uneasily quiet ship. Paul ordered the remaining crew members to arrange a meal. It had been hours since they had eaten and there was no way of knowing when his men would return with news of the land they had reached. Mimi and Paul agreed to eat their meal together on deck. The cabin, still damp, was less than comfortable and Paul wanted to keep the lanterns lit and an eye out for his boats.

Sitting in the dim glow of the lanterns Paul wrapped an arm around Mimi and placed her head upon his shoulder with a gentle hand. No one knew better than Paul what the past experiences had done to his beloved Mimi.

He began to chuckle lightly. "You make an outstanding figure of a seaman." He played with her.

Mimi gently slapped him in mock anger. "What would I wear if it were not for these?" She stood and strutted around jokingly, as she imagined a weathered seaman would do, and they both laughed at her clowning. Then, she playfully threw herself beside him pulling his lips to hers. They kissed and embraced lovingly as the quiet and peace of the ship fell upon them.

Paul caressed her body slowly, softly. Her breasts stood out voluptuously in the tight shirt and he kissed and caressed them. Unbuttoning her shirt he laid bare her breasts. Mimi stood and released the waist of the sailor's pantaloons. She stood completely naked in the light of the lanterns. Paul stared at her beautiful body, reaching up to touch her thighs. Relaxing, she slipped to the deck and laid full out, pulling Paul upon her. He pressed his manhood hard against her, fumbling with his waist buttons. Finally he entered her body smoothly. They writhed with ecstasy until the roar of passion settled upon them and their bodies went limp together.

Now, fully clothed, they lay in each other's arms. Mimi could think only of her love for Paul, and he thought only of his beloved Mimi. There under the warm, dark sky sleep overtook them.

## Chapter Six

Paul opened his eyes cautiously. Mimi, still asleep, lay beside him. He had been awakened by a slight but unnatural noise above his head. The captain, familiar with every groan and creak of his ship, every heavy step of his crew, knew it was none of those sounds.

He removed his arms from Mimi painstakingly, so as not to awaken her. He felt his waist to ensure that his dagger was secure in his belt. A quick tinge of despair rushed through his veins when he found it gone. Paul looked around and spied the blade shimmering on the deck as it caught the first rays of the early morning sun.

Whoever had boarded his ship meant harm to them and there could be more than one. Paul was sure of it, having heard sounds simultaneously on both the port and starboard. Paul felt helpless, unarmed and virtually alone. He could only think of Mimi's safety, but could conceive of no way to protect her, lying there so vulnerably.

Suddenly a shrill warhoop pierced his ears. He was overtaken from behind and boldly hauled down the steps to the deck. At the same moment Mimi was awakened by a rough-skinned hand clamping over her mouth. A strong arm seized her around the waist dragging her down to the deck beside Paul. She was held in a vice-like grip by two painted, bare-chested natives.

She wanted to scream, but felt like she was being smothered by the hand holding her so tightly.

The red-skinned natives wore bands across their foreheads, over jet-black, stringy hair, and leather loin wrappers. From their waists hung weapons of stone wrapped to hand hewn handles.

The two savages holding Paul hauled him against the mast twisting his arms as they tied him with leather thongs, pulling him stiffly against the pole. It was impossible for him to observe anything more, so tightly was he lashed. A fierce native held his weapon to Paul's throat, waiting for a signal to use it. As they spoke to each other in an unintelligible tongue, it was evident they intended to kill the two of them.

Mimi's eyes glared with fright, the strength slipping from her body as she fearfully studied the huge mountain of muscle who appeared to be the leader. In his native sounds he ordered a leather thong tied around Paul's neck and lashed to the mast. Mimi's body slumped in her captor's arms as she watched the Indian dip the leather in the salt water on the deck and pull it unmercifully tight around Paul's neck. Paul moved his head in an attempt to prevent it and was struck violently by the infuriated savage; his unconscious body fell against the mast.

Mimi's screams never left her lips, still clamped with the muscular hand. Bewildered and wide-eyed she viewed her lover's body hanging there as the native leader moved toward her. Everything inside her went limp as she watched him approach. Her heart pounded wildly against her ribs and she had never felt so helpless or so without hope as she did that moment.

The man grinned as he pointed at her breasts protruding in her tight sailor shirt. "This is a squaw," he said moving close, looking into her pale face. With a quick hand gesture he ordered the warrior to remove his hand from her mouth. By then Mimi was much too fearful to scream.

"We will take this one back with us. Take her to the canoe," he ordered. "This one, we leave to the sun and insects." He gestured toward the figure tied to the mast.

Too terrified to fight, Mimi was forced into the waiting canoe. Several others drifted on the waves as a lone Indian sat in each. Mimi was desolate and numbed with anxiety; a crazed look glazed her eyes.

The canoes headed for land, moving silently through the water as she struggled to a sitting position. The leather cut into her wrists and the warrior, at the head, paddled the canoe staring at her in silence, his eyes engulfing her body.

Up ahead, Mimi could see the ocean narrowing into a river where the tree-shrouded shores were visible on both sides as they quietly slipped along. It was no longer the endless, vast ocean. Directly behind her was the canoe of the hulking leader of the band. He motioned and the small boats headed for a small bay in the river. As they drifted slowly toward shore the Indians deftly guided them along using their paddles as rudders.

Jumping to land, the Indian in Mimi's canoe hauled the boat effortlessly to shore. Fear pulsed through her veins and her head reeled. She wondered what Providence held in store and how much more she could endure. Her thoughts wandered back to her beloved Paul and that last horrible glimpse of him. She could no longer contain her grief. Her eyes filled with tears; she was sure he was dead.

Numbed as she was, the young French girl was hauled from the canoe and shoved ashore as her guard shouted in his tongue, making it clear that Mimi was to move ahead of him. Her hands, still tied behind her back, created a loss of balance and she stumbled over fallen tree trunks and through trailing wild grape vines. Perspiration dripped down her face and her breathing became labored as her guard quickened his pace.

Moving silently through the trees, pine needles snapped beneath their feet, sending a strong, sweet aroma to her nostrils. Tall pines rose above their heads creating a cathedral-like ceiling where their green tops clustered together high above the ground. Mimi stumbled over exposed roots again and again. The natives laughed at her efforts to pull herself up—shoving herself to a sitting position with her elbows, then to her knees, and finally to her feet. They seemed to take delight in her suffering.

Through the dark forest she caught the shaft of the early sunlight glittering across a small clearing of wild flowers. Having been pushed to the head of the pack, Mimi bent low to avoid the hanging branches of a young pine at the clearing's edge. As she rose to an erect position the blood rushed from her head when she beheld the most gruesome sight of her young life. There hung the decapitated heads and dismembered bodies of the crew of the *Premier*, stuck on crossed poles; their empty eye sockets and distended tongues were hideous gargoyles strung in a row.

This was the last atrocity Mimi's mind and body could withstand. She fell to her knees and, throwing back her head, she let loose with an insane scream. Numbness swept through her brain as she collapsed.

The leader of the band hauled her limp body to his shoulders, dragging her through the clearing to where bark huts and animal-skin teepees formed their village. Everyone in the camp stopped to watch, stone-faced, as she was dragged through the entrance of one hut and tossed on a bundle of furs.

## Chapter Seven

As the days turned into months there were only sporadic glimpses of reality for the ailing Mimi Pean. During these times memories of Paul Regis, her capture, and the horrible sight of the tortured sailors fed her insanity. Lapses into a delirium were intermittently broken by vague ghosts of reality, and during those moments she was aware of a kindly old Indian woman who knelt beside her, forcing her to eat. She remembered the woman bathing her face with cool water, but when she finally awoke from her long, fevered sleep it was all unclear and she was too weak to think of what had befallen her.

The months went on and the squaw continued to care for her captured white woman. One morning during the very early hours Mimi opened her eyes, fully aware of where she was. Gazing about, she saw the old squaw sitting quietly in the corner of the house of animal skins. Then, looking about, she recalled that in her delirium she had seen long poles ascend toward the hole above and a patch of blue sky. A fire burned on the ground in the center and smoke twirled upward seeking its way out.

Mimi felt something pressing on her forehead; reaching out her hand she traced beaded designs across the headband. She felt the leather dress she wore and the luxurious fur blankets beneath her. Strange necklaces of beads and shell hung from her neck.

The aged squaw rose and stood over her. There was no longer fear in Mimi as she recalled the brief, fleeting moments when the woman had tended her so patiently. Even so far from reality, Mimi had learned to trust her.

"Where am I?" she asked the old woman.

"Mississauga, Mississauga."

She repeated the word but Mimi didn't understand. "Is that your name?" she asked trying to puzzle out the native tongue.

The old woman looked at her, then bending low she took Mimi's hand. "Mississauga Village," she repeated in the best French she could speak. "You in village, Mississauga braves."

Mimi's eyes lit up. "You speak French!" She tried to raise up, but she was too weak. The woman spoke French, Mimi thought and a new hope rose in the young prisoner. She laid back rejoicing as she grasped the knowledge that soon they would communicate with each other.

"This Onguiaahra land. Many tribes," the old woman went on, making signs with her hands as she tried to explain. "Many moons you fever, maybe die."

"How long have I been here?"

"Many moons. Two seasons." The squaw held up two fingers before Mimi's eyes.

"Two years!" Her voice trembled with her weakness. "Have I been here two years?"

The old woman waved her hands sidewise in front of Mimi's face and shook her head, trying to make the white woman understand, with her little knowledge of the French language.

Mimi understood. "How long, then?" she asked with quavering voice as she thought of all the time gone.

Again holding up two fingers the squaw hobbled to

the door of the skin-thatched hut. She pulled back the hide cover of the opening, revealing a thick blanket of snow and more falling.

"Dear heaven!" Mimi muttered as tears filled her eyes. "It's the middle of winter. The last I remember it was August." Her head fell to the side as tears rolled down her cheeks. It seemed to her, lying there silently, that she was an old woman and had spent her youth within the thick walls of an insane mind. She really didn't know if she had been lying there for months or years and it suddenly didn't matter.

Still not strong enough to move, Mimi lay there for days trying to remember the past months. She learned through the Indian woman's smattering of French that a band from the Mississauga tribe had captured her; and French soldiers frequently came to the village, but she was still too frail to leave her hut and seek them out. She asked often if Francois Laloque was one of the soldiers who came, but the Indian woman could not tell her.

As the days moved on Mimi became strong enough to sit up. Her mind was becoming clearer on the events leading to this place and as she thought of Paul, sure in her mind that he was dead, her eyes would fill and overflow. She wanted to die right where she lay. She couldn't think of trying to stay alive with her beloved Paul dead. She refused to eat when the Squaw brought her food and with such a strong desire to die she refused to move from her bed to even try to regain her strength. In her mind, there was no other way, since it was impossible to return to France and her beloved Paul was already dead. Death, she hoped, would come fast.

As she lay there, her strength ebbing away slowly, the hide door opened and a huge Indian man stood over her. His arms were folded across his broad chest and he wore a look of grave sternness. Mimi slowly opened her eyes when, suddenly, he lifted her from the furs and hauled her through the entrance, out into the snow, where he dropped her at the foot of a pole. He shrieked at her in his tongue. Finally, in what seemed to be the end of his patience, he whisked Mimi to her feet and lashed her hands to the pole. Then, seizing a whip of leather straps from an Indian brave standing nearby, he ripped the hide dress from her shoulders and laid the whip across her white back.

Mimi shrieked in pain, her feet went out from under her, leaving her hanging by her wrists. Again and again he laid the whip across her back, long after she ceased to be conscious.

Mimi came to, lying on the same fur bed from which she had been dragged. She had learned in that brief span that her captors had strong ideas of what she would do and her death was not a part of their plan. She knew that she would no longer be allowed to languish, waiting for it. She would have to struggle to her feet and gain her strength or the beatings would continue. The tears no longer flowed. Mimi would slowly become hardened to the wild ways of the new world she had fought so hard to reach.

There would be no peace for her anywhere, she thought. The Mississaugas refused to let her die. Indeed, they removed the choice from her. And yet she wondered why she hadn't just let them beat her to death. It all would mean the same. But now, she realized, they would stop just short of her death with each beating, prolonging her agony until she raised herself to her own feet. She had no recourse; she must either gain her strength and learn to pull her weight in that Indian village or suffer untold agony under leather whips until she learned. Considering everything, Mimi felt she had better be strong, for this life in the New World was beyond anything she knew or could imagine.

## Chapter Eight

There had been a ceremony, little of which made sense to her, but Mimi took it to mean she had been adopted into the Mississauga tribe. She was given the new name of Wild Flower and moved to a bark hut to live among other young Indian women. It wasn't long before she realized that she had been placed among the unmarried maidens of the tribe; she was now an available squaw, to be taken as a wife by the chief of the tribe or, if not him, then as a wife of a brave. Sometimes there was more than one wife for each brave, and the thought repulsed Mimi making her vow to kill herself before it would happen to her.

Young women braided her hair and Wild Flower was relieved to be able to move about in soft beaded moccasins without the encumbrances of petticoats and the usual voluminous skirts. Her reflection in the thin coating of ice on the streams surprised her. The soft look of a child had faded and Wild Flower was a full-blown adult woman now, a far cry from her genteel French upbringing. Although the life was more difficult than she could have imagined, Mimi slowly worked into a place among the Mississauga tribe in that fertile valley along the Hudson River.

She learned the women's work of the village, fashioning moccasins with beads and skinning and butchering meat along side other squaws as hunting parties returned with their kill. She began to speak their words and use effective sign language and saved her French for her tirades when she lost her temper. She found she could say whatever she thought and none of them knew that her words were of such vile strength. At least she could give vent to her anger without fear of punishment.

There were times when she'd laugh inwardly as her tongue venomously laid out a brave, and he'd stand there smiling along with her. It was a source of great amusement to the hardening Mimi.

Her life was too busy to allow room for loneliness. She entered into their entertainments and feasts and learned their dances. Mimi loved to dance, but she could hardly compare their gyrations to the graceful French waltzes she enjoyed at the balls at Uncle Nathane's estate.

Although Wild Flower soon fit in with the tribe and their ways, she knew in her heart, she'd never cease to attempt escape and her eyes and ears were ever alert. Still, it had been eight months since she had been torn from her place with Paul on the *Premier* and there were times when she felt escape would be impossible. And, thus far, no French soldier had come to the camp.

The snow melted into the ground creating soft, dark earth for planting; the bitter winter cold gradually softened into balmy spring, then into hot summer. It would soon be a full year since Mimi set foot in Niagara Country. She spent long, drudging hours in the fields alongside her Indian sisters planting corn and other vegetables. It seemed to her that this was to be her life for eternity, but she had not grown to like it now, any more than before. Then, too, she was constantly beseiged by young braves with lustful looks and wondered when she would be drawn from the hut and dragged before the chief to be told she would marry. Mimi tried to hold herself aloof from them all, never giving them a look or word to indicate she had interest. Her main fear was that her attitude would be ignored and she would be married against her will. She had already seen it happen to her sister maidens. And Mimi could not erase the face of Paul Regis from her memory no matter what happened. She made up her mind she would never become an Indian wife, and she constantly wore a knife-sharp stone beneath her deerskin garment for the day when such an eventuality arose. Mimi was sure that she could use the weapon without qualms.

It was late in the afternoon when all the women's chores, save the corn husking and grinding, had been finished. Mimi sat beside a row of young maidens talking amiably as they worked. Each in turn dropped their work as they recognized the young brave approaching to be the messenger of tidings that one of the unmarried women had been selectred.

Mimi stiffened as his gaze narrowed in on her. She knew his strong stride and determined expression indicated that her time had come and she pushed back against the others in an effort to avoid the inevitable.

Jostling aside the other women, he worked his way to Mimi and seized her by the arm, hauling her toward the hut of the chief. Mimi's pulse rose rapidly and her mind raced as she tried to think of a way out, but there was nothing she could do. Standing before the chief she understood when he pointed a finger at the strong brave, White Rider, who watched from the corner of the hut. "I will never be an Indian wife!" she screamed in French. "I'll die first."

Her words fell on deaf ears as she was taken from the

hut by the older squaws with solemn resignation imprinted on their ruddy features. Mimi was led to the marriage hut, dressed in the ceremonial clothes, then left to wait for the entrance of all the married women, whose lot was to train Mimi in her wifely duties to White Rider.

Instead, and to her great surprise, the hides parted and in stepped White Rider. He looked at Mimi with unusually gentle eyes for so rugged an Indian, and his touch was soft. Still, she cringed as he swept his hand down her arm and even he appeared somewhat uneasy. He, above all, knew he shouldn't be there before the wedding ceremony.

Mimi pulled from his touch. "This cannot be, White Rider. I save myself for my own kind, my own countrymen," she pleaded as he became more amorous.

"You are one of us now," he said.

"Never!" Mimi answered fiercely, her French blood rising in her temples.

White Rider's gentleness unexpectedly left him and falling upon her he attempted to assault her. Mimi had learned the silent, stoic ways of the Mississauga women and the instinct to scream no longer entered her mind. Instead, she reached for her hidden blade, but the warrior saw the movement and secured her hands above her head.

Since the marriage ceremony was to take place in the morning, after a great feast, White Rider had broken all the Indian laws by being in the maiden's hut. Struggling to free herself Mimi glanced over her shoulder and saw one of the older squaws standing above them, her face carrying a strong warning. Mimi knew she was suspected of complicity in this immoral act. When White Rider became aware of the squaw's presence he pulled himself up and ran from the hut.

Indian punishment was swift, for women, when adultery was commited. It was considered a woman's crime among the Indian tribes. The man was never punished, it being his privilege to take the women of his choice.

As the squaw left the hut Mimi knew she would shortly be dragged from her home and whipped. She lay there awaiting the inevitable, for she had learned that the Indian allowed no opening for explanation and all punishments were meted out with haste. With little hope of escaping, she rose to her feet and stood waiting for the village women to lead her to the hanging post, where her already scarred back would be stripped bare to meet the leather whips.

Standing there waiting, the hides across the entrance suddenly parted. An Indian warrior seized Mimi's hand pulling her through the opening and down the path away from the village. He quickly pushed her down behind a row of sumac bushes. So fast was the move, Mimi had no time to change any of it. She lay there panting, trying to get a better look at the brave.

As he peered around cautiously, he spoke to her. "If we make a run for it I think we can hide in the woods till nightfall."

"Who are you?" Mimi had never seen this man in the village before. Strangely, his French was perfect and she could hardly contain her excitement.

"Time for that later." He pulled her along into the dense woods.

It was long after that he stopped to rest and Mimi fell at the foot of a giant oak tree, panting. Trying to catch her breath she looked closely at the man who had saved her. "You're French!" she exclaimed, hardly able to control her glee.

"Indeed, madame, French!"

"But, who . . ." She stammered trying to overcome her great surprise. "Who are you? Where do you come from?"

"Sergeant Mileaux, at your service, madame." He looked incongruous in a low bow of the French gentry, attired as he was in full, vibrant Indian paint and dress. "Word has reached our quarters at Lake Erie of a French maid captured by the Mississaugas. We had to be exceedingly cautious in your rescue. Since the Mississaugas are our fighting allies against the British much care had to be taken. Thus you see the costume of their tribe." He flourished a hand from his neck to his feet. "You see, my lady, it was my officer's wish that you be taken from these natives, but we also had to keep our peace with them. So we devised this plan. I was able to enter the village unnoticed and was just about to enter your tent when your Indian lover walked in. I was anxiously waiting nearby for his departure."

"He is *not* my lover," Mimi said adamantly. She thought of how long and hard she had fought to keep from having an Indian lover, and the heat of rage surged through her body. She was about ready to give this Sergeant Mileaux a piece of her mind when he broke into her tirade.

"No need to explain. I know these savages." His implication was Mimi was trying to cover up her duplicity and she became even more annoyed.

"But, I swear, I have never taken an Indian lover." Mimi's face reddened with rage. "Sergeant, if you had even a snippet of an idea of how hard it has been to remain untouched by these savages you wouldn't have the heart to speak to me like this."

"Be thankful then . . ." He looked about cautiously to be sure they were not followed and completely disregarded Mimi's injured feelings as he tried to explain the circumstances. "For I hear these warriors are less than gentle with their women. Now, madame, if we are to travel together I shall have to know your name."

Mimi puffed with anger and frustration. The exasperating man hadn't listened to a word she had said. "Mimi Pean is the name, monsieur, and it's *mademoiselle*, if you don't mind." She said it haughtily, having lost none of her French aloofness.

"Indeed! I would think it would be *madame* by now," he replied sarcastically. Her high airs had not been lost on him in spite of his obvious disinterest in her opinions. "But, it is of no consequence to me. It's merely my task to bring you to the French camp as ordered by my superiors."

She had difficulty making up her mind whether to be grateful or indignant for her rescue. Sergeant Mileaux appeared to be less gentle than the Frenchmen she remembered. But she was also beginning to realize that this wild land could erase all traces of gentleness. She had only to look at herself for proof. She needn't be so hard on Mileaux. Her newfound tolerance had already begun to mold her into someone quite different from the fragile girl she once was.

It was always dark in the dense forest, but as the small animals and birds darted about in preparation for sleep, Sergeant Mileaux knew it was dusk and time to begin the trek toward their destination.

Mimi had rested as they waited. She wouldn't be sitting around in such a relaxed fashion if she were still back in the Indian camp, she thought. There she would still be at the height of the day, looking forward to sleep many hours later, after the squaw's work was done, and her thoughts were full of the many unanswered questions she would have asked had Mileaux not cautioned her to be silent.

After a year with the Mississaugas, Mimi had learned to snap into action at the mere movement of a finger, and Mileaux had pressed a finger to her lips; that had been sufficient to silence her. And Sergeant Mileaux had added his own picturesque comments: "These savages are light-footed. They can be upon you and have your scalp hanging from their belt in a thrice—and the pain of it would not shatter your nerves till long after death set in."

Mimi hadn't needed the vivid explanation. She had seen Indian torture methods and the swift death they administered.

Placing a finger on his lips once more, Mileaux pulled her to her feet. "We will move out now, madame," he whispered ever so softly. "Keep your eyes on me. I shouldn't want to lose you in this darkness, and the forest is deceiving. One can wander in circles for days."

Their moccasined feet snapped small twigs as they ran through the dry, silent trails. Mimi followed closely behind, but a new nagging began in the pit of her stomach. She wondered if her trust in this man was sensible; perhaps he wasn't who he pretended to be. She felt beneath her dress, checking her weapon, lingering behind him just long enough to do so. Then yet another wave of insecurity swept over her as she thought how quickly she had believed this man's story and how willingly she had accompanied him, but at the time, waiting as she had been for her unappealing wedding to take place, she would have gone with the devil himself. Uneasy as she was, she was taking no chances with this one, she thought. One suspicious move and he would be dead.

The deer runs were well worn and their footing was secure, but as Mileaux took on speed and Mimi tried to stay close behind she found herself cutting through small areas, bringing herself even with the Sergeant. Her zigzagging in and out amused Mileaux. However, he was unexpectedly brought up straight as a crackling of broken limbs stopped him in his tracks. He glanced back to find Mimi sprawled on the ground entangled in wild grape vines.

"*Sacre du lievre*! Keep to your feet or we'll never reach Lake Erie."

"Really, Sergeant! I don't have wings. How am I supposed to keep up with you?" Mimi puffed.

"Sorry, madame. It has been some time since I've run through the woods with a fair damsel. I fear I have lost all knack for such elegant playfulness." His sarcasm was not lost on Mimi.

If ever he had the chance to attack or kill her it was now, entangled as she was. Whipping a knife from its sheath he loomed toward her. Mimi's reflexes caused her to whisk her blade from beneath the leather flap at her waist. She raised her hand, ready to plunge.

"Aha! I see you don't trust me," he laughed.

"That's certain, Sergeant. I trust no one."

"But, I only meant to cut you from those vines that hold you."

"Then do so," Mimi replied in anger and humiliation.

Together they cut away the twisted vines from her feet. Mimi rose, brushing herself off. "May we rest?"

"Of course. Climbing up hills and sliding down ravines since yesterday, hasn't exactly been a soiree."

This extracted no sympathy from Mimi. "Humph!" she said looking around for a comfortable spot to sit.

"I expect a rest will do us both some good," he went on. "Besides, the dawn is beginning to appear and it would be well to lay low for a while."

Sergeant Mileaux assisted Mimi to a large fallen log

which brought a look of surprise to her face. Mileaux thought he had touched some vital nerve. "Is something bothering you, mademoiselle?" he asked with a puzzled expression.

"No, monsieur," she replied still with surprise registering in her voice. It had been too long since she had been treated like a lady. If she intended to return to France it would do well for her to restrain herself. Looks of surprise at a man's chivalry was hardly the proper approach. Besides, it was ridiculous to think that after only one year of life on the frontier she would forget twenty years of French manners. She would have to reverse the process. Mimi's hopes of returning to her homeland were now heightened with her rescue from the Mississaugas.

As she lazily gazed around, each tree looked much like the next. Mimi had never had reason for being alone in the forest, but she remembered thinking of escape and she knew it would be certain death to try it through unfamiliar woods. She silently thanked the French militia for sending Mileaux, otherwise she would have been an Indian wife, a thought which struck a senstive nerve whenever she considered it.

## Chapter Nine

Chattering birds took flight as the frosted shaft of the dawn's new light flickered through the foliage. Mimi slumped against the log and closed her eyes. Lying quietly she opened one eye surreptitiously and studied the face of Mileaux. Beneath the paint she detected strong features, his beard now beginning to show through the makeup. He was perhaps in his late twenties, Mimi thought. Although he was not large in stature, he was muscular and well built. His face and hands were weathered by the harsh winters and hot summers and she wondered how long he had been in Niagara. Looking at her own hands, she discovered they were not too far from the leathery appearance of the sergeant's and it was really the first time she had taken notice. While it hardly amused her, she did think how such a thing would have upset her, beyond reason, as the mistress of the Marchamp estate.

"Sergeant, how far must we travel to reach this Lake Erie?"

He sat against the tree beside her. "First we have to reach Albany, madame. My French comrades are camped there awaiting our return. We took a great chance since the British occupy Albany."

This statement meant nothing to Mimi. "The French army is in Albany too?" Albany meant no more to her than Lake Erie and armies and their ways were even more mysterious.

"Just a fragment. We devised this plan for only one man to rescue you. Any more and we'd surely have been detected and none of us would have succeeded."

"But, how did you know I even existed?" No Frenchman had ever come to the Indian camp and it struck her as being impossible for anyone outside the village to know that she was there.

"Our Mississauga allies told us. You see, they were not aware that they were amiss in kidnapping a French woman. Indeed, they did not know you were French when they took you. I suspect, just between you and me, that when they discovered this they thought it wiser to make it known to the military, lest their punishment be quite severe if great harm had come to you."

"That can't be so, Sergeant. Otherwise, I would have never been chosen for an Indian brave to marry."

"Why not? Many of our French soldiers have married Indian women."

Mimi was taken aback by the statement. Now she knew why she hadn't been turned over to the army, she was marriageable and would probably be considered somewhat special if one of the braves got her for a wife, if for no other reason than she was white. She didn't like the idea no matter how she turned it in her mind.

The sergeant went on. "Anyway, to them a squaw is a squaw no matter what nationality or color."

Mimi was not about to argue it. She had lived among the tribes long enough to know that Mileaux was right.

"Each one is more or less alike, for their purposes. When the Indian runner came to our camp at Fort de Portage and announced it to the officers, they thought nothing of it. However, our captain insisted that we make this attempt."

"Your captain?" Mimi's ears perked up. "Who is he, monsieur? What is his name?" she looked at him expectantly.

"Laloque, Captain Francois Laloque," he replied. "What is it, madame?" Mileaux saw the color drain from her face.

"Your Captain Laloque is the man I have come so far to see."

"You mean . . . you are the captain's fiancee?" Mileau was a trifle more than surprised, as nothing of this had been told to him.

"*Oui*, Sergeant, the captain and I were to be married."

"I did not know, madame—ah, mademoiselle. Forgive me, I had no idea."

Mimi was amused as she thought how the sergeant might have treated her a little differently had he known. But now it hardly mattered. Her treatment in the sergeant's hands, however rough it may seem to her, was far more gentle and caring than she had had since her capture.

"I had no way of knowing. I . . . I," he stammered in his embarrassment.

"Yes, Sergeant, I understand." She leaned her head against the tree. "There is much to explain when we arrive at your camp, Sergeant."

"Mademoiselle?" he inquired.

"It's all right. Francois Laloque and I shall never be married now. When he hears of the misadventures of his Mimi he shall have a quick change of heart."

"*Oui*, white men are not anxious to take a bride once touched by an Indian." The words were no sooner out of his mouth when he realized how thoughtless was his remark.

"Is that all you can think of, Sergeant? I have *not*

been touched by an Indian. It is not what you think at all. *I* have had a change of heart," she said, beating her fingers against her chest angrily. "It shall not be Francois who shall decide such things."

"If it is as you say, then why have you come so far— if not to marry?"

Mileaux had really gone too far. "Sergeant, I don't think I'm obligated to explain my actions to you. And I'll thank you to kindly put a little more thought into your remarks to me. I'd dislike having to pit my word against yours when we reach Lake Erie. Whom do you think the officers would believe?" Mimi had regained her station of a genteel woman speaking to an enlisted soldier. She wasn't as far removed from her former attitudes as she had thought.

"I beg your pardon," Mileaux bowed his head mockingly. "One must forgive the likes of me. My kind are but to serve." He rose and walked toward a clump of birches, nestling among them.

Too late, Mimi realized the mistake of her attitude. She was indebted to the sergeant for saving her from an awful fate, a whipping at the post, and only the Mississauga tribe knew what else. But his attitude regarding her association with the Indians was annoying. His assumption that she had allowed any one of them to make love to her was revolting and more than she could bear to think of. "Sergeant, please forgive me. I had no right to speak to you as I did."

"It's of no consequence. It's my duty. Now, if you are rested we must resume our travels." He began walking on before she could get to her feet and was almost out of sight when she had risen and collected her things. It seemed that he intended to lose her in the forest. Flashes of his colored paint could be seen through the underbrush as he ran. Finally, he reached a clearing where she caught full view of him and was about to call out when she saw him jumped from behind and hurled to the ground. As he and the native grappled, Mimi managed to silently move closer. A large arm rose above Mileaux's head; she swept her knife from her waist and with a lunge inbedded it in the attacker's back.

Sergeant Mileaux threw the limp body from him. "Now, I'm indebted to you, mademoiselle." He breathed vigorously. "You are quick." He pulled her toward him. "We must make haste. The Mississaugas are onto us; others will follow."

As he pulled her along, Mimi stumbled glassy-eyed and unseeing. She had killed again and the horror was just as great as when she had gaffed Jacque. Mimi wondered if she'd ever be as unfeeling as Mileaux had become. He, no doubt, watched men die often at his hands, but Mimi still didn't have the fortitude for it.

The low branches whipped their faces and arms. Only the sergeant was fully aware of the dangers ahead, although Mimi was learning that every tree and bush hid some new hazard that must be dealt with. They had moved but a hundred yards when the sergeant whipped her into the thicket, throwing her to the ground. "There's someone ahead," he whispered as he strained to see.

For a long time he said nothing and Mimi followed his move. "Thank the saints!" he said at long last. "It's my French comrades." As they crawled ahead Mimi could see shadowy figures crouched in the underbrush yards beyond.

"Beaver," Mileaux whispered, then waited.

"Is that you, Sergeant?" one of them asked.

"Beaver," Mileaux repeated, missing through clenched teeth.

"Oh . . . racoon," the soldier finally replied.

Mileaux ran toward the others, crouching close to the ground. "My God man! Doesn't anyone here know the password?" He was whispering as loud as he dared. "I was ready to blow your head off, you idiots!"

"Sorry, Sergeant," mumbled a private.

"You could be much sorrier, Private." The angry sergeant had difficulty keeping his voice civil and quiet.

"Get down, Sergeant," another said, much too loud.

Sergeant Mileaux pulled Mimi along side and inched closer to the others. "Segeant, I should think you'd keep your men on their toes. What seems to be the problem? No password—someone shouts for me to get down when my head is already buried six inches in the dirt. Don't these greenhorns know anything?"

"If you're through with your lecture, Sergeant, we have Mohawks ahead." The man in charge crawled out of the shadows. "They've been on our tail since we were ordered to follow you. Now, if it's more important to read us the rule than take care of these savages, who have already killed Maynard, then get at it," he said derisively.

"What are you doing here?" Mileaux was still angry.

"Major LaDue thought we should back you up, but we got no farther than here when Mohawks killed Private Maynard. They haven't shown themselves since, but we know they're out there. Stay low and keep that wench quiet."

Mimi could hear the conversation as she lay there, still holding her breath. "Wench!" she mumbled under her breath, taking note of the sergeant's tone. This man apparently had no more feeling than the Indians. The niceties of the gentle Frenchmen were definitely fading, at least in this wild land.

Mileaux crawled back to join her. "Trouble,

mademoiselle."

"Yes, I heard. What are we going to do?" she asked unemotionally. Whatever had to be done, Mimi was ready, no longer too frightened to hear the truth. She had pulled herself together quickly after the killing. It wasn't that she was any the less disturbed, it was that the ruggedness of staying alive allowed no time for dwelling on what had been done. One second later was the future and each minute presented another threat which had to be dealt with.

"Wait, they will show themselves," Mileaux reached into his belt and, removing his pistol, handed it to Mimi. "Keep this, and—use it."

"Aren't the Mohawks your allies also, Sergeant?"

"They are British allies and they mean to kill us all. We've already had battles on the Niagara frontier."

"I don't understand any of this."

"I don't have time to explain, either," he said impatiently. "Be alert; they are devils when they attack. And if you don't shoot them first, I suggest you turn the gun on yourself. They are fierce fighters and will torture a captive mercilessly."

Mimi had felt terror before, but the sergeant's remarks held a more ominous tone, too meaningful to ignore, and she had never forgotten the horror of the tortured crew from the ship.

The deadly quiet surrounding her slackened her fear and let the young woman succumb to a needed sleep. She had no more than shut her eyes when she was jerked to life by a large hand seizing her by the braids. She was face to face with a wild-eyed, warpainted native. He pressed a blade against her forehead, ready to scalp. Instinctively, she brought up her knees catching him in the groin. As he rolled in anguish she unhesitatingly aimed her pistol and blew a hole in the savage's head, shattering the forest silence.

Within seconds, a pack of natives, far outnumbering the French emerged from the bushes and with hawk-like cries besieged the soldiers, stirring them into frenzied action. Mimi, caught in the center of the foray, whisked her knife from her belt and slashed wildly, still fumbling awkwardly with her pistol. Seeing an opening, she rolled under a bush grasping a heavy limb as she went. She jammed the limb between running feet so the attacking men stumbled and fell; the soldiers picked them off as they went. Keeping an eye about her, Mimi loaded her pistol with black powder from the metal flask and rammed a lead ball into the barrel. The young French woman was hardly an expert with guns and she spilled powder every which way.

There were two Frenchmen lying dead across the path while others still on their feet were bleeding from their wounds. In horror, she watched them fall, one by one, hideously scalped or ripped apart by tomahawk blows. As fast as it began everything went still—except the deafening thud of her heart. Lying motionless beneath the bush, her face pressed in the ground, there was no sound more desolate than the roar of the silence now ringing in the ears of the panic-stricken woman. Her heart shook her body with its ceaseless pounding.

Seized with the chilling thought that she might be the only one still alive, and totally alone in the forest, she gripped her pistol and crawled along the ground, easing herself toward the bodies.

A low moan rose from the heap. Rising to a crouched position, Mimi saw a hand rise above the dead. Her view was blocked by the mound of bodies. Rising, she stretched as far as she dared, trying to see who was still alive. As she moved she silently prayed that it wouldn't be an Indian playing possum.

For what seemed like hours she carefully scanned the dead men, trying to discern a movement, a blink of an eye. She could see nothing. She wanted to call out, but knew the savages were skilled in the art of remaining perfectly still, hardly breathing, like animals waiting for the right moment to spring.

In desperation, Mimi found her voice. "Sergeant." She tried to keep her voice down moving over the bodies toward him. "Sergeant."

Mileaux turned his head toward her.

"Sergeant!" she said louder, her emotions heightened by the realization that he was still alive. "Thank the Lord you're alive. You're alive!" Mimi chanted rocking his head in her arms.

"But just barely." The man looked up at her managing a slight smile.

"Where are you hurt?" Mimi pulled at his uniform.

"Madame, please! I hurt everywhere. Don't pull at me like that," he snapped. "My worst injury seems to be my right arm. I can't move it." In shock and pain Sergeant Mileaux didn't know that he was pinned to the ground by the body of one of the Indians.

Like a frenzied madwoman Mimi began to haul the dead native away, tugging and grunting with the exerted effort. Mileaux's arm, severely slashed, was wedged beneath the body. With every ounce of strength she possessed Mimi hauled the dead man off of Mileaux. She turned to the dead soldiers and tore strips from their shirts to bind his wounds, then began to pull him from the wreckage toward a rock, where she propped him. She slipped slowly beside him. "*Mon Dieu*! I thought you were dead!" she panted excitedly. Mimi wasn't sure if she would faint as her head reeled, but she fought it knowing she had to help her wounded friend. Alone now, and her companion wounded, Mimi knew that the burden of their safety was placed on her as her friend passed in and out of consciousness, mumbling incoherently. "You can't die," she pleaded on her knees beside him, tears running down her cheeks. She continued to mop up the blood as it seeped through his bandages. "You can't die." Mimi kneeled beside the unconscious solder sobbing uncontrollably.

"Mademoiselle, it is not my intention to do so if I can possibly avoid it." His old flair returned and Mimi pressed her head close holding him to her as he fell into a coma.

She spent the rest of the night holding him, shuddering whenever she thought of the other dead men lying just a few yards from where she sat. And, as the pitch-black forest moved in she imagined everything was out there, watching and waiting to attack. She struggled to keep her eyes open. Every crackle, every whisp of wind sent new chills up her spine. She expected another attack any second, or worse, a bear, a wildcat. She would get no sleep and dared not shut her eyes even for a moment.

To her great relief the daylight began to drift through the trees just before the weakened Mileaux awoke. Mimi was cleansing his face with cool water.

"Can you get me a drink?" he asked through parched lips.

"I found a stream just a ways over. I don't know how I ever got down to it in the dark. I was so scared my bones almost rattled, but I was so thirsty I had to have a drink. I'll get more, be right back." She ran off with a collection of canteens from the battleground.

As Mimi came over the rise from the stream, Mileaux took a long look at her. Bedraggled as she was, in the torn Indian dress, he could still see her beautiful face and penetrating dark eyes. "You know, you're quite a lady." He spoke aloud as she approached with filled canteens. "Are you wounded?"

"No, just scared."

"You don't present a picture of one who is scared."

"All the same, I am. Scared that I would be the only one left alive. Sergeant, do you know that if you had not survived I would probably have died out here in this wilderness. I have no idea of how to manage in a forest like this. I don't know which direction is which, and I would die, just plain die. I thank my lucky stars that you are still with me."

"You can't be as happy about it as I, mademoiselle." Mileaux siled at her as he made an effort to sit. "You know, young lady, you could teach the army a few things. How you came out of a melee like that one, unscathed, is a miracle. This weaker sex is quite something after all," he teased.

"Sergeant, save your strength and your compliments. We've got to be on our way before we are discovered." Mimi felt a little embarrassed. It appeared their roles had been reversed. Now she was issuing the orders.

"They won't be back, at least not that tribe." He winced as he raised his hand to his wounded arm. "Far as they know we're all dead. That, however, does not exempt us from other attacks—and you are right, we must move along. You lead the way." Mileaux was, in fact, pleased that the woman was taking charge. She was toughening to the situation. It would certainly make his job all the easier without a wailing, screaming woman on his hands.

He moved to rise, but fell back, still too weak to muster to his feet. Lying back against the tree weakly he studied Mimi's face. "I'll bet you're something to behold in the proper clothing."

"Whatever that is! It's been a year since I've had

proper clothes. The last of mine were hanging from the rails of the ship that brought me to this horrid land."

Mimi's remark set her to thinking about her appearance. She found it difficult to make a decision whether it would be wiser to remain an indian or trade the garb for a French uniform. It seemed to her, each was equally dangerous in this unsettled country. The only clothing nearby was on the dead men sprawled before her. Mimi began to walk among the bodies. Mileaux watched her stop to remove the breeches from one, a coat from another, finally a shirt. He wondered how such loveliness had grown so hardened to be able to touch the dead men she had spoken with only hours before. Still, he thought, why should it be a mystery, only strong breeding had sustained her through the rough life she had been forced to live thus far, totally different from anything she had known. He admired her spunk and tenacity. Mimi was a fighter in spite of her frail exterior, and Mileaux suddenly realized he was beginning to feel strong affection for this French girl.

Mimi decided her moccasins would have to do since a quick look guaranteed that none of the men's boots would fit and she darted behind a clump of trees and stripped.

"*Mon Dieu*! Mademoiselle, you take advantage of my condition." Mileaux managed a smile, pulling himself up a little higher. As she turned her back, he gasped at the red welts of scar tissue across her white shoulders. He couldn't believe his eyes; even more, he wondered how such a small girl had survived such severe beatings. He had known men who had been unable to withstand Indian torture.

"Be quiet!" Mimi playfully replied, pulling on the breeches. She stepped into full view, picking up a musket from the ground she walked toward him.

"What are your orders, sir?" she said jokingly.

"Mimi, you are really something." He raised his hand, pulling her down beside him. Looking into her eyes he painfully pulled her face to his and pressed his lips upon her warm, sensuous mouth.

"You are too injured for such ideas, sergeant." She gently pushed him away.

"You're right but, the good Lord willing, I shall recover quickly to take up where we leave off."

Mimi laughed as she snuggled beside him. They rested till nightfall.

## Chapter Ten

Mimi was awake the instant she heard Sergeant Mileaux move. Sound sleep was a luxury to Mimi. Back home, at Uncle Nathane's, Elaine used to have great difficulty waking her before noon most days. Here in the wilds it was all different; she had learned to snap to alertness and to keep her weapon within reach.

Mileaux caught her quick action and was reminded of a soldier in battle, so fast were her moves. "We've got to get going," he said gently, his weariness showing in his voice.

"Are you well enough?" She stood beside him as she slapped her stone dagger into her belt.

"I must be, mademoiselle. Besides, we don't have time to find out. It's like another two days to Albany. There are miles of mountains west to Lake Erie before you are delivered to your captain."

"Oh yes! Francois!" Mimi's voice fell. She had certainly lost all eagerness for that meeting. The most it could ever mean now was return passage to France. She was definite on that.

Mileaux offered her a handful of wild strawberries. "This is all I could find. I have a pocket full of hickory nuts when you want them. I'm afraid the forest doesn't give up much in the way of substantial food—except game, and I don't dare take the chance of shooting my musket. This will have to be it for the time being."

"But, when . . . where did you get these? Are you telling me I slept as you went about collecting strawberries? I must have been unconscious not to have heard you."

Mileaux laughed lightly. "You deserve the sleep after all you've done. But, now we've got to be on our way," he said.

"Well, Sergeant, I hadn't thought much of food," she lied. "Why don't you finish them?"

"I have had my share. These are yours. He was completely aware that she was giving up her food thinking he was being chivalrous, which was not at all the case, but he admired her for it.

"Are you sure, Sergeant? You have eaten? You must keep up your strength."

"Of course, mademoiselle. It wasn't exactly a feast, but then neither is yours. Come on, now, let's go," he said impatiently.

"It seems like days since we last ate." She stuffed the berries into her mouth.

"It was." Sergeant Mileaux took her free hand and they continued their cautious walk. Mileaux, still terribly weak from loss of blood, made their progress slow. They stayed along the established deer runs which entailed a risk of being seen that much easier, but he knew it would be fruitless to try to hack new passage through the forest, having such little strength left. At the moment it was all he could do to stay on his feet.

Sometimes the two walked side by side in the wider areas of the runs, always speaking in whispered voices, and Mileaux kept a watchful eye in all directions. He was completely mindful that, in his present condition, another attack would finish them off. He also suffered the nagging realization that his orders to bring Mimi back had become a personal desire, one which he would have to shake. He had no right to entertain such ideas regarding this beautiful woman, under any circumstances, and particularly since her reason for being in Niagara was to marry his commanding officer.

The night continued to hang silently and heavily, making their travel more dangerous. Fallen branches and trees were a hazard, unseen until they were already upon them. The bushes rustled as wild animals darted off, each time reminding them of their need for caution.

Mimi had her own reasons for keeping Mileaux alive, and they were selfish, she knew, but she was more frightened to be alone in the forest than almost anything else. She frequently insisted that he sit and rest, bathing his wounds with water. He leaned on her when he became too exhausted, stretching their tiring trip one step closer to their destination. It seemed to be an exercise in selflessness as each made a determined effort to see to the comfort and safety of the other.

Their bodies ached from the pressure and the need for caution as they wended up the country side toward their rendezvous with the detachment at Albany. Mimi was utterly fatigued and her stomach growled with hunger pangs. It was only when Mileaux stumbled, unable to get to his feet, that they finally lay side by side on a bed of leaves where sleep overtook them again.

Mimi awoke before Mileaux. Her first thoughts were of food. Pulling herself from the uncomfortable place on the pine needles and leaves, she stretched her aching muscles, then began to wander through the trees looking for some kind of nourishment. She smiled as her eyes fell upon a huge bed of mushrooms in a dark pine grove. Dropping to her knees she filled the pockets of the uniform and was back before the sergeant awoke. "Breakfast is served," she said playfully, as he opened his eyes.

Mileaux still had his sense of humor despite his pain and went along with her game. "And, what shall we partake of this lovely morning?"

"A great delicacy, monsieur." Mimi answered with all the aplomb of a hostess, comfortably ensconced in her grand living room.

"Of course! We French indulge in the delicacies. Ah! Champaignon!" he exclaimed with delight as she handed him a hat full of mushrooms and popped one into her own mouth.

Mimi stood and brushed herself off. "Come, Sergeant. It's dawn." She bent to help him to his feet. "As you would say to me: 'We've already dallied too long. The night is gone.' We'll have to travel during the daylight now."

As he struggled to his feet, she took him by the arm. "No need. I'm all right now. That long sleep served me well. I feel we can make good time today. We have, perhaps, a day or more to go. Unfortunately it is daylight and we will have to be extremely careful." He looked about as if estimating their distance from Albany.

"Are you really feeling better?" Mimi was glad to hear a new strength in his voice.

"I do, indeed, mademoiselle, and you shall not have to dawdle awaiting me to catch up or rest so often. My strength is back, thanks to you." He looked at Mimi lovingly. "I would not have made it if it weren't for you." He bent to kiss her.

Mimi weakened as his lips touched hers. It was the first time she had been kissed since her last embrace with Paul Regis. It was the most tender thing that had happened since her capture by the savages. "Sergeant, this can not go on." Her voice was a little firmer than before.

"Forgive me. I've rather overstepped my bounds, I fear." The sergeant became serious. "I have no right, I know. I only thought that if you feel as I do . . ." His voice trailed off as he hurriedly prepared to move out.

Mimi seized his arm. "No, Sergeant," she said laughing. "I can't go on calling you 'Sergeant.' Do you have a first name?"

Mileaux smiled with relief; his initial thought being one of total rejection. "My name is Jean."

"Jean," Mimi repeated. "You can call me Mimi then, monsieur. With what we've been through I think it's time we forget formalities."

Relaxing from his stiff stance, Jean threw his arms around her and kissed her again. Mimi pulled back. Then, reconsidering, she threw her arms around his neck and returned his kiss with enthusiasm. At that moment Mimi wanted Jean to make love to her, but she fought it. "We must be going," she said reluctantly pushing him from her.

Jean could feel the rejection again. "And, we shall," he said with a forced lilt to his voice.

Mimi knew his nonchalance was studied, but laughed as the two again picked up the trail through the forest.

Jean was much stronger, pushing his way ahead of Mimi, constantly surveying the thick patches of brambles and trees. She followed him carrying her musket, her pistol and knife secured tightly in her belt. They had reached the foothills that would lead into higher peaks, and both were panting on the uphill climb under the weight of their small arsenal. Walking in silence they attempted to cover as much ground as possible, until they needed to find shelter and rest for the next leg of their journey. It seemed to Mimi that the Creator had made nothing but stress as she stopped to catch her breath.

"Even finding a cabin, preferably abandoned, would break the monotony of all this, Jean." Mimi had leaned against a willowy young white birch, puffing from the rugged climb. "And, with a bed, of course. As long as I'm dreaming I might as well wish for the best."

"Ah, dream on, my sweet, and include me. Nothing would be more welcome than a soft bed." Mileaux had dropped to the ground beside her.

"I fear they are just that—dreams. There hasn't been a decent bed between this spot I now stand on and my bedroom at home in France." Her breathing was beginning to become more normal as she rested. "I truly miss France, Jean. I don't know how you have managed to stay in this country so long with all this hardship."

"I'm afraid the military doesn't give me the choice."

"Yes, I don't suppose they do, however I doubt very seriously that I would strive as you have to reach my post. I would think that, alone like you are, you'd abandon the whole idea and try to find some method of getting out of Niagara."

"The idea has occurred to me, but you forget there is nowhere to go and no way to get there. Further, the French army would never forget and would hunt me till they could watch me rot in some dungeon. There is nowhere to go but back to the regiment."

"You're right! Where would you go? I haven't seen anything remotely resembling a seaport since my arrival here in America. She leaned back against the tree and peered up through the high limbs over their heads. "Pay no attention to me, Jean, I fear my fatigue is prompting my cynicism. Forgive me, it must be difficult enough for you without all this."

"We'd best be moving on, Mimi. We still have quite a ways to go."

As they again began to ascend the steep incline Mimi thought she heard the sound of falling water. "What is that?"

"There is a creek up above which falls into a small lake. Wait till you see it. I stopped here on my way to your rescue to fill my canteens and clean up a bit. It is well to reach it now; we can camp here while the sun shines." Elatedly he said, "This means we're almost to Albany—one more day or less, Mimi. And, I can tell you, I'm eager for that."

Mimi knew it had been a very bad trip for the sergeant, wounded as he was. Although much of his strength had returned she knew his exuberance was faked at times for her benefit. She often watched him wince as he pulled himself over boulders and through thickets, and admired his strength immensely.

"Unfortunately," he continued, "we shall only encounter more of the same when we reach Albany. I dislike having to break this to you, Mimi, but we are to hook up with the rest of the regiment and continue west to Lake Erie."

"You're very encouraging, Sergeant." Mimi slumped to the ground. "*Mon Dieu*, this is a hard country. I haven't had much time to think of my home, until now, and at this precise moment I would give my soul for a restful sleep in a soft bed in the peace and quiet of my uncle's estate."

"Amen to that," he replied. "It has been three long years since I left France."

"Yes, I almost forgot it is also your home."

"One loses all perspective in this savage land. A minute seems an hour, a day seems a year. There is nothing that changes enough, nothing that makes the morning seem worth the awakening, and life is so pointless and demanding. It takes not only a strong back but a very solid mind. If one dwelled on it, one could go mad."

"It makes one come of age quickly," Mimi added thoughtfully thinking of how Uncle Nathane always castigated her for her childish demands.

"You may call it 'of age.' I think of it more like 'aging.' " Mileaux laughed lightly. "Well, we have certainly become very philosophical haven't we?" He stood, brushing the seat of his breeches. "Can't stop now, we're almost there." He raised a hand to help Mimi to her feet.

The sun caught the drops of water as it cascaded over the narrow precipice into the clear lake. Mimi thought she could see clear to the bottom as she stood at the edge dipping her hand and squealing with delight. Remembering where she was she caught herself and covered her mouth to silence her gleeful sounds.

Jean lagged behind painfully easing himself down the ravine while Mimi removed her clothes and stood naked at the edge of the pool; then she dove in. She came up beside Jean, pulling herself on shore; her dark hair clinging to her shoulders. Jean looked at her full naked beauty. Although marred by the whip welts on her back, it was almost too much for him. He pulled her close feeling her smooth thigh with a wandering hand, the heat rising in his own body. In his emotion, Jean fumbled with his buttons, frantically tearing at his clothes. Then, siezing her again, he clutched her and their bodies pressed against each other. Mimi found she didn't want to resist and, slipping to the ground, they rolled in passion as he caressed her skin and soft breasts. When his emotions rose he entered her body and she relaxed to his desires. She moaned lightly under the writhing of his body and stirred him climatically to the heights of ecstasy.

The day was still warm and they lay there naked and wrapped in each other's arms. Jean remained strangely silent.

"What is it, Jean?" Mimi sat up and spoke softly, but he didn't answer. "Jean, are you all right? Why don't you speak?"

"Yes, Mimi." His voice was controlled and quiet. "This isn't right."

"Dear Jean, why do you say that?"

"I'm an emissary sent to bring you back to your intended husband." His voice was full of reproach. "This is hardly the way to fulfill my commander's orders."

"I'm not going to marry Francois, Jean. I told you that."

"But, he doesn't know that, my love. Not yet."

"What difference does it make? He will soon know."

"Mimi, don't you understand? I have taken his fiancee."

"Fiddlesticks! I shall choose whom I want to make love to me, not Francois. He doesn't own me."

"It will mean the firing squad for me when they find out."

"How shall they find out? Do you think I'll tell them?" Mimi looked at him as he lay on his back, arms under his head staring up at the sky.

"I couldn't help myself, Mimi, and I will do it again and again—if you are willing." He rose, leaning close to her. "Mimi, I want you now and forever. I love you."

"Jean," she whispered as he kissed her soft white shoulders. "That is the wilderness speaking. We are both lonely, both tired and both wishing for much more at this moment."

He kissed her again. This time her passion burned more strongly than his, and she forced him upon her.

Feeling his manhood hard against her, she wrapped her limbs around him, forcing him to enter her burning body. She smothered his face with kisses until the boiling spring of desire bubbled to the brim. Then she fell back to accept his burning body, writhing under his touch. Jean molded her breasts with warm, loving hands, adding coal to the fire of fervor. Mimi thought the thrill of it too much to bear and, caught up in it totally, her nails clawed at the back of her lover until the pent up passion spilled from her as the water spilled into the lake, submersing her in the white heat of it.

## Chapter Eleven

The pair awakened to the early movement of the wilderness. Jean kissed Mimi as she began to dress, all the while watching as she drew on each piece of uniform. She returned his kiss while she fastened her breeches. He bent to kiss her breasts again and again. As each piece of clothing went on they kissed and played until she was fully clothed. Then he grabbed her passionately, pressing his lips hard against hers. Again the swelling emotion gripped them, but Mimi withdrew, and both silently agreed there was no time.

"Where will we find breakfast this morning?" Jean felt much better, his wounds healing more each day, his spirits were brighter than they had been in some time. He felt as though his life had begun anew, and in his frolicsome mood he sprang for Mimi who charged toward the woods.

As if pulled by an unseen rope, Jean was snapped stiffly to a halt. His hand flew to his chest and he twisted in a fall. Mimi shattered the air with a scream that ricocheted from boulder to boulder, tree to tree, as she saw the feathered shaft of the arrow in his back.

Some hours later, the French girl was unceremoniously heaved atop a pile of animal furs in the long hut where men, women and children stared at her. She pulled herself up, curling against the wooden wall.

Down the center of the house fires burned on the dirt floor, the smoke filling her eyes.

The acrid odor of body sweat, hanging meat and manure permeated the entire building. Bundles that looked like bodies wrapped in fur were piled in corners throughout the room. Mimi could see women removing dried and decayed flesh from bones, already partly bare. It was as if they were cleaning the flesh from the bones of their own dead. The strength of the stench was unbelieveably strong. Along the sides of the squalid long house were wooden beds covered with putrid smelling animal hides.

Mimi made attempts to talk to her captors in the Mississiauga tongue and sign language, but they just stared at the frightened girl with questioning eyes. She tried speaking in French, but they didn't appear to understand.

A mumbling from the back of the room turned Mimi's attention as a tall, beautiful Indian woman dressed in the most elegant clothing entered the cabin. With deliberate strides she walked toward Mimi spreading her hands and smiling kindly. "I am of the Onondaga tribe," she said softly.

There seemed to be an unusual benevolence about the woman and totally in contrast to Indians Mimi had known before. She was surprised when she could understand a bit of her language, it being somewhat similar to the Mississiauga she had learned.

"I am Princess Liliyana. My father is Chief of the Onondagas," she said quietly. She sat at the edge of the fur bed beside Mimi. "The warriors thought you were a French soldier. Why do you wear these clothes?" She plucked at Mimi's soldier jacket.

"It was a matter of necessity. I had nothing else to wear." She found that she was not at all frightened by the woman. She was glad that the question of clothing was dropped and didn't have to explain further; the less she had to say about her capture by the Mississaugas the safer she felt.

Princess Liliyana beckoned, silently, to several women standing on the perimeter. In sign language, she instructed them to dress Mimi in the Onondaga costume. Several of the squaws returned shortly with their arms full. Mimi offered no resistance, and when she emerged from the flurry of hands she was beautiful in a white-beaded deerskin dress with flowing strips at the sleeve and hem. Her long hair was caught with a headband covered with small white and red feathers which had been meticulously sewn to the band. She wore necklaces of bone and sparkling silver and a heavily beaded sash was thrown over her shoulders. Mimi had never seen Indian clothing quite so rich.

"These are the clothes of a princess," said Liliyana as she walked around Mimi. "You will be taken to meet my father, Chief Red Feather. Come, we shall go now." She beckoned Mimi to follow.

A short distance from the long house she found herself standing before a very old man handsomely attired in fine leathers and breeches and feathers. He sat upon luxurious pelts and addressed his daughter in sign language bringing laughter to both he and Liliyana.

"What did he say?" Mimi asked.

"He said you were as lovely as the Maid of the Mist."

"Maid of the Mist?"

"Yes," said Liliyana softly. "Not long ago it was the custom for some tribes to offer the fairest maiden to the gods of the Onguiaahra falls. It was believed that the thunderous roar of the falling waters was the anger of this god. Maidens were dressed in the finest skins, with flowers in their hair, and put into canoes filled with rich, ripe fruits and vegetables from the harvest. The canoe would be launched into the water above the falls where it drifted toward the giant flow and the maiden would be swept over the brink. They sacrificed one maid each year, but when the time came that the daughter of a most beloved chief was chosen he was filled with grief. As her canoe reached the brink of the great falls he drifted from his hiding place at the edge of the river. He was willing to leave his tribe and die with his daughter. Not until then did the tribes discontinue their sacrifices, so beloved was this great leader."

The old man in the teepee nodded with a pleasant smile. He gestured to his daughter.

"Come, we must not tire my father," Liliyana said.

Outside the house she directed Mimi into a smaller hut. "This is where I stay. Here, you will share it with me and sleep and eat. We bring you no harm. Our nation is a peaceful nation. Our country is becoming overrun with white men and we have found that some are not as friendly or honest as others. It has caused much upheaval among the tribes of Niagara; breaking them into groups who sympathize with the invading nations from across the great sea. My father fears we may be the last of the great nations who have survived for so many centuries." Liliyana suddenly caught herself. "I am getting too morbid and serious. Come, we shall eat."

It came as a surprise to Mimi that the Indian had, somewhat, the same fears and concerns as the white men. For a moment, she even felt the shame for the white men having invaded the Indian country. She felt the guilt for all foreigners who had usurped the land from its rightful owners. In the midst of her contrition she was overcome by Liliyana's hospitality.

"You look hungry, my sister. Why don't you eat?"

Not until then did Mimi realize that young women had brought the food and placed it before them. "I am, Liliyana," she said gratefully. "It's been a long time since I have had anything but wild nuts and berries."

"Then why do you hesitate? Eat!"

Mimi was uneasy. She had to know why Sergeant Mileaux was not taken captive and alive. She knew the only way to get information from an Indian was to come right to the point. They would either tell you the whole uncluttered truth, or would make it clear that they had no intentions of revealing anything. "Liliyana, please." Mimi hesitated. "Why, if you were willing to save me, did you have the sergeant, who had been my companion these many weeks, killed? He was a good man. He was trying to help me to my destination."

"Your companion?" Liliyana asked in surprise.

"Yes, Sergeant Mileaux was my friend."

"But, you had only an Indian warrior with you, and one from an enemy camp. We thought you were his captive. We are sympathetic with the French, my friend. We were saving your life." There was no question in Liliyana's answer that she had done the white woman a service. It was then that Mimi remembered Mileaux was dressed as a Mississauga native.

Since Mimi felt it would be wiser to not reveal that she was held captive by the Mississaugas she deferred to Liliyana's explanation accepting it as gracefully as her heart would allow; she had learned to feel a strong kinship, if not love, for Jean Mileaux.

Mimi was dumbfounded by the abundance of food and she ate the tender deer meat, squash, beans and delicious fresh peaches, pears and apples. She relished every bite and with renewed strength she no longer feared her captors, talking freely with Liliyana.

"Is this camp near Lake Erie?" asked Mimi as she

nibbled on her food. She found she could eat less than she thought and supposed it was because it had been so long since she had a full meal.

"Lake Erie is many days from here. Why do you ask?"

"That is my destination. I left France many months ago—or perhaps it is years, I have lost all track of time. I have been traveling by foot for such a long time."

"How do you happen to be in Niagara Country?"

"I have come to marry my intended." Mimi had already considered everything that had happened before she spoke. She was still much too untutored as to the relationships of the many frontier tribes and never quite knew what would be the right words to keep herself out of trouble. She was truly alone and never felt safe, even as kind as Liliyana had been.

Liliyana smiled. "I, too, am to be wed. My father and I plan our travel west to Seneca Country. There, our tribes will become as one when I marry Chief Black Bear. I shall then make a home for my husband where the thundering waters fall. I shall request of my father that you travel with us, if that is your desire. We must pass quite near Lake Erie."

"Thundering waters?" Mimi questioned.

"Yes, the falls I spoke of before. This falls flow between the great Lake Erie and Lake Ontario. Many French and English soldiers trade with the Indian tribes near this waterfall. Perhaps there you will find your husband to be."

"I hope so. It has been an arduous trip." Mimi's only hope was to reach a French camp where she might find a means of returning to France. She was also concerned with Francois and his acceptance of the news that she no longer would be his wife. "When do you leave for this waterfall, Liliyana?"

"Seven moons." Liliyana gestured gracefully with her hands. My father and I have stopped among this small band of neutrals so that he may rest before we continue. Tell me, my sister, can you ride a horse?"

"A horse! I—that is, my Uncle Nathane has a full stable at his estate. I have ridden since I was a child. Is that how we are to travel? I hope so, I am footweary and it will be such a delight to ride again."

## Chapter Twelve

Mimi's week at the Indian camp passed quickly. She found the natives to be friendly, even gentle, but they were a far different tribe from that of her hostess. So tranquil were the days spent among these people, Mimi almost regretted having to leave them, but before long she and her Onondaga companions were fully prepared with food and water, and the local tribe had rounded up three beautiful stallions and saddled them with colorful blankets woven by the women of the tribe.

Mimi's only problem was becoming accustomed to riding without a saddle or stirrups. Two days into the trip, however, she was handling her mount with ease. The route was treacherous—over high mountain peaks, then fertile valleys where fruit trees grew in abundance. The orchards brought back memories of those in France. Indeed, her uncle's estate had acres of them. Waves of loneliness seeped into her thoughts again.

As the small group traveled they encountered occasional bands from other tribes but passed without incident. She was happy to be in the company of a chieftain and his daughter. Mimi knew she would have no such safe passage had Sergeant Mileaux still been her leader from the valley. She felt no fear of being ambushed as long as she was with them and it never occurred to her that, as an Indian, she might be attacked by soldiers from her own country.

Cool pine glades became their campgrounds; the nights were frosty, but days were still hot and sunny. Mimi lost track of time, having no idea as to what day or even what month it was. Now, sitting by the campfire, Liliyana mentioned that she would be married during the season of the autumn festival. Only then did Mimi know that she was entering into her second year in Niagara Country.

The two young women grew close during their long journey west. Their many hours together were productive, at least for Mimi. She learned many things about the tribes and listened carefully as Liliyana and her father spoke their words of wisdom regarding the wild land in which she now lived. Since Mimi had no way of knowing when, if ever, she would find a way to return to her homeland, she wanted to know as much as she could for the day when a decision would have to be made. She never harbored any delusions that she would just walk into a French camp and there would sit Francois. She considered it a miracle that she had lived through the experiences so far.

The leisurely pace of the Indian caravan gave the young French girl many hours to do her thinking. Even though she was, in a sense, traveling with enemies—after all Liliyana's warriors had killed Mileaux—she had learned to feel affection for the young princess and her father.

It was a strange land, Mimi thought, friend and foe lurked behind every bush, and yet these very same people could become her greatest aid for reaching her destiny, or the worst obstacle to hinder her.

They were two days from their destination when the warriors set up camp for the chief and princess. They had been riding since early morning and Mimi was ready to dismount and find her legs again. Liliyana remained high, her back beautifully arched and in perfect control of her horse through the action of her legs against the animal's body. Mimi had never learned the "art" of riding except side-saddle and watching Liliyana control the large animal intrigued her. As fatigue from the long ride set in her thoughts drifted back to Nathane's estate and the comfort of a carriage drawn by horses, where one could relax and take in the scenery without the low branches in the face, snakes slithering across the trail and everything else that kept this ride from being pleasant in Niagara Country. She was definitely uncomfortable but still, in spite of her fatigue, she found she was taken with the wide expanses of uninterrupted hills and forest unmarred by man. The more Mimi thought of it the more deeply impressed she became with the virginity of the new world, a subject which had interested her little, if at all, in France. The contrast of the two worlds were impressive and Mimi Pean was in the midst of history being made. Until now, it had meant very little to her, but suddenly she realized she was part of a mere handful of people to observe the wilderness as the Creator had made it.

After camp had been set up Liliyana and Mimi sat near the fires watching the setting sun. "This country of yours is truly quite fascinating, providing one can overlook the immense dangers." Mimi caught her breath. She had already said it and there was no way to recall her words. But, Liliyana found no particular meaning in what she had said.

"Overlook?" Liliyana said a little puzzled.

Mimi laughed. "I know that must sound rather foolish to you. My country has many streets and houses, wagons and carriages, and people fill the streets every hour every day and all night. There is always the theater or the opera or shops."

The Indian girl sat combing her unbraided hair with wonder on her face.

"Yes, I suppose you wonder what I am talking about, don't you?"

Liliyana understood nothing of what she said. Yet, Mimi couldn't help reminisce. It was the first time she had the opportunity to do so; it seemed that she had been away from France most of her life. Tremendous waves of loneliness for Uncle Nathane and her home rolled over her.

"I cannot even envision the things you speak of. We consider our lives very full here."

"Yes, your life is full." Mimi didn't dare continue with what she intended to say. Her life was "full," well into the dark hours of the night, when she was one of the Mississaugas. But that was still a subject she felt wiser to keep to herself.

"And your country? Is it not also beautiful with all these things you speak of?"

"Oh yes, especially my uncle's estate. It is really glorious there."

"Do you miss your country?" It was an innocent enough question for Liliyana, not being aware of Mimi's capture from her ship and the year that followed. Liliyana only knew that Mimi was traveling toward the lake where she would find her intended husband, and she still didn't know Mimi's relationship with Sergeant Mileaux. He had merely represented an enemy to Liliyana's warriors and to them Mimi was his hostage in need of help.

"I do, yes, I do Liliyana. I miss my country very much." She fairly whispered the words as she thoughtfully watched the flickering flames.

"Soon you will arrive at the land of the Great Lake.

Perhaps seeing your intended will cease your longing."

Mimi could say nothing.

Liliyana glanced toward the sky and Mimi knew their conversation had ended. "We must retire early. We are on the last of our journey. I am happy for my father grows weaker and I worry about him. Let us retire to our shelter for the night."

As the remaining embers flickered out Mimi and Liliyana covered themselves in fur and fell into deep sleep.

Hours later, Mimi opened her eyes as if awakened by a crack of thunder. There was a hushed quiet and an eerie forboding as Mimi smelled smoke. Above her head a fiery arrow pierced the hide, burning toward the top. She rolled from her sleeping place and shook Liliyana, but she didn't move. When Mimi turned her over she saw a sharply honed stone blade in her breast. Her hand went to her mouth in shock but she didn't scream.

She crawled through the covered opening as the flames consumed the tent above her. Outside, she saw the sprawled figure of Liliyana's father; a spear pinned him to the ground in front of his still-smoldering shelter. All around lay the dead bodies of their accompanying warriors. Rising to her feet she dashed toward the thick of the forest, little knowing where she was going, and stumbled to the ground, panting.

Her pulse quickened as the air shrieked with hawk cries and the painted natives surrounded her. In a flashing thought she wondered why she hadn't been killed along with the others, when out of the blackness strode a French officer. He bent over the huddled woman, her hands covering her face, afraid to look at what she might see.

"Mimi," someone whispered softly.

Disbelieving, the astounded woman slowly removed her hands and stared into the face of Francois Laloque.

He threw an arm around her holding her close, whispering softly to quiet her. "Come, Mimi we must hurry," he said. She was speechless. Seeing Francois and the death of Liliyana was more than her mind could accept.

Francois slowly lifted her to her feet. She clung to him, not knowing why, as she viewed the painted, half-naked savages gathered around her. It was almost unbelievable that this man was her own Francois, for the shifts from tranquility to trepidation had reached the boundary of what her mind could withstand.

Francois mounted his horse drawing Mimi up behind him, where she clung to his midriff as sobs shook her.

Many hours later the group dismounted, setting up camp in a clearing near a small lake. Mimi still had not spoken, her eyes vacant and glazed as she stared into the distance, unseeing. Francoise talked to her in futile attempts to bring her back to reality, but he was unable to penetrate the wall between her eyes and her mind.

She refused to eat and Francois feared her mind had gone completely as she remained in the state of emptiness. They finally reached the French quarters on the shores of Lake Erie, but Mimi had lost all will to know or care.

## Chapter Thirteen

Francois set up his bride-to-be in her own bark hut near the French trading post, where he arranged for Indian squaws to bring her meals and water. Day after day he looked in, spending hours trying to recall their lives in France, but Mimi never reacted to his touch or his voice. As the months went by, and the cold Niagara winter again set in, Francois was sure that his beloved was lost to him forever and he knew of nothing to bring her back to reality. He ordered the women of the small village to keep the fires of her hut going and to be sure she slept under heavy furs. Beyond that, Francois could do nothing more.

The French trading post, Fort de Portage on the upper rapids of the Niagara River, was like a beehive. Its main building, where the soldiers and their friends conducted their business, was just a few hundred feet from where Mimi lay, her mind still in the land of unreality.

Francois involved himself in his duties—keeping peace among the tribes, and observing the movements of the English army which was edging closer to the French territory. It was not the dream of France to settle permanently in the Niagara Country; they never would willingly leave their homeland for such a wild country, except for the lure of adventure and the bounty of its valuable furs. Captain Laloque's commanding officer, General Pouchot, had placed him in charge of getting the Indians to bring their furs to the French and not to trade with the British and the Dutch, who sneaked into French Territory from Albany.

General Pouchot had made his words clear when he ordered the French military to keep the Indians in a friendly frame of mind. There was always the chance that they would interfere with the plans of the French king. At the moment the natives were content with the profit from the trade.

These problems of duty, and the apparent amnesia suffered by his intended bride, did little to ease Francois's mind. The long hours of haggling with the traders; his daily trips on horseback with the Senecas, their backs loaded with furs, kept Francois on the rim of tension day and night. The banks of the Niagara River were dangerous and Laloque had to be constantly on guard to repel raids by marauding tribes from other areas. The Indians had their own wars between themselves, each tribe vying for jobs as porters along the route between Fort de Portage and the castle on Lake Ontario. The payment of trinkets and whiskey was much sought after and the Indian would kill his own kind to have them. And, as the beaver, deer, bear, lynx fox, squirrel and racoon skins piled up at Fort de Portage, so did the red man, either awaiting payment for his pelts or his labor.

Francois had learned to dread the journeys through narrow paths of thick forest from the fort to the heavily embattled post at the mouth of the lake. Chabert Joncaire, owner of the trading post, had watched the decline of his weary friend, as he suffered with the illness of his beloved Mimi and with the tension of his army duties.

One morning before the drained Laloque mounted his horse, he approached Chabert. "I must have a word with you," Francois said anxiously.

"*Oui*." Chabert was checkng beaver pelts with his storekeeper, Monsieur Martel. "What can I do for you, my friend?"

"I have been thinking, perhaps it would be better if I transferred Mimi to Lake Ontario. There is an army doctor there. These Indian women here can do nothing more for her."

"*Oui*, Monsieur Captain. I think that would be a very wise move. The young lady hasn't seemed to improve these many months. The trip to the French castle would be a very difficult one for her though."

"There's not much I can do about it, Chabert. I expect all the difficult trips she has had since arriving here had much to do with her present condition. I doubt if one more will change much and a doctor would be of help. I must try to get her there."

"Does General Pouchot give his permission, my friend? With all the talk of the British attacks I suspect you will be based at the castle soon anyway, no?"

"I'm quite sure that will happen. There is an order that more troops will be moved to the lower river because of the constant attempts of seige. The British are setting up encampments close by and along the lake shore. I am sorely worried, Chabert, but I feel Mimi will be safer inside the walls of the castle. If she is ever to be safe from harm it will be there," he said emphatically.

"Ah! Well then, Monsieur Captain, by all means take your lovely Mimi and go with God's blessing. It cannot harm her and at least you will have peace of mind."

"Chabert, will you have one of your runners take a message? Mimi will need her own room."

"Of course, I will see to it, but finding room is going

to be difficult. Already they are overcrowded with soldiers and their Indian friends and families."

"I know, and I'm obliged for your help and concern. Please let me know when you receive an answer." Laloque left the post heading for Mimi's lodge.

It was January, 1759; the annual thaw had come and gone and the bitterness of the cold winter set in more fiercely. As Francois plodded on snowshoes through the drifts toward Mimi's hut he tried to devise a method to get her to the castle. It was impossible to think of her on horseback in her condition. And only a few daredevils had attempted the trip in wagons, most unsuccessfully.

"She speaks of Paul." The Indian squaw said when Laloque entered the cabin.

"What of this . . . Paul?"

"I do not know. She speaks only his name, over and over."

"Is there no change, Mara?" Laloque asked the woman, disregarding her last remark.

"None, Captain. She is eating better, that is all I can say." The squaw left the cabin leaving Francois and Mimi alone.

As he sat on the edge of her fur bed he stroked Mimi's long, lovely hair and looked into her vacant expression. "It's Francois, my love." It seemed to him that this phrase was all he had said for months.

Mimi slowly turned and looked, for the first time, at his face. "Francois," she said, without expression.

"Yes, my darling. How do you feel?" He bent low, excited by her apparent recognition. It was the first time she had fully said his name and his pulse quickened with hope. "You remember?" His voice rose with excitement.

"Francois is in Niagara Country. I go there to meet him," she said, still without expression.

The dejected Francois sat beside her holding her pale hand, but Mimi didn't respond. Crestfallen, he rose and left the cabin.

The sound of the closing door stirred the young woman. Had Francois remained one moment longer, or spoken one more word she might have responded, but now she awoke as if from a hundred year's sleep and the cabin and all the surroundings were strange and new to her. Pushing aside the furs she stood wavering from the weakness of her long illness. A fire hissed and popped in the large wall fireplace, but Mimi shivered from the chill in the room. As she shuffled toward the window, the door opened and Mara entered. "Mademoiselle!" She rushed to Mimi's side.

"I'm all right, I am just weak."

"But, you remember?"

"Yes, I remember," Mimi said hesitatingly.

"Mademoiselle, you had better get back to bed you are still too weak to walk."

"I must regain my strength. I don't have time to waste." As quickly as Mimi's sanity had been swept from her she regained it and now everything that had happened was clear. The only mystery remaining was where she was at the moment.

"Is Captain Laloque nearby?" she asked of the Indian.

Mara rushed out into the snow, calling after the captain. Francois, who had just reached the edge of the portage road, wheeled around at her call. "What is it, Mara?" He rushed toward her as she struggled in the deep snow.

"Captain, she has recovered. She calls for you. Hurry!"

He plodded toward the cabin, impeded by the cumbersome snowshoes driving his already high anxiety to fever pitch. "Mimi!" he shouted, rushing through the door. Falling to his knees he grasped her around the waist. "Oh, my darling," he sighed as he kissed her still feverish forehead. "My darling, I thought you would never return to me." He picked her up and whisked her to the layers of fur pelts.

"Francois." Mimi touched his hair lightly. "I am still very weak but I do remember now." She lay quietly as if collecting her words. She haltingly began several times, hestiated, then finally summoned her strength. "I remember the horrible death of my friends, Liliyana and her father. I don't understand it. I don't understand why they had to be killed just for me." Her voice was rising. "Why? Why, Francois? Why did you have to have them killed? They were bringing me to you. Why?" Mimi was now crying and struggling to sit up. Leaning toward Francois she almost screamed, "Why Francois?" Again and again she asked the question, tears streaming down her cheeks.

"Mimi, not now. You need your strength." Francois's blood ran cold, thinking of what he must tell her; of how he and his scouts had thought she was being held captive by Liliyana and her father.

"Francois, why?" Mimi was insistent.

"Darling, you must listen to me carefully." Laloque began to relate the events leading to his finding her with the Onondagas. "We had only received word of your capture by an Indian tribe. A group of soldiers were dispatched to release you, the plan being that Sergeant Mileaux would travel alone from Albany."

She interrupted. "Sergeant Mileaux made it, Francois. He saved me from the Mississaugas, long before I met Liliyana. Mileaux and I had traveled many hundreds of miles before the neutral tribe killed him and took me to Liliyana and her father the chief."

"There are many tribes in this country, some friendly with the French, others not."

"And the Onondagas?" Mimi questioned. "Are they not friends of the French? They were bringing me to Fort de Portage at the upper Niagara. Is that not sign enough that they were friendly. How often do you kill traveling Indian chiefs and their princess daughters. It was evident that we were not a warring band of Indians."

Francois wondered where Mimi got all her strength, her temper was so high and her reaction so violent. "My dear, you must quiet yourself and let me explain. The English are making great strides with the Indians. They are seriously moving into this territory, French territory. We can take no chances. It is difficult to distinguish friend from foe when it comes to the red man, and he has the unhappy talent for changing his loyalty from one to the other without a moment's notice. Their alliances drift so quickly one must distrust them all. It is a miracle that I have found you at all—and alive."

Mimi didn't listen to his explanation. She wasn't hearing him at all. She had only one thing on her mind and that was to tell him about of her change of heart. And, too, she would never forgive him for asking her to come to Niagara, after all she'd been through. All her hatred for him and Niagara came rushing up within her.

Disregarding all he had said she began. "I was a Mississauga squaw for a year and I know the hardships of their life and their torturing ways. I have seen things I shall never forget and, Francois, I have had to do my share of killing. I am not the young, innocent girl you left behind in France and asked to join you here to make a home." She gazed at him with bitterness as she described their attack by marauding tribes while she and

Sergeant Mileaux made their way north, of his death and her recapture and how Liliyana and her father befriended her. "And now, for all that . . . for all I've been through to reach here, to reach you . . . all I have to show for it is a searing brain that refuses to accept any of it."

Francois stiffened as he listened. "Do I understand that you are castigating me for having seen to your rescue?"

This was an attitude she had never seen in Francois before. "I am telling you that these past years have been a nightmare. I would never have believed such a life existed. I have lived through too much horror to ever be the same woman you knew in France. We shall never marry." Her voice was firm and strong, leaving no doubt. Mimi sat up. "Francois, you and I cannot be man and wife, now or ever. I want to go back to France."

"I see." He paced slowly in the small hut. "Your feelings for me have changed, then. Is that it, Mimi?"

"Yes, for you and this awful country. I could never live here as you wished I could."

"And what do you think you will be now, if you return to France?" His remarks reeked with implication.

"What do you mean?" Mimi's eyes glistened with rage.

"It's simple enough. Having been a *squaw* for a full year, as you have said, can you imagine how the gentry of France will receive that news?" His voice was as honed as a saber's edge. "I see you in a different light, my dear Mimi. You are right, of course—we cannot marry. I could never take a defiled Indian squaw for a wife."

"No Indian has ever defiled me!" She screamed with

a sudden, strong surge of fear and anxiety.

He raised a hand to quiet her. "You need not explain to me. I have lived among these tribes for five years. I know what they are. You would be as a pearl among lowly seamen—to be passed from hand to hand, pawed and admired." His voice rose to near crescendo. "Never fear, *madame*, I shall not have you as my wife now."

His emphasis on the word "madame" made Mimi feel faint. Her strength was spent. Francois now knew what she had to tell him. She cared not where she would be sent. Without Paul Regis, Mimi felt her life was over.

## Chapter Fourteen

Chabert Joncaire had, long ago, received word that a place would be provided for Mimi at the castle, but Francois had dropped the matter and even cajoling by Chabert never rekindled his desire to see Mimi to safety. Chabert decided he would pursue the matter no further.

When Mimi's health warranted she walked to the trading post and for the first time she met Chabert Joncaire. He was younger than she had imagined, having heard of the many heroic episodes he was involved in. She judged him to be in his early fifties, but much younger looking.

She made it her business to learn the routines of the portages and to keep abreast of Francois's movements when he was out of the village of Lewiston. She had no desire to lay eyes on him ever again.

During these times she would be entertained by Chabert's affable personality and listen to his tales of the life in Niagara. They quickly became friends. It was difficult not to become Chabert's friend, for he seemed to find something to like in everybody and everything. Mimi hadn't laughed so much for years, and without him she would have starved for companionship, since Francois had so detached himself from her. Chabert was the one who finally saw to it that she had everything necessary to remain alive. The fur jacket and high fur boots for protection against the cold and snow were gifts from him. Mimi hoped someday to be able to repay him, but he asked for nothing and made jokes when she swore her uncle would send him money for the help he had given.

As trappers arrived loaded with pelts she took pleasure helping his storekeeper separate them tying them into bundles for transport to coastal areas and shipment to France. Many of these valuable furs found their way to the shore where Joncaire would fill batteaux for secret shipment across the Niagara to Mont Real. It was while helping at Joncaire's trading post that Mimi learned of these trips and she and Chabert devised a plan whereby she could reach Mont Real and return to France.

Joncaire, aware of the seriousness of the rift between the captain and Mimi was not reluctant to help her. If Francois could just walk away from this young woman, after asking her to come so far, then Chabert would willingly take on the matter as his own. And Mimi tried her best to pay her way, working long hours in the post beside him. Joncaire was quite irate that Francois would not escort the young woman to the castle; and since she would have to wait until warmer weather before her trip, he considered her work at the post a welcome distraction for the impatient Mimi Pean. The work was hard with long hours, but she had nothing better to do and no better friend with whom to spend the time, although the scowling Senecas almost drove her mad sitting silently along the wall and outside the door.

Many of the shipments from Europe, which she unwrapped, contained bolts of colorful cotton and muslins for bartering. They weren't the fine satins and silks Mimi had at home, but nonetheless she wished to make dresses for the warmer weather and found

Joncaire receptive and encouraging when she asked if she could use pieces of the material. The kindly trader didn't have the heart to tell Mimi he'd rather see her at woman's work than trying to do the work at the post. She was a different "sort." Not the kind of woman one would ordinarily find at a rough post. Actually Chabert was uncomfortable having her about, with all the rough talk among the men. He was most enthusiastic with regard to her request for the dress goods.

Mimi spent her evenings fashioning her frocks and hours embroidering fancy stitches on the bodices. It recalled her life in France, where Nathane hired tutors to teach her the fine arts. She thought of her uncle again, longing to see him. Even the insipid young men she thought so distasteful when first she left France began to look good to her, so willing was she to be back home.

As she quietly mused about all that had happened she felt the urge to write to Nathane, something she had not been able to do until now. She ran to her small table and, taking her quill and parchment, jotted a letter.

> *My dearest Uncle Nathane:*
> *Forgive me, Uncle, for waiting so long to write to you. It has not been my doing entirely. This is my first opportunity, and the first time I have had the parchment, to pen a letter to you. I have had occasion to think of your strong arguments for not coming to this wild frontier, Uncle, and I willingly admit that you were right all along. I should never have left you and France. I would never have believed that this country could be so wild and so bewildering. You cannot believe the terror I have lived through. But, at this moment, I couldn't be safer or among better friends.*
> *Francois and I have finally found each other, after almost two years. But, Uncle Nathane, we have agreed that we can never marry. I am presently trying to make arrangements for my return to France. I hope to be there*

*by the time summer arrives, but, Uncle, this country is so unpredictable one can plan nothing. So, until I arrive in France I am respectfully,*

*Your loving niece,
Mimi*

There was much more Mimi wanted to write, but she thought better of it; there would be time enough for that when she returned. Not for a moment did she give pause to the thought, that her dear Uncle Nathane might not receive her letter. She had long ago forgotten that night when he tried to tell her his thoughts—that he would not live long enough to see her return—and she had refused to listen. Even as she folded the letter, ready for the sealing wax, it didn't occur to her that he might not be alive.

"Mademoiselle." Joncaire greeted Mimi as she entered the post. "Spring is upon us. There are only patches of snow in the forest where the sun refuses to shine. I think you should begin your arrangements for your departure for the castle."

"Chabert, do you mean it? We can leave?" Mimi's elation was childlike.

"How well do you sit a horse, mademoiselle?"

"I think I can ride. I am familiar with this new style. I probably will have to learn to use a saddle again when I return to France." She laughed.

"We are not Indians. You shall have a saddle. Several of the French military and I will be riding along the portage trail in two days. They have agreed to see you safely to the castle."

"Not Francois?" Mimi questioned breathlessly.

"No, mademoiselle, I have made sure of that. It would not do under the circumstances, *oui*?" Joncaire gave a little chuckle. "We Frenchmen are more gallant than that." He gave a wide flourish of his hand and laughed vigorously. If something was amusing to Joncaire, and much of life was, it needed laughter; there was little in the man's life that could pass with a mere smile.

"I will be ready when they are," Mimi replied and pure glee forced her to join in her laughter. She was suddenly reminded that she had found little to amuse her, to bring her to laughter, since she had arrived in Niagara, a sad commentary for the last two years of her life.

"Ah, but one thing, Mimi." Chabert turned as serious as she had ever seen him. He touched her arm lightly with his finger. "I must warn you, this trip is a treacherous one. True, it is made many times, but the path is fraught with dangers. I cannot stress it enough."

"I understand and shall prepare myself."

As Mimi left the post and ran to her hut, Chabert looked after her wondering if she truly did understand the danger she was to embark upon. He wondered how much of the conversation she had really understood when the traders spoke of the English movements and the threatened attacks on the great fort on the Ontario.

Swinging inside her hut, Mimi leaned against the door; her eyes closed as sheer joy engulfed her. Just thinking of this step, which would bring her closer to home, rejuvenated her. When she opened her eyes she was shocked to see Francois silently observing her from the small wooden chair in the corner.

"Francois!" she gasped in surprise.

"Forgive this intrusion, but I know of your plans to leave soon."

"Joncaire!" Mimi became infuriated. She knew it was clear to Chabert that she didn't want Francois involved and she was angered by the thought of his betrayal.

Francois raised a hand to quiet her. "Don't blame Joncaire. I made these arrangements many months ago. Joncaire is only seeing that it comes about. I shall not interfere, whatsoever. I simply stopped by to give you this pistol." He drew it from his waist. "Mimi, keep it close. I fear you may need it often before you arrive in France." He strode toward the door, turning toward her as he opened it. "You did say you learned to kill?"

There was a tinge of something in his voice that again infuriated her. "Yes!" Her eyes became slits. "And, I sincerely hope I never have to use it again."

"I can guarantee you nothing. It is many miles to the French post by the portage." He again closed the door, slowly walking toward her. "But, much has been known to happen in those few miles. Mimi, forgive my poor reception to you. I spoke harshly, but you are right, I am quite ready to admit marriage is not for us. Much too much has happened. I don't condemn what you did, but neither can I accept it. I bid you a safe journey and please convey my respects to your uncle when you arrive in France."

Mimi was again angered by his implications. "Indeed, Francois, you have a nerve to come back simply to reiterate your stupid insults to me. You *will* make sure that I understand what you mean when you say what you do, won't you? It is apparent, sir, that you think you are speaking to an illiterate." Her eyes flashed with fury. "There is no need for repetition of something you have made exceedingly clear the first time. I will convey no messages to anyone. When you insult me you insult Uncle Nathane. How could you possibly think he would be interested in your solicitudes after the insensitive things you have said to me. And why do you bother to repeat these infuriating allusions to what are only your suspicions, springing from your narrow mind? My dislike for you has increased beyond all bounds. I hope never to have to see or hear from you again."

Francois's face dropped with astonishment. He had difficulty believing that Mimi could speak so harshly—his mild, sweet Mimi who had never so much as raised her voice.

Mimi noted the strange expression on his face as he fumbled for the latch to make a hasty exit. She was amused to find that Francois was unable to handle her acid tongue, however well he may deliver his own abusive remarks.

Leaving Fort de Portage, where this man was stationed, was inviting, if for no other reason that she would not have to face the possibility of meeting him again. She waved her hand as if to dismiss the entire affair. Her mood was too high to let herself dwell upon Francois's vile attitude toward her.

Elation again swept over her. She twirled, flopping backwards on the thick fur bed and a smile broke across her face. She could leave on her journey, shed of all the venom she had held inside so long. From now on every mile would be a mile closer to home.

## Chapter Fifteen

There was little for Mimi to do to get ready for her journey; it had all been done when first she spoke to Chabert. If she had learned anything from the harsh life in the new frontier, it was to be prepared at a moment's notice. Since it was early May and still cool, she planned to wear her fur parka but made ready a lighter wrap for the warmer days to come. Her fur boots would do as protection against the horse's hide and Joncaire had also provided her with a more delicate style boot to wear with the dresses she had made. She would forever be grateful to Chabert; no one had delighted her more since she left the shores of France. As she packed them in the leather pouch she held them a moment thinking of the day when she would again wear the clothes of a lady. It had been two long years since she had really felt like a woman and she was more than ready.

"Mademoiselle." A young private rapped on her door.

"I'm ready, monsieur." She clutched her bag and threw it over her shoulder swinging out the door, for indeed, she had been up waiting and pacing for hours.

"This way, please. Our mounts are tied by the trading post."

Mimi followed him down the rutty path toward the portage, Corporal Sovie was untying a horse; backing it away from the pack he held it for her to mount. "Joncaire will be right along, mademoiselle," he said as he mounted his own horse.

Inside the post, Chabert pulled on his jacket and beaver hat. "My sad friend." He placed his hand on Francois's shoulder. "Do not be bitter. This poor girl has had a rough time in the colonies. But," he gave a flourish of his hand as he sympathetically intoned, "*Mon Dieu*, she is tough, no?" He looked at Francois questioningly, as if seeking some slight tinge of regret or remorse, some feeling for Mimi and her plight.

Without answering Francois adjusted his tricorn firmly on his head and left the building. He is a sad man, thought Joncaire as he shook his head and strode toward the waiting horses.

Mimi felt comfortable in the saddle and was glad she had it as the path was pitched with steep areas that barely allowed room for horse and rider. There were times when she ducked under low branches; other areas required the horses to file through singly. Mimi stayed between the corporal and the private, with Chabert bringing up the rear. The steep, narrow path made it necessary to keep their steeds at a slow trot. There were the narrow ledges along the very edge of the river and boulders, worn smooth by the sliding hooves and many work animals, protruded along the way. The loud, rumble that Mimi had noticed some time back began to obliterate all other sounds as they moved closer. "What is that I hear, Chabert?" she shouted behind.

"It is the river, Mimi. The Niagara River, and soon you will hear the thunderous falls. It carries across the still air for miles."

His words reminded her of Princess Liliyana. She had told about the falls called "thundering waters." "Will we see these falls, Chabert? She raised herself in the saddle as she shouted back.

"It is out of our way, mademoiselle. Our path veers northeasterly."

"But, I must see it. Oh, Chabert, please. I know it is much to ask but can't we go just a little out of our way? I will never get the chance again."

Chabert Joncaire hesitated. This young maiden has not grasped the gravity of the situation at all, he thought. His first impulse was to refuse her request, but Chabert had always been a man to take chances. Besides, the affable man could never resist a woman's pleas. "There is no such thing as 'a little out of our way,' " he laughed. "But, since we have come this far without incident, perhaps we can. However we cannot dawdle endlessly. Time is valuable, you understand?" He was inclined to diminish the danger of the route, not wishing to alarm his young companion. It wasn't too long ago that she had recovered from a shocking episode that left her near death.

"I do, Chabert, and I am grateful." Mimi could already hear the roar as their path took them up to the great river's edge. The rapids were incredibly fierce as the water boiled in the direction of the cataract. A mist rose high into the air at the brink of the falls, joining the swirling clouds overhead, as the early morning sun hit the mist a perfect rainbow was created, spanning the width of the falls.

The path veered again into the dark woods where old oaks were thickly clustered, their gnarled branches twisted and turned, growing close to the ground then sweeping up to where the leaves shut out the sun. Reaching a small clearing, Mimi beheld the most magnificent sight she'd ever seen.

"Can't we stop here, Chabert?" She didn't wait for a reply; slipping from her saddle she threw the reins over a low limb and ran to the edge where the roar of the water was deafening.

"Be careful. Don't go too close," Chabert shouted after her.

Mimi almost had to read his lips over the roar of the water. The heavy mist rising from the formidable spill of water glistened on her face and hair. She wiped it from her eyes as she drank in the exalted spectacle. Tons of blue-green water cascaded gracefully over the rounded arch of the brink, now smooth from centuries of the water's action. It fell from a colossal height where the weight of it forced it into a deeply recessed pool at the base. Rising again to the surface in boiling rapids, it slammed against smooth boulders, then rotated into the widened river in foamy white circles. The currents from the gargantuan thrust forced the foaming water between the high cliffs toward the lake where it rolled and gyrated around boulders of great height. Mimi was transfixed by the movement.

She clutched an outcropping by the bank to steady herself and to cease the feeling that she was moving along with the water. Breathing laboriously she pulled herself back from the brink to regain control. Never before had she witnessed such a moving experience. She could almost understand the Indian belief that the thunderous roar was some hidden giant whose voracious appetite needed constant appeasement.

She breathed heavily as though she had just performed some strenuous feat, and threw herself on the ground, still mesmerized by the experience. "*Mon Dieu!*" she exclaimed breathlessly as Chabert seized her arm drawing her back from the edge. "Chabert, I am undone. To think I might have missed this had I not insisted. I am truly grateful for your patience." Mimi leaned over and kissed his cheek lightly.

Chuckling at her impulsiveness, Chabert helped her to her feet. "One never ceases to be captivated, mademoiselle. It is no small wonder that the natives of this country pay such high homage. It is, indeed, awesome, no? It has been some time since my travels have brought me to this great falls, but the thunderous roar continues to beckon, always." Taking her arm he eased her back from the edge toward the horses. "We must make haste now. The castle is still some distance."

She had difficulty relinquishing the view and even more difficulty accepting it as real. It took her some time to adjust to her surroundings and for miles she was still absorbed with the great falls, so much so that the real danger along the portage escaped her thoughts entirely. It was quickly brought to mind, however, when a herd of deer bounded across their trail sending Private Lauch's horse rearing up on his hind legs beating the air with his front hooves. Once again, Mimi stiffened in her saddle and was again alert.

"Will we reach the fort by nightfall, Chabert?"

"It is to be hoped, my friend." Chabert Joncaire's lifetime on the frontier taught him never to state anything flatly, there being nothing certain about life along the Niagara. The only reason they wouldn't reach the castle that day would be another ambush and such things he kept to himself, knowing his highstrung young companion.

They continued to move in and out of treed stretches along the river, sometimes high atop cliffs and then straight down steep trails alongside the rampaging rapids where the horses precariously stomped over rocks and loose shale which had fallen from above. Layers of variegated stone could be seen on the rising wall above them, and sparse, scrubby bushes and stunted pines grew from the side.

The roar of the falls became more distant as they progressed and the river unexpectedly cut back into the land. Down below Mimi could see a large eddy of water and the huge recess it had worn into the wall of the cliffs on the distant shore.

"It's a whirlpool." Corporal Sovie anticipated her question. "This is the Onigara Trail where Indian religious rites are held. These are treacherous waters." He pointed a finger towards the swirling circle of water. "A canoe will spin for months before it hits the current which will throw it back into the flow. Sometimes it never does and sooner or later is dragged down beneath the water."

"I'm beginning to understand the need for the portage trail. It is certain death to attempt navigation isn't it?"

"Navigation is impossible, mademoiselle, between the upper and the lower river. From the falls you saw back there to the heights of Lewiston there is nothing but rapids and certain death for anyone trying to navigate it. Of course, once past Lewiston it is a quiet, peaceful canoe trip to the castle."

"How long have we been traveling corporal?" she asked.

Sovie pulled his collar around his neck; though the sun shone brightly the coolness of the forest remained and clumps of snow covered the ground amid the trees. "It's long enough for us to stop and have something to eat. I brought along wafers and dried fruit. The sun's already in the west so we'd better stop at the next clearing."

The path again took them below the cliff to the crushing water's edge. Corporal Sovie reined and tied his horse and pulled a packet of wafers from his saddlebag. The narrow ridge of land along the shore allowed just enough clearing for tethering the horses. Finding a smooth rock, Mimi sat in the sun where Chabert joined her.

"Hasn't it been peaceful for so dangerous a trip, Chabert?" Mimi asked with a good deal of question in her voice. Her other treks through the forest had taught her a wariness only seasoned frontiersmen possessed.

"Be thankful, mademoiselle. We have had an exceptionally good day. The Senecas have been momentarily satisfied since more porters have been hired at the post."

Mimi nibbled on her wafer. It occurred to her that Chabert had employed more porters thus enabling their party to reach safety, and she wondered if he would have done so if she were not along. However, Mimi didn't persue the idea. She was too intent upon reaching the security of the fortified castle to want to know of the inconvenience she might have caused. She quickly changed the subject. "Is this the route to Lewiston?"

"Not really, mademoiselle. This is an Indian route; the portage we take is up above us and more direct. We should reach it shortly. I think it would be wise to get back on it." With a wry smile Joncaire continued, "We lost time with our detour."

Mimi flushed with embarrassment. These were the first words that resembled a rebuff from Chabert and she was glad she hadn't questioned him further about the porters. "I hope it doesn't mean trouble for us."

"Joncaire plays with you," he said laughing. 'We are not that far off. Just above is the connection."

"Well, I'm ready." Mimi stood, brushing her hands on her breeches.

Joncaire stood, stretching his arms above his head and groaning with a pleasurable sound. "*Oui*, mademoiselle, that is a good idea. It is too delightful sitting here. It makes one forget one should be more wary."

Once again mounted, the group began to rise steadily up the slope. The way was narrow and dangerously steep. The horse's flank muscles rippled as they hauled themselves and their riders up the incline, hooves kicking small stones, sending them hurtling down where they resounded on the boulders along the river, the echoes reverberating from the opposite shore. Reaching the regular portage route they rode down into a well-worn flat ribbon of road.

Mimi was unexpectedly shaken with fright when Private Lauch jolted his horse with his sharp spurs, speeding the animal off ahead of the others.

"What is it, Chabert?" her heart skipped.

"We've reached the heights. Don't worry, little one. Private Lauch is just scouting ahead a little."

Mimi couldn't quite settle with Joncaire's answer. She knew his way of hiding dangers from her and for the first time she felt for her pistol. She was reminded that it wasn't a pleasure trip she was about, even though she had treated it as one, insisting, as she did, upon stopping at the falls. The private's action brought back visions of other ambushes she had seen and she vowed that she would act more realistically in the future.

Joncaire reined his horse beside her shouting instructions. "Sit your horse well, mademoiselle, we have reached the heights. This is a dangerous downhill ride. Give the horse his head. He's made it before so don't rein him in. If he slips try to release your feet from the stirrups and roll off."

Such instructions were beyond Mimi. Never before, had she been told to roll from a moving horse. Almost before she was prepared for it, her steed began slipping and sliding as the earth tore away from its hooves. The horses panted as they worked their way down the incline. Mimi's impulse was to pull her horse up tight but remembered Joncaire's admonition and it took all her concentration to stay in the saddle and the reins loose.

Private Lauch's horse lost its footing and fell sidewise against Mimi's lathered steed. She swayed in the middle clinging with her knees as she had seen Princess Liliyana do. Mimi's brain reeled from the excitement and the danger. Reflex action caused her to pull the reins hard and her horse whinnied as the bit cut deep.

"Loosen the reins. Give him his head!" shouted Chabert.

The horses broke into a fast clip across the open flatland where they all pulled to a full stop at the base of the heights.

"Well done, my dear—it's over!" Joncaire sat in his saddle laughing gustily. He thoroughly enjoyed the thrill of it all.

Mimi, on the other hand, was shaken, though it hadn't been nearly as dreadful as she had anticipated. "That's it?" she questioned.

Joncaire waved a hand through the air, indicating the land. "This is Lewiston. We shall stop awhile at the trading post before we continue to the fort."

"How much farther is it?" Mimi's excitement was rising. She never dreamed they would reach the heights without some encounter; especially after what Francois had said when he gave her the pistol. Even going out of their way had caused no problem. And now she realized that she could have been the cause of someone's death had it been different.

"Just a slim mile, mademoiselle, to the Lewiston trading post and once again at the water's edge."

Mimi recalled a brief glimpse of the winding river

through the trees on the arduous descent, but she was too busy to appreciate it fully. "I'll be happy to reach this trading post, monsieur. Not until now did I realize that I am beginning to feel the horse's backside. I could use a rest from this animal."

Joncaire laughed. "Here we go, then." He spurred his horse ahead of the others down the wide muddy road toward the river.

As Private Lauch collected the reins, Chabert escorted Mimi into the large bark hut. There were other huts around the village occupied by Indians, the children playing and women working in the doorways. Inside the post, more Indians sat on the floor in rows against the wall. At the rear of the building a figure was busy stacking furs and hides.

"Daniel!" Chabert called out. "Come, Mimi, and meet my brother."

This new country had been just one incident after the other for Mimi Pean, but here and now, she could not be more surprised to learn that Chabert had a brother. Never in all the months she had worked with him at his post had he once mentioned his family.

## Chapter Sixteen

At the sound of his name a short, stocky man with full beard turned from his work. "The Mademoiselle Pean has arrived I see—and all in once piece." He laughed loudly, much like Chabert. "I trust your journey was not too much for you, young lady?" He extended a rough, calloused hand toward her. "Ah, forgive me, I forget myself. I should kiss your hand, no?"

"It hasn't been done for some time, monsieur." Mimi smiled.

"That is a shame. Such a beautiful lady should always be kissed." His eyes twinkled mischievously. "Allow me to be the first then." He bowed low, taking her small hand and planted his bush beard against it. "*Enchante*, mademoiselle," he said in the fashion of the gentry of France. "Welcome to our humble establishment."

"I certainly never dreamed that I would have the pleasure of meeting another Joncaire. Chabert, you have been keeping secrets." She waggled a playful finger at her friend.

"What's to tell—he is nothing!" Chabert waved his hand toward his brother and boomed with laughter. "You have already met the greatest of the Joncaires." He placed a hand on his chest.

"Ah huh! You believe this one and you will believe

that it snows in July." Daniel played along. "I have taught him everything he knows," he tossed back.

The three laughed at their clowning. Mimi had no difficulty believing the two were related; the same affable personality displayed itself as they amused each other.

"It is good to have you here." Daniel returned to Mimi, ceasing his horseplay with Chabert.

"I'm afraid it will be a short stay, I hope to make the castle before dark."

Daniel turned to Chabert and frowned. How had she gotten the idea she would be at the castle before dark? But he said nothing when Chabert indicated he should remain silent, by a slight wink. He returned immediately to Mimi. "But yes, my father's castle." Daniel smiled proudly.

"Your father's castle?" Again Mimi was surprised.

"*Oui*, if it were not for my father the King of France would not have built this fine castle."

"I'm really impressed." Mimi looked at both men. "Chabert, you are full of secrets, first a brother, and now a famous father."

Chabert laughed. "There is too much to tell about the Joncaires, and it is boring—besides, I would not know where to begin."

"You've really piqued my interest now. You're going to have to find somewhere to begin, I want to hear it all."

Daniel threw an arm around his brother. "Speak to this one. He knows more than I. After all, is he not the eldest?" He threw a look at Chabert, his eyes twinkling with his delight in the insinuation that he was so much younger.

Chabert took it in stride. He and Daniel were always joking with each other in this fashion. But it was apparent that they shared a great respect for each other.

"He was a great adventurer and soldier in His Majesty's service, mademoiselle," Chabert began, becoming more serious. "Our father, Louis, was one of the first white men to live among the Indians in this country. If not for him, I would not be here today, nor would Daniel." Chabert smiled devilishly. "Come to think of it, that wouldn't be all that bad." He laughed loudly as he slapped Daniel on the back. "But, back to our father. When his troops were set upon by the Indians he went into a rage as a savage tried to tie him to the stake for burning. You see, the red man attacked Louis's fighting outfit, and he was the only one to come out alive, but only because he fought and gained the red man's respect. His fighting comrades died but the Senecas adopted our father into the tribe." He laughed again spreading his hands before him. "He is responsible for all this—this trading post and the village around it and the post Fort de Portage from where you have come. Daniel and I merely carry on what he began years ago."

"Don't tell me I am to meet another Joncaire when I reach the castle?" Mimi laughed.

"No, mademoiselle." Daniel smiled broadly clapping a hand on Chabert's back. "We are the last of the Joncaires here I'm afraid." Chabert made a playful lunge toward Daniel and the two danced about in a mock fistfight, feigning blows that purposefully missed their mark. Then, throwing their arms around each other, they laughed at their game.

"You two are really a pair." Mimi shook her head. "You *do* enjoy life don't you?"

"*Oui*, is that not what it's for—to enjoy?" asked Daniel.

"I used to think so, before I came to Niagara, now all I can think of is getting back to France."

"First we get you to the castle," Daniel said, rubbing his hands together. "Your intentions are to then try to find passage home, no?"

"Yes, I must," she said forcefully.

"I am to have the pleasure of escorting you to the great stone house as Chabert has arrived at his destination."

Mimi's expression contorted slightly at this news. She hadn't learned that Chabert would be leaving her group when they reached Lewiston. She wondered, but even if ordinary politeness kept her from asking she would not ask anyway. Now, after two years in this country, she had learned that much was military and most was secretive.

Chabert took notice of her furrowed brows. "No fear, my friend, Daniel will lead you through the savage territory." He gestured toward the row of Indians against the wall.

"Monsieur, they will hear you." Mimi was astonished that he would speak so bluntly before them.

Daniel's booming laughter shook the cabin. "I have lived among them since birth and now follow my father's footsteps. Like him, I tell them only what I want them to know. They understand me and I them." He changed the subject abruptly. "Now then, remove that heavy jacket and sit for a while." He motioned to a small wooden chair by the open fire. "I will be but a moment."

Daniel placed his arm around Chabert's shoulders and the two men walked out the door toward the waiting soldiers. Mimi felt strangely uneasy as the rows of men silently stared at her. She could hear the Joncaires continue their clowning as Chabert mounted his horse and Daniel boomed loudly all the way back to the trading post. Mimi's troubled expression hit him directly as he entered; the glaring faces of the natives conveyed various ideas of intent regarding the lovely French woman. Flailing his arms in anger, Daniel screamed at them in the guttural sounds of their language, ordering them from the building.

"I'm sorry. It is my fault. I should have thought."

"You don't seem to worry about retaliation. I know they can be exceedingly dangerous. Surely I am not telling you something you don't already know." She shifted uneasily. "I would as soon have nothing to do with these people. The sooner I am away from them, the better."

"This is so. And the truth of the matter is—they retaliate, as you say, for everything that displeases them. And, mademoiselle, much displeases them. They are not to be trusted." Daniel cocked his head to one side in thought. "If one stops to think of it, one can not blame the native Americans for what they do. We would not like it either if some other nation took our land—conquered us as we have them. Anyway—" He waved his hand to dismiss the thought. "They know Joncaire. His bark is much worse than his bite. I am the second generation to live among them and they know we treat them well. They show me respect as they did my father. Oh, we have our differences and we settle them with strong measures, but that is the way it has to be." Daniel pulled a chair beside her and sat down. "Don't worry, little one, everything will work out."

Mimi wondered about the man's brashness. She judged him to be in his early forties, and he possessed a strong appearance, a ruggedness that spoke of his many years out of doors. She knew no man could live his life on the new frontier without spending a good share of it fighting with hostile tribes. Daniel had done this, it was clearly written on his face. Still, he had an easy way about himself, as did Chabert; she was relieved to know such a man would escort her the rest of the journey.

"Now, mademoiselle, about the trip to the fortress—" Daniel abruptly stopped as a loud bustling noise from outside interrupted him. He charged to the rear of the building seizing his pistol from a shelf and as though knowing what he would encounter on the other side of the door, he ran out. Mimi watched from the open doorway.

Pushing himself through the crowd he wrapped his muscular arms around the neck of one of the fighters. The muscles rippled as he pulled the man from his opponent, choking off his breath. Daniel's feet were ruggedly planted on the ground and the cords of his neck protruded with his effort. The Indian dropped to the ground, gasping and clutching his throat. Placing a hand on his pistol in the belt of his homespun breeches, Joncaire shouted in French, interspersed with the Seneca language, as he waved his arms to scatter them all from the area.

The onlookers shuffled toward their huts as Joncaire hauled the prone man to his feet. Shoving him down the path Daniel walked slowly to the trading post, keeping his eyes constantly on the man.

"What was that all about?" Mimi asked as he entered.

"You, my friend."

Mimi gasped.

"It is to be expected. These savages know great beauty when they see it," he laughed. "But, don't worry, Mimi, they will not try anything as long as Daniel is about. However," he said seriously, "I think it would be wise if we did not attempt to get to the castle tonight. It grows late and these people do not forget quickly. It would not do if they attempt retaliation along the trail. You can stay with me and my wife. One more day will not hurt, *oui*?"

Her mind was swept with terror at Daniel's words. She wished she had more control over her own destiny, but knew she was totally dependent on Joncaire's protection. There was nothing else she could do. So, reluctantly, she agreed to stay the night, silently cursing Francois for his part in her being in this savage land.

## Chapter Seventeen

Daniel Joncaire's wife was a seasoned woman. To Mimi's surprise she was an Indian and behind her somber face were traces of her fading beauty. She welcomed Mimi with little explanation from Joncaire; her attitude was one of acceptance, as though used to strangers putting up the night in her cabin. But she was quietly friendly. After the meal she hoisted a lighted candle to escort Mimi to a small room at the back.

It wasn't until Mimi sat on the bed that she was totally aware of her fatigue, and for the first time since leaving Fort de Portage she felt she could relax and get some rest. Mimi had hardly removed her outer garments and stretched across the bed before her breathing became steady and deep.

Hours later she was aroused, unexpectedly, by the feel of a hand on her arm. Mimi's reflex action coiled her into the corner of the bed, coming face to face with the fighting savage of the previous day. Before she could react, he clamped his hand on her mouth; she could feel his breath on her bare shoulders. Her struggling was ceased by the weight of his body across her own. Tearing at her night clothes he threw a leg over her, straddling her body. Mimi was prepared for the worst. She knew she must relent or loose her life resisting. Everything in the room began to spin; she was ready to faint. But she was shocked back to the present as a pistol shot shattered the air, the impact sending the man backwards to the floor.

Mimi screamed. She could see Prisella Joncaire's smoldering pistol, her face strong and serene. Silently, the woman walked off leaving the disheveled Mimi alone with the dead intruder. Her impulse was to run but there was no way out except over the dead body. She again curled into the corner of the bed like a small child. Muffled voices emanated from the front of the cabin. Two soldiers entered the room and hauled the body from the cabin. Mimi rose, still shivering from the attack, and threw the fur robe from the bed over her shoulders. She followed the body bearers to the front of the cabin watching as Prisella closed the door on them.

"You are not hurt?" There was still no strain or strong reaction expressed in the woman's voice or manner.

"No, just frightened." Mimi's voice quavered. "Where is your husband, Madame Joncaire?" Now, more than ever, she wanted to leave and get to the safety of the French haven on Lake Ontario.

"Trouble on the portage route," answered the Indian woman. "He left hours ago. There is no saying when he will return."

Mimi's heart fell as hope faded. Prisella's indifference was mysterious to her, and she thought she'd cry at one more discouraging word from the Indian woman. "How did that man get into my room?" Mimi asked.

"I fell asleep. He walked right by me."

Mimi was aghast. "Is there nowhere where one can be safe in this country?"

"No, there is nowhere."

The woman was so matter of fact that Mimi wrung her hands in frustration and paced the floor of the small room. Finally she sat on the bench on the other side by the fire, studying the Madame Joncaire. "It doesn't bother you to kill, Prisella?" she finally asked.

"No."

For what seemed like an hour she continued to rock before she went on. "It is part of my life. I had to learn to kill very early. You live with a man like Daniel and you must learn. I was a young woman when first I killed. One grows used to living this kind of life. Death occurs frequently. I had to choose between that or my Daniel. As you can see—I kill when it is necessary."

Mimi drew her wrap tightly around her and shuddered as the woman spoke with such lack of feeling. "Well I shall never be used to it."

"If you stay in this country you must learn a different way of life. One cannot escape it."

Mimi covered her ears to shut out the woman's words, but nothing helped. They seemed to be seared in her brain. She remembered those men she had already killed to arrive at this point of her journey. Still, she was sure she would never reach the time when she would take human life for granted as did this woman. "When will your husband return?" Mimi asked.

"It is difficult to say. When trouble arises on the portage he could be gone for days. I just wait."

Mimi grit her teeth and silently seethed. Prisella Joncaire may be used to the awful life on the frontier, but Mimi had only thoughts of returning to France, and in no way was she ready to abdicate the idea. Reaching Lake Ontario was uppermost and she felt absolutely drained of hope since she was totally dependent upon the Joncaires for help.

"I think it best if you go back to your bed and get some rest." Prisella slowly rocked in her chair.

Mimi watched her and thought, *Mon Dieu*! Will that

be me in a few years from now? Then turning to Prisella she said, "I can't go back in there again."

"Very well," the stoic woman replied. "Stay by the fire. It is but a few hours till dawn." She closed her eyes and continued to rock.

Mimi sat staring into the flames, fuming with the delay in her plans. Of course she couldn't blame Daniel. She had great respect for the man and the hard life he had. Again her thoughts turned to the woman sitting beside her and Mimi realized that Prisella had had a very rough life—in many respects, worse than Daniel. He loved the wild land and the challenges it presented, even delighting in the danger of it, while Prisella's life had an entirely different meaning. She could only sit and wait and protect the home in her husband's absence. Thinking about it all, Mimi found herself respecting Prisella more. She stretched out on the long bench pulling the fur blanket snugly around her, and after a little fighting she succumbed to sleep.

When she again opened her eyes the cabin was eerily silent. The sun was just coming up, it's warm rays glistening through the single window of the cabin. Mimi knew she was alone. She called to Prisella but received no answer. Dashing to her room she drew a dress from her leather pouch and pulled it on. As she re-entered the main room Prisella came through the door.

"There's cornbread on the hearth." She pointed to a heavy black metal pan.

"I'm not hungry right now. Has your husband returned? I must be on my way." The words spilled out in her impatience.

"What do you mean you are not hungry? You must eat."

The woman meant business and, obviously, Mimi was going to get nothing from her until she had eaten. So she cut herself a slice of corn bread and slumped on the bench to eat. "Your husband has not returned?" she asked again.

"No. I have been to the trading post. He has not yet returned."

As little as it was, it presented some hope to Mimi. "What am I to do, Prisella?"

"You must learn patience. Daniel will be back." She busied herself around the cabin.

"I won't wait!" Mimi burst out in an act of childish frustration.

"A tantrum?" Prisella looked at her with those dreadfully unfeeling eyes. "There is no one in this village to appreciate your difficulty."

Mimi was stunned by her uncompromising attitude. Why was she so insensitive to her plight? Mimi pulled herself up full height. "This life may be all you could ask for, but as for me—"

Prisella swung around facing Mimi, her eyes fierce. "You are not in France."

Mimi knew she had gone too far. Prisella Joncaire had a breaking point in spite of her hard exterior.

The older woman's voice softened as she went on. "I know of your trouble. I still say—patience. Now, come with me. You will help at the post until Daniel returns." She left the cabin with Mimi falling in behind.

Prisella had always said *when*, never *if*, Daniel returns. This must be where this woman gains her strength to go on, thought Mimi. It was her faith that had sustained her all this time. And, with this new insight, Mimi began to realize that her loss of hope would be more fatal than any of the other dangers on the frontier. Her admiration of the older woman increased."

Prisella, even at her age, could heave a bundle of

heavy furs on a pile and hit her mark. She swiftly slit the leather thongs, separating the heavy furs into piles on the long table. Along side the Indian woman's bulky frame stuffed into a man's heavy shirt and homespun breeches, Mimi's dress was incongruous. To say the least, she felt overdressed as she watched the older woman and listened to her big boots clump back and forth on the plank floor of the hut. Mimi began to feel encumbered as her dress began to get into her way when she bent to lift the bundles. But she was adamant in her desire to return to France and she struggled along as best she could. However, it wasn't long before she again appraised the older woman who stood beside her. This is nonsense, thought Mimi. If I am to survive any of this hell I must show some common sense. She whipped her skirt up, wrapping it around herself, exposing heavy knit stockings. Her slim, shapely legs extended up from her boots presenting a humorous study, which didn't go unnoticed by the expressionless Prisella.

Late in the morning, the quiet of the small village of Lewiston was broken by the clatter of horses beating down the rough dirt road. Prisella hesitated a moment in her work, never changing her expression. Both women hurried to the post entrance. Daniel dismounted while several Indians and French soldiers tethered their mounts to the rail.

"Ah, Prisella!" Daniel threw open his arms as he approached and gave his familiar laugh.

"You're wounded," Prisella said quietly.

"It is nothing. Don't fret, woman. We are hungry. It has been a long ride." Throwing an arm around his wife, he walked with her toward their cabin.

Mimi remained behind watching the soldiers talk among themselves. She strode to the hitching rail where Corporal Sovie leaned as he talked to the others.

"Corporal, what happened? Was it the portage route again?"

"Yes, another fracus on the route, mademoiselle." He touched his hat lightly. "The British have set themselves to take over the Niagara frontier. Anyway, for the time being it is settled."

"The British?" she asked in surprise. "Then it wasn't Indians?"

"Well, it was and it wasn't." Corporal Sovie shoved a hand into his pocket as he leaned against the rail. "It was Indians, except they were fighting for the British. Them redcoats haven't really shown themselves yet, but they're behind all the trouble. Some of their Indians tonight were our own just yesterday. You can't ever be sure about 'em."

"Do you think I will get to the castle?" Mimi had convinced herself that her only safety would be there. She held the illusion for some strange reason, that it would be a piece of France, a haven and immunity from the plague of hostilities which surrounded her wherever she went.

"I would guess that you would get to safety soon, mademoiselle," Sovie replied. "We are riding there today after we get some rest. The French militia from Fort de Portage will arrive some time later, and then we are to join General Pouchot at the castle. It is probably wise to prepare to go with us. Have you talked to Joncaire about it?"

Running for the cabin she bounded inside interrupting Daniel and his wife who abruptly stopped their conversation. Again it appeared that Mimi attached little meaning to their actions. "They are going to the fortress today, Prisella."

"I know," the woman answered.

"Can I go too, Daniel?"

"Oh, *oui*, Mimi. They must go, and it seems you should take advantage of it, no?"

It almost went unnoticed that Prisella was cleaning a wound in Daniel's shoulder. "Oh! Daniel, I didn't realize you were hurt."

"One more scratch to add to my scarred body," he laughed.

Mimi could see healed wounds covering his back and chest. She wondered at the man's tolerance and at Prisella as she tended his wound so tenderly, yet so dispassionately. She couldn't believe that she would ever become so hardened.

When his wife had finished Daniel reclined upon his bed in the front of the cabin. "Awake me in an hour, Prisella." He immediately fell into a deep and heavy sleep.

Mimi approached the older woman, watching her poke up the fire. "I want to apologize for my behavior before. It's just that I can't reconcile to this harsh life. My desire to return home confuses my wits."

Presilla looked up from her kneeling position, her face somber as ever. Pushing herself to her feet she wearily slumped into the chair beside the fire. "I remember when first I came here," she started slowly, eyes steadily on the flames. "I was much younger than you, just thirteen. Daniel's father brought me from my father's land, far north of Mont Real. My father promised me to Daniel when I was five. There were many times when I felt as you do now. I bore my children alone, as all Indian squaws do. Daniel and I had thirteen children—none of them lived. I learned patience. You must too, if you are to survive. You must cease your childish ways. They are of no use to you here in this land." The woman's voice took on momentum as she talked. "It has been your own strength which has kept you alive. Is that not so?" She looked piercingly at Mimi who was, indeed, listening closely.

"Look at your hands." She pointed toward Mimi's folded hands with a wooden spoon. "They are already calloused, are they not? What makes that so? Tell me how you have survived long enough to reach this village. Tell me how you are in this land. Tell me."

Mimi could feel the strength of her questions. They were not idly asked; she wanted Mimi to think of how much it had taken to reach this very spot where she now sat, still straining toward a goal she had set upon herself.

Mimi looked at her hands, turning them over. "Yes," she said softly. "I had not realized. I have been here but two years and already I have been taken captive and made to live the Indian life. I have fought and killed." She again looked at her hands. "You are right, Prisella, I am stronger than I think. I have become hardened. I was not carried here, I had to walk, fight, crawl and kill to get this far." Her voice became stronger.

Prisella stirred the boiling pot over the fire, confident that she had, at last, inspired the young French maid by forcing her to gain strength from the strength she had already expended. She looked firmly at Mimi. "Rest and be ready when Captain Laloque arrives."

## Chapter Eighteen

"Francois!" Mimi was jolted to her feet by Prisella's words. "He is coming here?" Her voice was shrill. "I don't wish to see him." She threw her hand in dismissal, as if by doing so she could rid herself of the whole event.

Prisella looked at her sternly. It was clear that her constancy could give way to a violent temper if she was provoked. "You flit like the birds, here and there. You cannot decide. You try my patience." Prisella walked away from Mimi showing her total disdain for her and her fleeting attitudes.

Mimi tagged after her. "But, this man, you don't know how he has treated me, Prisella." She was trying to retrieve the woman's respect. "If it were not for this man, I would not have suffered all that I have—nor would my hands be so calloused—nor would I have killed." Mimi's voice was at it's height of shrillness.

"Aark!" Prisella waved a hand showing her irritation with the girl. "You must learn to be patient—and to be quiet."

Stiff-backed Mimi stomped into the small room where she had slept. Her anger rose to fever pitch. Again she wanted to scream or throw something in her anger. How dare this woman speak to her like that? How dare she? Mimi threw herself on her stomach across the bed and kicked her feet until she had unwound, then relaxed she rolled over on her back staring at the ceiling. Her expression had changed from one of anger to one of tranquility. "You are absolutely right, Prisella," she said aloud and yet to herself. Mimi rose abruptly from the bed, stomping determinedly to where Prisella sat. "You are absolutely right, Prisella," she said firmly. "It makes no difference who arrives at this post nor who accompanies me on the trip to the fortress. You are absolutely right." She said it with such fervor Prisella shook her head at the waxing and waning of this spoiled young woman. Mimi stomped out, returning to her room and began to pack her trivial possessions.

At last her common sense took control. Mimi removed her dress, folded it, and donned the breeches and jacket she knew would be more practical for her trip by horse. As she packed her shoes and dress her hand fell upon the pistol Francois had given her at Fort de Portage. She stuffed it into her waistband with determination. Then with strong, deliberate moves she twisted her hair into a chignon, pushing it up under her cap. Picking up her saddlebag she re-entered the main room where Daniel still slept and Prisella quietly rocked in front of the fire. Mimi dropped her pack to the floor and sat on the bench to await the hour of departure.

"No dress this time?" Prisella looked at Mimi.

"No, not this time. I have decided to be practical. That should please you."

"It's of no matter to me, one way or the other."

"Madame Joncaire, my only thought from this day forward is France. And, thanks to you, I shall earn it for myself. You have given me the best advice I've had since my arrival."

The older woman was perplexed, but wasn't about to question the girl. "As I have said, if you learn nothing else here you learn patience." Leaving her chair she walked to where her husband slept and shook him awake. "Daniel."

Daniel Joncaire rose immediately, stretching his arms above his head. "A short sleep, but a good one." He laughed as he rubbed his stomach. "You are ready, I see, mademoiselle." Daniel looked at Prisella and gave her a wink. Apparently he was not as soundly asleep as was thought.

"Then we shall go. Prisella will keep the fires burning till I return." He walked to his wife and putting his arm around her shoulder gave a tight squeeze. "She is a good woman, this one," he said to Mimi. "Now, we must go. The others will be waiting."

Prisella stood at the open door as they headed toward the trading post. Mimi couldn't help but admire the woman's courage and wondered how many times she had stood there, watching her Daniel leave, never knowing if he would return.

Approaching the mounts, Mimi saw Francois among the saddled soldiers. He lightly touched his hat as Daniel assisted her onto her horse but made no special move, as one might expect of a gentleman who had pleaded with this woman to come to Niagara to be his bride. Mimi managed a brief smile in his direction, glad that they had greeted each other without rancor.

The group reined their animals down the road toward Lake Ontario. Private Lauch and Corporal Sovie rode ahead with several other soldiers; a group of six Indian allies followed. Joncaire instructed Mimi to ride between, and he and Captain Laloque brought up the rear.

Mimi heard the two men behind as they spoke in hushed voices. It was apparent that they intended she should not hear their conversation. She obligingly moved her horse closer to the men in front, giving Francois and Daniel their privacy.

"It is well past noon, Daniel." Francois said in an authorative tone of voice.

"*Oui*, still plenty of time before dark." Joncaire was not subject to military orders or discipline.

"That skirmish above the heights last night—I see Corporal Charpente was killed," Francois went on.

"*Oui*, this is so, but the Iroquois did not fare too well either. But that you would know had you been with your men." Joncaire let go with his familiar laugh, which he sometimes used as a ploy.

Mimi knew their whisperings were intended to keep her from hearing and she realized that Daniel, especially, didn't want her to know of the perils ahead. He had purposely declined discussing the events of last night when she entered their cabin as Prisella tended to his wounds. Mimi had been aware of that then, and just as happy not to hear. She had seen enough to be able to imagine what went on and the less she had to hear the better she felt, since each encounter seemed to be a step backward for her.

The two men continued to whisper. "We must be very careful, Captain. I fear they are not done with us yet and we have the maiden along."

"She will have to fight along with us. This is no place for chivalry, Daniel."

" 'Tis true, my friend, but she is such a small one, no? We must see to it that she reaches her destination. Especially you, my friend." Joncaire looked sternly at Francois. It was rare for him to take someone to task, but he was well aware that if it weren't for Francois's insistence Mimi would not have been on the frontier. It was Daniel's opinion that, regardless of what had come between them after her arrival, Francois owed her a safe return.

"You speak like a father, now Daniel. I don't need your lectures on my duties."

"Oh, Monsieur Captain, have I offended you?" Daniel's voice was slightly tinged with sarcasm. "I think it is time someone talked to you. You are shirking your responsibilities. Someone owes Mimi that much." He punctuated his clipped words with quick movement of his hands. "If not you—then I and the rest will take your responsibility."

The man's words were meaningful and were not falling on deaf ears, but all the same, Francois resented Daniel's remarks. "Mimi Pean made her own decision and arrangements for going to the castle. Now, that she has succeeded I don't see how any of it becomes my problem, Daniel, and I'll thank you to stay out of my business. I don't need your preaching."

Daniel Joncaire didn't change his tone of voice as he leaned toward Francois. His words were direct, as were his eyes. "Francois, I want to say that you are a disgrace to the French explorers, *oui*, even to France. I am greatly disappointed in you, but this discussion will have to wait until we have seen this journey to its end. Have no fear, Captain, you will not have to worry about the destiny of this young woman; it will be taken care of, but Daniel does not forget. He forgets nothing!" he emphasized.

"Taking it a little personally aren't you, Daniel? I didn't say that I would not help in Mimi's welfare. I don't see how it should affect our relationship." Laloque backstepped in his attitude, softening the edge of his voice.

He suddenly sounded simpering to Daniel and it added to the disgust he now held for the man. "Your lack of courtesy toward any woman will affect my relationship with you. How much does it take for a man to be stronger and meaner than a woman? Officers are supposed to be gentlemen, but you, Monsieur Captain, are a disgrace." Daniel whipped his horse to move ahead where he joined Mimi, leaving Francois alone to bring up the rear.

Inside the dark and sinister forest the wild life had made itself scarce; the unnatural stillness was intense and Mimi shivered with forboding.

Corporal Sovie's horse had been reined far ahead of the rest and Francois and Daniel seemed to be riding stiffly and uneasily. The tense atmosphere was heightened as the horses whinnied and snorted with warning instincts. Mimi placed her hand on the grip of her pistol as she studied the animals' behavior.

In a flash, the forest shattered as tree limbs cracked from their mother trunks and warhoops and rifle shots sounded ahead. Daniel slapped his horse, dashing past the group to the front.

"Go!" screamed Joncaire whipping Mimi's horse into violent action; her head jerked back with the unexpected lurch of the animal. It took all her conscious effort to control the steed and stay in the saddle as the horse bucked, its feet slipping in the wet mire of the forest floor. The animal nervously spurted through trees where Mimi caught flashes of red and white uniforms. Behind her, shots ricocheted from trees and rocks.

The horse sped on out of control, bouncing her in the saddle. Then the animal's front legs slipped and went down. She grasped the reins, forcing it back to its feet, regaining control. Suddenly, without warning Mimi was thrown from her horse by a burning thrust. There was a loud crack as she rolled, falling against a large boulder. She had been hit by an arrow, the shaft breaking as she rolled; blood spurted from the wound. The shock and pain of it diminished as she drew her pistol, breathlessly waiting for the as yet unseen foe.

She caught brief views of darting Indians, and ahead hand-to-hand combat began between the French soldiers and Iroquois Indians. Mimi checked her pistol. She was only slightly conscious of her own wound as the blood soaked her jacket. Disregarding her injury she wondered how she would distinguish which Indians were French allies. Since she had no better method, she decided to aim for those who fought with the French uniform.

Leaning against a rock to steady her hand she took aim on a savage in combat with a Frenchman. Her hand wavered, but with concerted effort she steaded it and shot. It hit its mark, slamming the Indian into a nearby tree. Reloading, she steadied her hand again and squeezed the trigger. The British soldier screamed as the burning pellet hit him. The action around her abruptly stopped. She seemed to be alone, but the firing continued down the trail.

Inching her way along she moved toward others, still locked in battle. Twenty feet from the foray she stopped. Like a seasoned soldier she readied her pistol and waited. She was unprepared when a body came crashing beside her. Not daring to move she saw the open eyes of a dead Seneca. She crawled toward the dead man, all the while keeping her eyes on the battle, and seized his musket. Then pulling herself slowly around the body she grasped the flask of powder from his belt. Filling the musket barrel she drove the ramrod home.

In the flurry of battle and through haze of powder in the air she could see a savage attacking a Frenchman. A tomahawk was poised for scalping and the soldier, who had lost his musket, was quickly losing ground in the test of muscle against muscle. Mimi raised her gun and fired, flying backwards from the recoil. The lead ball slammed the Indian against a tree. He pitched forward, a gaping hole in his chest. The soldier rose to his feet and charging into the bushes it seemed to Mimi he was running away from the battle. As she fell back to the ground she recognized Francois. Storming through the underbrush, he was dragged to the ground by a British soldier.

For the first time Mimi saw the full brilliance of the British uniform. Without time to think she charged the Englishman with the bayonet. She felt it crunch through his ribs and Francois rolled away from the dead man, his eyes wide and crazy. He threw his arm across his face, barely glancing toward Mimi, and ran up the trail toward Lewiston.

Panting furiously from it all, Mimi leaned against a tree; she could see no one from her party nearby. It appeared she was now alone. Pulling herself to a crouch she moved back behind a boulder and headed toward the road; at the same moment she became aware of sounds behind her. Swinging around she gasped as a tatooed savage stood above her ready to spring. Through the thicket a musket ball pounded into his back. A loud scream puffed from his lungs from the force and the body rolled to her feet. At that same moment Daniel Joncaire ran from behind underbrush with a smoldering gun, signaling her to follow. With only a brief glance up the trail she followed and Daniel swiftly pulled her to his side behind a row of huge boulders.

"We wait," he whispered.

Mimi said nothing. She became aware of the burning pain in her shoulder and the blood-soaked jacket. Raising her hand to the wound, the splintered shaft of broken arrow sent a pain shooting through her side.

"Now we go!" Daniel clasped her hand pulling her through the small opening in the brush. Quickly, he darted into a cluster of huge boulders forming a natural cave where he shoved Mimi inside and knelt at the entrance, musket ready.

"Joncaire, Joncaire," came voices from without.

Daniel waited silently, never making a move. There was a rustling of dry leaves and snapping twigs before Captain Laloque crawled beside him. Joncaire reached out, pulling him in swiftly. Francois took one brief glance at Mimi nestled in the corner, but said nothing, which Joncaire noted with a smirk. The woman saves his life and this coward has nothing to say to her, he thought. *Mon Dieu*, such a tarnish on the country of France.

"Is there anyone else coming?" Joncaire asked Francois.

"I don't think so," he replied tersely.

"You mean . . . this is all?" Joncaire spread his hands.

"Our Indians are all dead and I had to jump over Corporal Sovie's body as I made out," Lalóque said.

"But, what of Private Lauch. Did either of you see him?" Daniel was unwilling to leave for the fort if others were still out there needing help.

"I saw nothing of the private," said Francois.

"Neither dead nor alive?" said Daniel grilling the captain with his eyes. "You saw nothing of him at all?"

"I told you, I did not see him." Francois raised his voice.

"Then don't you think it would do well to scout out and see if he needs your help, Captain?" Daniel was deliberating baiting the cowardly Laloque.

"If he were alive he would be here by now with the

rest of us." Francois spoke nervously, trying to hide his fear.

"Would he? Are you absolutely sure of this? How would he know we are here? Do you suppose he was hiding in the bushes as you were and watched us seek shelter here?" Daniel was unrelenting in his disgust for this man. The Frenchman was totally diminished in Joncaire's eyes.

"If you're so worried about him why don't you go out and find him?" snapped Francois.

"I fully intend to," said Daniel. "It's just that I have great difficulty believing that you are a French soldier." His voice reeked with disgust for the captain. Daniel left the entrance of the cave and crawled out to the portage route.

Within half an hour Joncaire and Private Lauch crawled through the entrance. Mimi, who had remained silent all the while Daniel was gone, smiled and spoke weakly. "I'm glad you are all right, Private."

"*Mon Dieu*! This is terrible," Daniel said. "Only the four of us survive." He crawled back into the cave wearily leaning against the damp boulders. "We wait awhile. Maybe others show up." He looked at Mimi, huddled against the wall, silent and quiet. "A great fight, my dear. Prisella could not have done as well." With a muffled laugh he quietly moved beside her tapping her hand consolingly. "*Oui*, mademoiselle, you are a credit to France."

As he touched Mimi the warm blood flowing from her injury covered his hand. "What's this? You are injured? Private, help me." Laying his musket aside he examined her shoulder. He gasped, "Oh! little one, I must remove the arrowhead. I must push it through. Do you understand me?"

"I understand," she gasped.

"It must be pushed through the back of your shoulder. Do you think you can bear the pain?"

"I don't know, Daniel," she said weakly, avoiding the sight of her own blood.

"You understand why I must do this?" Joncaire wanted Mimi to understand completely that it was either immediate removal of the arrowhead or blood poisoning. He wasn't sure if she was conscious enough to know the gravity of the situation.

"I understand," she grimaced.

"Private, hold her tightly." He motioned Lauch to get behind her.

Joncaire tore the jacket from her back. On seeing the scarred whip marks he gasped, glancing knowingly at Lauch. "This will hurt, I'm afraid, my little one." Joncaire pushed with all his might, forcing the arrow slowly through the skin. There was nothing else he could do. "Do not scream. Do *not* scream," he said, almost too loud, as he forced it through.

"*Mon Dieu*! Joncaire!" Mimi tried to muffle her painful moans.

"There, I have it."

It was the last Mimi remembered as she slipped into unconsciousness.

"She will be all right," Daniel said, picking up his musket again. "I will crawl to the trail to see what I can see. If there is nothing I will whistle, like so." He gave a low cooing whistle. "When you hear you must come at once and bring the little one." He motioned toward Mimi. "She will have to walk since we have lost our horses, but that is all we can do. Now, listen carefully, Private." He stealthily crawled away from the entrance of the cave.

On his signal Private Lauch touched Mimi. "Mademoiselle, we must leave now."

Mimi roused. "I'm ready, Private." She struggled to her feet with Private Lauch's help while Francois played possum in the corner, lest he might have to carry the woman. Francois wanted no part of anything which might hold him up and make him more vulnerable to attack by enemies still hiding out there somewhere.

"Hurry, mademoiselle. Can you stand?" Helping her to her feet Lauch crept through the thickets to Joncaire on the trail. Francois came up behind.

"All seems to be clear, my friends. We have lost many comrades." His head swiveled in every direction as they hunched together close to the ground.

The sun had already set and darkness had closed in the trail. Daniel and Lauch flanked Mimi, helping her stay on her feet. She was still dazed and the full shock of pain was setting in. She dragged along as they increased their pace.

"Now much farther," Joncaire encouraged her. "Soon you will see the great castle." He swiftly swept her into his arms and almost ran as they came closer.

Through dimming eyes Mimi could see the trail widening, trees thinning as they reached the large clearing where the great stone fortress loomed.

"Mademoiselle, as I promised, no?" Joncaire broke the eerie silence with a booming laugh.

"It's . . . it's beautiful . . ." Mimi lapsed into unconsciousness.

## Chapter Nineteen

When Mimi re-opened her eyes Captain David Palmatier, the French militia physician, was standing at the foot of the high wooden bed. The room was small with a large open and barred window on the opposite wall; the breeze from the lake whisping through. In a far corner, beside a large heavy chest, stood the French tricolor. The walls were of heavy stone, and arches overhead were of brick laid in unique patterns.

"How do you feel, Mademoiselle Pean?" Seeing her awake the captain moved to the side of the bed.

"I'm a little shaky, but comfortable. Thank you."

"Good. I am Captain Palmatier, the troop physician. You've got a pretty bad wound there, young lady, but Daniel did a good job removing the arrow. In a day or so you can get up and move about." The doctor walked toward the door to leave.

"Captain," Mimi called

"Yes, what is it?" He moved from the door to her side.

"Is this the castle?"

"It is, indeed, mademoiselle. In a few days, when you're on your feet, you can see it all." He again moved toward the door.

"Captain, is Daniel Joncaire still here?"

"I believe so. Would you like to see him?"

"I'd be grateful if you'd ask him to come."

"He is downstairs in the trading room, I believe. Now, you get some rest. I'll send him up."

Knowing that Captain Palmatier had other patients and duties, Mimi thanked him again as he closed the heavy door behind him.

Even the weather had changed. It was a glorious May day with winds warm and gentle, a contrast to the cool wind of yesterday. Mimi lay still as it wafted through the window. She remembered the events of their trip down the portage, and her thoughts roamed again to the day she began her journey on the *Premier* heading for this land, and to Paul Regis. A sadness filled her as she remembered how much she loved him and how she would never feel his touch or hear his voice. Her spirits were as low as they had ever been and thinking of Uncle Nathane and her beautiful home and gardens was sinking her lower into the well of despair as the memories flooded over her.

A loud rapping on the door broke her reverie.

"Mademoiselle, it is I, Daniel. May I come in?"

"Yes, Daniel. Please come in."

"Well, my little one." He burst into the room. "You are not so bad off." He laughed as he grasped her hand, planting a kiss on it. "You would make an excellent soldier. Excellent!" he exaggerated.

"You know how to make me feel good. But, I wasn't a good enough soldier to remember how I got here. I remember very little after the cave."

"There is not much more to remember, then. We managed to get you here to safety. You will be about in no time. I have the doctor's word for it."

"I know and, Daniel, I am so anxious to get around and see this beautiful place. Her voice was returning to the lilt of the old Mimi and Daniel was glad to hear it.

"Large, maybe. Serviceable, perhaps. But Beautiful?" He laughed heartily. "Depends who looks at it. It is surely a fortress, mademoiselle, and it serves its purpose well. But don't hurry your recovery. True, you could have been more seriously wounded and it will heal but—I must warn you—you will need all your strength."

There was that tone in his voice, the one Mimi had grown to know meant his fatherly concern was about to exhibit itself. "What is it, Daniel? I know that worrisome tone of yours. What are you trying to say?"

"Well, I do not want to worry you, but you should know that the British are making plans to attack and you will need to be well."

"Attack us? Here?"

"*Oui*. Unfortunately it is our last stronghold."

"But, what of Fort de Portage and Lewiston?" Mimi showed great concern.

"Yes, Mimi, they will fall." This was the first time she had ever heard defeat in Daniel's voice.

"But, I can't believe this. Where are all our soldiers?"

"Little one, don't excite yourself. They are on their way, don't worry." He stood to leave. It was becoming more difficult for the usually optimistic man to continue.

Mimi's hopes for peace and rest on the last leg of a long, long journey back home, were shattered. "They can't occupy this castle, Daniel. We must stop them."

Joncaire threw back his head and bellowed unreservedly. "We will stop them. *Mon Dieu*, you are a tiger. Now, my dear, I must return to Lewiston and my Prisella."

"I expect you must," Mimi said dejectedly. She had grown to rely on him, placing all her trust in this man, forsaken as she was by others. But now her hopes of immediately returning to France were dashed by Joncaire's story of the British attack. She knew there was no one else she could trust and new waves of misgiving seeped through her already exhausted brain.

"Don't worry, mademoiselle." Joncaire could see that his tale had upset her. "You have the French army and General Pouchot has sent runners to Presque Isle for more. They will arrive soon enough. Now, I must go." He lightly kissed her hand once more. "*Adieu*, little one." He left. Mimi held his hand until she no longer could, as he slipped out the door.

The following morning Mimi stood beside the bed, wavering with weakness from loss of blood. The large bandage on her shoulder was cumbersome, but aside from the soreness of the injury she felt capable of moving about. Someone had seen to it that her torn and bloodied shirt had been replaced and the new garment lay beside her breeches and boots. She found it difficult to bathe in the porcelain wash basin, and arranging her hair seemed hopeless with the limited use of her arm, so she finger combed it as best she could. Then, cracking the door of her room, she peeked out cautiously.

She first glimpsed the vestibule and as she wandered out slowly she could hear low murmurings in the room to her right. Easing herself along the wall she crossed the vestibule to the open door. Mimi was surprised to find it was a small chapel where Father Claude Virot, the Jesuit priest, was conducting Mass; the room was filled with soldiers. She knelt quietly on the floor behind them. At the moment it seemed like years since she had attended Mass. Indeed, she had not been inside a church since leaving France.

As the priest droned through the last of the Mass she

stood aside waiting until all the men had filed out. Each took up his musket at the entrance as he left.

After intoning the final blessing Father Virot approached Mimi. "You must be the young lady they brought in wounded?"

"I will be all right, Father."

"Yes, I can see you have done well. Tell me, have you had anything to eat today?"

"No, I haven't."

"Then wait till I remove my robes and I shall join you." He passed through hides draped over an opening behind the altar, returning in seconds wearing a frockcoat. "This way, my dear." He took her arm leading her to the head of a narrow staircase. "Just downstairs we shall find the kitchen with fresh fruit and hot cornbread for our breakfast."

Mimi was astonished to see another French woman working about the large kitchen, issuing orders to Seneca Indians and army privates who were chopping meat and rolling dough for bread. The heat from a large open fireplace was staggering in the warmth of the May day. Irons were hung with heavy pots, some filled and cooking over the flames, others hung overhead on long metal racks.

In the center of the large room stood a long oaken table, slick from years of use. Long benches flanked it and in one of the corners stood a deep basin, carved from a huge oak log. It was filled with water. A young soldier dipped his arms to the shoulders as he cleaned heavy pots and pans, his feet in inch deep water on the floor. In the far corner, beside the fireplace, stood a well-worn butcher's block, a cleaver piercing the top.

"Sit here, mademoiselle." There was no questioning the authorative tone as the cook indicated the bench in front of the open window. Mimi loosened her jacket from the oppressive heat and was glad she had been assigned a seat near the window.

"Father, you sit at the head of the table." The huge woman indicated a chair at the end, beside Mimi. A large smile broke across her face when she addressed the priest. Slicing fresh fruit the woman set it on a plate before them. "Eat. Keep up your strength."

Mimi wondered how this heavy-set masculine woman happened to be at the castle. Her voice was loud and course and it appeared she never spoke below a shout. There was no telling her age, but her face had a thousand years of lines. Yet Mimi had the feeling that the woman was not all that old. A certain vigor in her walk and movements, lead Mimi to think she was a good deal younger than she looked. But, she must have, indeed, lived a rugged life and her attitude was quite unladylike. Mimi had never had any relationship with such a woman and had no idea what to expect from her. She reminded Mimi of the women who swarmed the seaport that dark night when she and Uncle Nathane sought her passage.

After eating, Father Virot blessed himself as he had before and pushed his chair back from the table. "I must be on my way, but you take your time and enjoy your breakfast. Madame Gereaud here will see to your wants."

Mimi wondered about that. It didn't appear to her that this Madame Gereaud would willingly see to anyone's needs, much less a stranger's. The woman seemed to be very much at home among all these men. The strange thought crossed Mimi's mind, that she probably would even resent the presence of another woman at the castle. As she nibbled her food, disinterestedly, she watched the bustling woman slam about the kitchen, bellowing orders to the poor wretches under her command. The woman was merciless in her rebukes and she shoved and pushed the young men hither and thither in what one must suppose was her effort of getting things done. Although, as Mimi watched, it seemed that she hindered the work rather than helped it. Mimi failed to see the rhyme or reason for the doings of this bulky woman, except it showed a certain authority she held over the others and she was making sure that they remembered it.

Finally, wiping her hands on the large apron, the generously endowed Madame Gereaud plunked herself beside Mimi, placing a huge hand on her hip.

"You are this Mimi Pean, no?" She spat out the name as if she were cursing.

"Yes," Mimi answered rather meekly.

"Well, you were pretty sick when they brought you in. That portage is dangerous, eh?" She raised her eyebrows; a gesture Mimi had difficulty interpreting.

"Where are the others who were with me?" Mimi wondered why she was asking the cook, but she was so intimidated she hardly knew what to say.

"Joncaire? Oh, he left." She waved a brisk hand through the air. "The other soldiers are around somewhere. They have other things to do besides escort young girls down the portage."

There it was. Mimi knew now, why she was being given the treatment. Madame Gereaud *did* resent the intrusion of another woman. Although exactly how it would affect the big cook was a mystery to Mimi. She had no intentions of even making an attempt to usurp her duties in her kitchen.

Gereaud leaned uncomfortably close to Mimi. "This may not be the best place to be, my little friend. The British are already at Four Mile Creek, a short way from here, making plans for their attack. Did you not know?"

Such a blunt woman, Mimi thought. She obviously said exactly what she thought and without pretentiousness. "Not until Daniel told me." Mimi looked at the curious woman. She had watched her long strides and her skirts hampered her not in the least. She wore soldier's boots which clumped annoyingly when she walked. The very way she threw herself on the bench was much like a rough soldier would do.

"Keep your pistol close, mademoiselle," Madame Gereaud said secretively. As she leaned closer Mimi caught the hint of whiskey on her breath. "It will come in handy." She pulled up her apron and patted a pistol in her waist band. "This has been my friend many times. I am undressed without it." Then, removing her eyes from Mimi, she screamed: "Stir those pots, you savages." She threw a warning glance at the Indians then turned back to Mimi. "These British people think they will conquer our Niagara Country. The devils!" She stood as she shouted. "Who do these damn Englishmen think they are? They want to own the whole world. Already they fight in our homeland."

Mimi gasped at the last announcement. "You mean there is a war in France?"

"Since almost two years," the cook answered.

"There was no war when I left," Mimi protested, hoping against hope that this woman was wrong.

"How long ago, mademoiselle?" Madame Gereaud fairly spit out the words. "When did you leave the French shores?"

"It was June, 1777." Mimi was thoroughly intimidated by the loud woman. And, in her weakened condition she had no desire to get into a debate with her. At the moment, she felt outweighed, outmuscled and certainly behind the news of France. Her dizziness returned.

"Oh, you see! You left just in time." Gereaud then hesitated and leaned close again, contorting her mouth when she spoke. "If you think leaving one war to enter another is good timing."

Gereaud pushed herself from the table and moving to the fire she began stirring a boiling stew in a huge pot, flames crackling around it. She used her apron to wipe the perspiration from her face then looked at Mimi with a scowl, pointing with the large spoon in her hand, "You and me—we are the only French women here." With the spoon still clasped in her hand, against her hip, she sidled up to Mimi, again leaning close as if to tell a secret. "Keep your wits about you, girl. If it isn't these damn Indians, it's the weary soldiers—stalking, always stalking." She twisted her mouth in disgust. "Keep your wits about you," she repeated loudly as she gave a knowing look toward the men in the kitchen. They totally ignored her and went about their business. They acted as if they had not the vaguest idea of what the woman spoke. It left Mimi wondering if it was all a fantasy conjured up in the mind of a very lonely woman.

With a sudden move she threw the spoon onto the table. Mimi jumped in her chair from the loud clatter. "Now, I've got to clean the general's room. Did you leave your bag there?" She looked over her shoulder with her sternest look, both hands on her huge hips.

"I didn't know I was in the general's room."

"Ha! Cute! When these men got a look at a beautiful girl like you, where did you think you'd be?" She grabbed the cornhusk broom from the corner and headed out the door.

Mimi sat there bewildered. She was almost afraid to move. Shoving her dish away, she left through the door and entered the large, slate-floored vestibule. To her left were double doors leading to the compound. Moving much too quickly, she felt the blood drain from her head and swayed as she walked. Steadying herself against the stone walls, she made an effort to control her movement, waiting till the spinning subsided.

"Are you all right, mademoiselle?"

She raised her eyes to a distinguished gentleman in French Uniform.

"You don't appear to be too sure-footed. May I assist you?" He put his hand lightly on her arm.

"Thank you, Captain." Mimi had hardly looked at the man. She was only aware of the uniform.

"I am General Pouchot, mademoiselle," he said mildly as he smiled.

"Oh, dear, please forgive me, General. I had no idea you'd be about."

"I hope you found my room comfortable. I fear a soft bed is all I had to offer. The cell is modest. Actually it is quite stark, but it serves its purpose, at least for me."

"Yes, General, I slept very well. I do hope I haven't inconvenienced you."

"Not at all. I didn't get much chance to sleep last night anyway."

"I understand the English have entrenched a short ways from here?"

"It's true, unfortunately. However, I have ordered other troops to join us here. They have been stationed at Presque Isle. Also, Captain La Beuf at Venango and his troops, along with those now stationed at Frenchman's Creek and the Alleghany River, are due to arrive shortly. We will give the British something to think about."

Even with the strong convictions of General Pouchot,

all the talk of attack was doing little to comfort Mimi, especially as weak as she was. The killings of the day before were all too vivid in her mind. She felt as though she was a war-weary frontiersman but, unlike them, she was alone, a stranger at the castle. The only other French woman was Madame Gereaud, a thought which gave little comfort to Mimi Pean. And now Mimi's insatiable desire to seek passage back to France was even stronger. Without the slightest thought to the contrary she seized the opportunity right then and there.

"General Pouchot."

"Yes, mademoiselle. What can I do for you?"

"I realize this is hardly the time to bring it up, but is there any possibility, do you think, that I may find some passage back to France?"

"You are quite right, Mademoiselle Pean, I cannot advise you at this time. There is no hope at this moment. However, when we have taken the British we shall discuss it again." He touched his hat lightly and Mimi realized it was with some annoyance that he walked through the heavy plank and iron doors into the compound grounds.

She silently reproached herself. If Prisella had you now she'd skin you alive. What must he think of me to bring up my safety at a time like this? Mimi had so angered herself by now she looked around for a place to run, and without thinking she charged through the doors.

Outside, the grounds surrounding the castle were crowded with scurrying military and their Indian allies and families. Senecas were moving kegs from the huge stone powder magazine and smaller huts stood around the perimeter of the fortification. At the very edge around the fort mounds of earth had been erected leaving troughs in the ground where a sluice controlled the flow of water from the river. Just below was the Niagara River where it flowed into the lake.

To Mimi, Lake Ontario seemed to be as sprawling and endless as the ocean had been. The waves rolled from the horizon, gaining momentum at the shore, crashing over it. Somewhere out there was Mont Real, the seaport where she hoped to obtain passage home. Mimi's reverie broke as she became mindful of the activity surrounding her, the tense atmosphere and the diligence of the soldiers and allies.

Best to get busy and help the others prepare for this attack, she thought. As she swung around vigorously her head swam. It was useless to think she would be of much help in her condition and she realized it. Rest, she thought, would be more appropriate at the moment, if she were to be of any use when the time came. She had pushed herself a little too far on her first day out of bed, and it was taking effect. She headed back to the castle in search of a place to rest. Only then did it occur to her that she had no bed to rest in, for obviously, it would be impossible to occupy the general's room again. However, at the moment, she had no choice, she must sit somewhere or fall in a heap.

As she ran through the doors she crashed headlong into a tall robust man, for he never budged in his tracks as she collided with him.

"I beg your pardon, monsieur," she said, embarrassed. It seemed she was only succeeding in getting in everyone's way at this point.

The man was dressed in rugged frontier clothes, which had seen their share of rough wear and weathering. A large black beard covered his front and long curly hair fell to his shoulders. His musket was strapped over his shoulder and on his feet were knee-length hide boots. There was no word from his lips. He just stood there staring at the woman before him.

Nonplussed by his continued silence she mumbled on. "I do hope you'll forgive my clumsiness, I felt faint and wanted to sit somewhere."

Still, without a word, he aided her to a bench against the wall inside the entrance way.

"I appreciate your help, monsieur. I am quite all right now. Don't bother with me." She leaned against the wall to stop the spinning.

"Mademoiselle," the man said softly, hesitatingly, still staring as if unbelieving. Then he said ever so softly as to be almost inaudible, "Mimi."

She sat erect looking at him. "That voice!" Her voice became stronger.

"Mimi, it's Paul," he said as gently as possible.

"Paul Regis!" Her scream brought stares from others milling through the building.

"*Oui*, my darling." He clutched her to him.

Mimi couldn't believe what she had heard. She pulled back, examining his face. "Those are Paul's eyes; I could not be mistaken. Paul, my darling, I can't believe this." Her hands groped at his chest. "Let it be so, please," she said prayerfully.

"We can't talk here, come with me." He helped her to her feet, leading her across the green to a small hut. "Come Mimi," he said as he opened the door.

She followed him inside where he swept her into his arms and kissed her long and lovingly.

Mimi almost swooned in the warmth of his embrace. "I can't believe this. I thought you were dead," she panted breathlessly.

He kissed her again and again, holding her close. "I know, darling, I know," he said between kisses.

Mimi was going limp in his arms. He caught her, placing her gently on his bed.

"I can't believe this," she repeated. "Is it true, Paul? How is it you are here? How did you survive?" Mimi thought of that last sight and began to cry from the excitement. "Oh, darling, please tell me," she sobbed.

"How did you survive?"

Paul held her close, gently rocking her, realizing that the shock of seeing him had weakened her further. He tried to be gentle when first he recognized her but there is no gentle way to rise from the dead, he thought. She struggled to sit but he gently forced her back on the bed, stroking her long, loose hair. "So, you are the girl they brought in wounded?" he smiled. "When I heard the report I thought of you, but I could not bring myself to hope it would be you. I, too, thought you were dead. Oh, my darling, I am so sorry you have suffered all this."

"Paul, it is none of your fault. It is a great surprise to me that I have not been wounded before this." She again laid back on the bed.

"It has been so long, so long," whispered Paul.

"You haven't found someone else?" Mimi sat up abruptly, searching his eyes.

"No, Mimi," he laughed gently, glad of her concern. "There could never be anyone but you."

Mimi threw her arms around him. "I knew it, my love. I knew we would find each other again. I never stopped thinking of you. Paul, I was trying to get back to France," she looked up at him. "That's why I'm at the castle, but you—how did you get here?" She spoke rapidly, excitement vibrating through her body.

"If you make a promise, I will tell you all about it."

"Anything, darling."

"Lie back and sleep. There are things I must do, but I will be back and when you are rested I will tell you all about it. Will you do that for me, my beloved?" He touched her cheek softly.

"Yes, I am tired. But, Paul, don't leave me for long. I couldn't bear to lose you again."

"I promise. I'll be back shortly." He drew his fingers across her eyes, closing them, then silently left the hut.

## Chapter Twenty

As Paul Regis stepped from the cabin he was confronted by Francois Laloque. "So, *you* are this Paul—the one Mimi spoke of?" His stance was firm as he glared at Regis.

"What do you mean, Captain?"

"Do you take me for a fool?" Laloque snarled at him.

"I'm afraid I don't know what you're talking about. Now, if you will excuse me . . ." Paul made an effort to move past the man.

Francois held Paul's arm unrelentingly. "You will not dismiss me that easily, sir. I am *Captain* Francois Laloque."

"Laloque?" Paul recognized the name. "Yes," he said calmly. "You are the man the Mademoiselle Pean sailed so far to see."

"It was much more than that, I assure you, sir. We were to be married."

"Yes, I remember." Paul stood stiffly before the captain. "I'm afraid things have changed a good deal, my friend." Paul said with a firm voice and another attempt to leave.

"And your part in this change . . . ?" Laloque again seized Paul's arm swinging him about.

Paul glanced at the captain's heavy hand. "I suggest

you release your hold, sir." His anger rose.

"In France, monsieur, this would be settled by a duel." Francois's eyes glistened.

"At your service, Captain. Whenever and wherever you say." Paul gave a salute.

"Well, time enough for that." Francois backed off. "For the moment I have more important duties to attend to."

"More important than Mimi, Monsieur Captain?" Paul said sarcastically, his eyes in a steady gaze at the man confronting him. "I think she is not important to you at all, sir."

"Watch your mouth. I shall have you thrown in the dungeon to rot. I won't tolerate your insubordination—you a mere frontiersman," he hissed.

"I think not. You have a loud mouth, Laloque, but your rank is too low. I suggest you watch how you threaten your superior officers."

Francois's eyes opened wide as he dropped his hold on Paul. He didn't understand how a simple scout could be addressing an army officer in such a manner. Paul walked away. As he passed a group of soldiers they saluted him and Paul returned it.

"Who is that man?" Francois asked of a passing soldier, toting a powder keg on his shoulder.

"Who, sir?" the amazed soldier asked.

"That man you just saluted, you idiot." Francois's exasperation was getting the better of him.

"Oh, him. That's Major Regis, sir."

Francois's chin fell as he stared after Paul. He realized the gravity of his talk and actions. While he may have been the highest-ranking officer at Fort de Portage, it was a different story at the castle. And to Francois's amazement officers wore clothes other than their regular uniform. He mounted his horse and spurred the animal into a fast gallop toward the portage road.

Mimi had been awake and active for some time when Paul entered the hut. She had straightened the cabin, folding blankets and clothing. As he entered she ran to him, throwing her arms around his neck. He kissed her tenderly and when he did, Mimi noticed his beard and hair had been neatly trimmed. He looked, now, as he had aboard the *Premier*, handsome, tall and strong.

"Now, Paul, you promised." She smiled endearingly. The mystery of how he had managed to reach the castle alive still had to be told and Mimi wasn't going to let him forget. She knew the horrors she had survived to reach this point.

Paul placed his musket in the corner of the room and slowly removed his jacket. He sat in a chair to remove his boots. "Did you get any sleep, darling?"

He was taking painfully long, too long to suit Mimi. "Yes I slept and I feel fine. Paul you are teasing me." Her eyes sparkled as she knelt at his feet.

He smiled at her looking so small and frail. With all she had been through she still possessed the childlike quality he found so refreshing when first he saw her. Paul laughed at her enthusiasm as she pleaded with him to tell his story of escape. Settling back in his chair he began.

"When I regained consciousness I had been cut from the mast and was lying on deck. Remember the sailors who remained aboard with us?" Mimi shook her head in reply. "They stayed out of sight as the savages took you from the ship, then they came from below to cut me down. They told me you had been taken to shore." Paul thought for a minute, looking into the distance. He rubbed his hands together in an almost embarrassed gesture as he explained. "Besides, my darling, sailors are not great fighters. Oh, they are good brawlers—there's nothing they like better. And they are great philanderers. But when it comes right down to it, their temperament is more suited to a stealthy attack on a stranger in some dark alley. Anyway, in the end they high-tailed out into the woods at our first encounter with a small band of Indians. Lord only knows where they are now. As it turned out, these very Indians were the people who led me here to the castle." Paul leaned back in his chair and put his hands behind his head. "Well, the weather had held calm and the three of us managed to bring the ship to shore. I imagine the English have it today. I had no way of knowing where you had been taken; it didn't seem to matter what direction I went, it was a rare chance that I would follow you or find you. When we finally disembarked, just below Four Mile Creek, where the British are now encamped, we swam to shore meeting no opposition whatever. Apparently, even at that time, the British were on their way up from Albany."

"That is probably why Sergeant Mileaux and his troops were able to get through," Mimi said thoughtfully.

"Sergeant Mileaux?" Paul asked.

"Yes, he's the one who saved me from the Mississaugas who had taken me. Without him I might be dead—or worse, an Indian wife."

"My poor Mimi." Paul put his arms around her. "Was there any sign of my crew when you reached land?"

Mimi grew pale. "Paul, it was hideous." She covered her face with her hands, recalling the horrible sight as she related it to Paul.

Regis had seen the work of the Indians and he spared

her from further recollection, pressing a finger to her lips. Then he went on. "When I reached the castle apparently Frenchmen were in great demand." Paul laughed at his remark. "General Pouchot greeted me like a long lost friend and immediately commissioned me major of the French army. In all my time here I have never heard of any French women, except Madame Gereaud, and everyone hears about her, eventually. Your name was never mentioned. I could only assume the worst, my darling. I thought you were dead."

Mimi sat silently. She was truly astounded by the idea that she and Paul had only been twenty miles apart when she was in Lewiston.

"And you, my dear, what befell you? Tell me how you have come so far."

"Paul, it is difficult to think of it," she said turning away from his eyes.

"Mimi, it doesn't matter. I love you. Nothing can change that—you know that."

Remembering Francois's reaction Mimi was hesitant. "It is not pleasant, my darling," she said as she looked up at him.

"If it is too unpleasant to speak of, I can understand. There's no need to tell me, if you don't want to." He held her hand tenderly. "I know this wild land and the savages who roam here. Believe me when I say that nothing you could tell me would change my feelings about you, my love." He kissed her hand and smiled.

"I do want to tell you Paul. I think it might cleanse my own thoughts if I could just say some of the things I feel." She lowered her eyes. "It's just that some people feel that I am defiled."

Paul lifted her face to his and kissed her warm mouth. "My love, no matter what, I want you."

Mimi began hesitantly. "They made me an Indian

squaw, Paul. I lived among them. I worked with other Indian squaws, but I was never defiled. Never! It was Sergeant Mileaux who saved me from becoming an Indian wife. I am so indebted to him."

"I too." Paul smiled. "Whoever this Mileaux is, I owe him a debt of gratitude. Perhaps one day I will get the chance to tell him."

"He is dead, Paul, killed as we made our way north. The sergeant and I were on foot for days, fighting Indians who ambushed us. He was badly injured. In the end, he was killed when French-allied Indians surprised us. That is when I met Princess Lilyana and her father, the chief. They were traveling north for Liliyana's marriage. The princess and I became close friends in that short time, before . . ." Mimi's voice cracked. "As we camped one night, we were set upon by another band and Liliyana and her father were killed. Only I was allowed to live. I couldn't understand this until Francois Laloque showed himself. He was the one who brought me to Fort de Portage at Lake Erie."

"Laloque," Paul said thoughtfully. "Yes, we have met."

"He is here, I know. And he hates me, Paul. He is so unpleasant. He said vile things to me. If it hadn't been for Chabert and his brother Daniel, I should never have reached the fortress at all. Francois would just as soon have left me there to die as not when he learned I could never marry him.

"Daniel Joncaire is a great Frenchman," Paul replied in a quiet way. "I regret that I do not know his brother. My travels on the portage only took me to the heights."

"You know Daniel?" Mimi asked.

"*Oui*, I have helped him many times along the route."

"You mean you have been to Lewiston?" Mimi

stood, staring with disbelief.

"I have been there many times."

"How could we not have met? Oh! There has been so much time wasted, my darling."

"It's over now. We have finally found each other. That's all that matters." He stood drawing her to him, kissing her soft mouth. "Oh, Mimi, I love you so. We will never part again." He swept her from her feet and placed her on the bed, then slowly slid beside her.

As he fondled her gently, she kissed his mouth again and again; the bottomless well of wanting flowed over the brim with their feelings. Mimi gently pulled him to her and their passion joined them in a fiery embrace. As Paul removed her bodice he silently gasped when he saw the scars across Mimi's delicate back and he kissed each one. Mimi moaned under the wonderful weight of his body and Paul entered her slowly. Suddenly, the fervor of their love coursed through them and they exploded as one.

They lay there taking pleasure in their closeness. "Now, we can go back to France, my beloved." Mimi looked at Paul anxiously.

"We will, but not yet. I must see this battle through. Then we shall think of returning to France. He gently pushed her from him. "Now, you shall stay here with me, at my cabin." He pulled her to him and kissed her long and tenderly.

"What will they say?" Mimi questioned, although she had no idea where she would stay otherwise. Certainly General Pouchot wasn't going to give up his room forever, and the castle was crowded to overflowing. Mimi had visions of sleeping on the floor like some urchin.

"What can they say? There is no other room in the castle. Besides, I have already discussed it with General

Pouchot." He took her face between his hands. "Mimi, we can be married right here if we want."

"Oh Paul!" She squealed in delight. "When?"

"Now, tomorrow, the next day, next week, whenever you say. The chaplain will perform the ceremony for us."

"Tomorrow. Oh yes, Paul, tomorrow." She hugged him tightly as he bent to kiss her again. Then Mimi pulled away. "No! I shall not marry you looking like this. I must have time to get ready." Her voice was suddenly firm.

Paul threw back his head and laughed. "My dear, any time you say will suit me." He continued laughing, watching Mimi dance around the tiny room.

"I must make a beautiful dress. I will plan it carefully, as I would in France. I am so happy!" Mimi threw herself beside Paul. "I must be beautiful for you. I have new shoes, a gift from Chabert Joncaire. I will get material at the trading room and make my wedding gown. We will invite everyone at the castle."

Paul sat there watching her, rejoicing in her happiness. "Mimi, my dearest, you are not planning the wedding for the Queen of France." He leaned back on the bed, chin in hand, laughing with delight at Mimi's happy antics.

## Chapter Twenty-One

In the bustling days that followed, Madame Gereaud took note of the particularly animated Mimi Pean. There was very little that escaped the inquisitive woman, even if it required pressing her ear to closed doors that might hide that which was intended to be hidden. General Pouchot often remarked, in the confines of meetings with his officers, that if Madame Gereaud wasn't so large and loud she would make an excellent spy for the French army since she was the first to discover rumors, spreading them so thoroughly and quickly that she was laughingly referred to as the "Fast-Talk Journal."

Before the British had indicated their determination to take over the territory in Niagara Country, General Pouchot would often conjure some ridiculous story primarily for Gereaud's listening ear, pressed against the door, only to have it repeated to him, in all seriousness by some young soldier as the general left the meeting where it was first originated and discussed. It served as relief for the serious business of maintaining an army. General Pouchot and the others were quite amused with the Madame Gereaud and the curious twists the tales took as she spread them. Within a day the original story would be so convoluted that it was barely recognizable. But such playfulness, however harmless, had to stop when the serious business of war became evident on the frontier.

Now they had to be exceedingly cautious when discussions took place to see that the same Madame Gereaud was out of earshot. While in jest they may have thought of her as a good spy, in serious matters she could be deadly with her stories, should any of their discussions be spread so loosely. She was a genuine threat to the French army when it came to war, and she was watched thoroughly.

On this particular day, however, Madame Gereaud could stand it no longer and sidled up to Mimi as they passed on the castle green, holding a large basket filled with freshly baked bread on her shoulder. "So, my pet, we are to have a wedding are we? I expect that means a bit more work for me? Do you think I have nothing more to do than fuss with fancies in that steaming kitchen?"

Mimi couldn't have been more perplexed by the barrage, having never mentioned anything about special fare for the wedding. She never could understand the woman anyway, always blustering about something and finding imaginary oversights on the part of others, supposedly causing her no end of work and hardship. "I don't recall asking you to do anything, Madame Gereaud." Mimi was no longer frightened by the woman, but she wasn't all that fond of her either. She mainly stayed entirely out of her way.

"Maybe not, but this one knows what you French gentry expect of us." Gereaud was surprisingly outspoken for one who, obviously, considered herself a mere servant.

"There will be no need for any fussing, madame. My wedding is more important than anything you could possibly serve."

Gereaud picked up on the tinge of insult in Mimi's answer. "Indeed, mademoiselle, then I say you underestimate me. I'll show you a feast fit for the king himself." She stomped off.

Mimi was undisturbed by the woman, but she wasn't the only one who was taking a strange attitude toward the upcoming marriage. She was beginning to believe encounters with Francois were deliberate on his part. He had appeared as she examined new materials in the trading room, then again as she left the chapel after a conversation with Father Virot. Saying nothing, he merely appeared, always watching.

One day as she crossed the green he approached her. "Mimi, I can't stand by and watch this mockery any longer."

Mimi stiffened. "I would be most delighted if you did not address me at all, Monsieur Captain. We have nothing to say to each other." She made an attempt to pass.

Seizing her arm he stopped her. "Please reconsider. Perhaps I was a little hasty in my judgment of you."

"Indeed! Surprised, no doubt, that someone else would have me. Your plea means nothing to me now." Her eyes glistened with hate and anger.

"How can you forget what we meant to each other?"

"I think it is you who have forgotten. It seems I wasn't good enough for you. I don't wish to discuss it." Again she attempted to leave but he clung to her arm.

"I can't let you do this," he ordered.

"You have nothing to say about what I do with my life, now or any other time, and if you don't unhand me immediately I shall see to it that reprisals will be severe."

The blood rushed to Francois's face as his venomous tongue went to work. "Don't threaten me, mademoiselle. I don't take kindly to such talk from sluts," he hissed.

"Sluts indeed! You have a nerve, sir. Where do you get the cheek to judge others when you, as an officer in His Majesty's service, runs like a coward leaving a woman to kill your enemy and pull him from your back?" Mimi's hatred for this man caused her blood to run hot. She reared back and slapped his face with all her strength. "Stay out of my life, you slinking milksop," she screamed.

Francois, who stood watching her go, was jerked around unexpectedly. A fist met his jaw, landing him on the ground.

Paul Regis stood over him. "I think our unsettled differences should be concluded now, Captain."

Francois rose, feeling his aching chin. "I beg your pardon, sir?" He feigned an attitude of disbelief for the attack on him. "It is not our quarrel, Major."

"It seemed to be our quarrel when you demanded retribution some weeks ago, Captain. I am ready now, as I was then. In fact, sir, I now demand it."

"Why, I see no need to upset ourselves over this wench, Major. As officers of the French army . . ."

Paul sent him sprawling to the ground. "We'll settle this here and now," he bellowed. The simpering excuse of a man had drawn Paul's anger to a peak. There would be no satisfaction until he had beaten him to his knees in abject disgrace—or to the death.

The captain rose. Drawing his saber, he hunched for action. Teasing the unarmed major, he flicked the long blade in his face; laughing at his opponent. He lunged, but Paul dashed aside avoiding the point. Again Francois lunged and again Paul slipped past the point. Groups of soldiers and Indians began to encircle them. Francois grinned with delight, jeering at Paul. "Come,

Major, put me in my proper place. My blade is anxious to run you through."

Sliding deftly past the blade Paul wrenched Francois's arm until the weapon fell to the ground where Paul kicked it out of reach. "Now, Monsieur Captain, let's see how well you fare on an even basis."

Maddened by the loss of his weapon, Francois dove for Paul, but was slammed to the ground once more. Again he rose, his anger mounting with his heightened disgrace in front of the men. He dove toward Paul who caught him by the shoulders, spinning him headlong against the crowd. They darted out of the way, letting him fall. The men gathered at the rim of the action shouted epithets at Francois while his own ineptness added to his already bursting anger. He crawled to his feet and as he wheeled around Paul hit him, crumbling him in a heap. Dragging him up by the collar, pressing him close to his face, Paul grit his teeth as he spat, "I should kill you right here and be done with it, but death is only for the brave. You will live with your disgrace for now, but if I see you near Mimi again I will squeeze the life's breath from you with no more thought than if I were squeezing a grape." He threw the beaten man into the throng and stalked away, leaving him to the jeers of the mob.

Aside from the hubbub of the coming wedding, the castle green was a mass of soldiers and their Indian allies, making plans for the inevitable attack by the British. Continual bombardments from both sides of the fortress had created a tense atmosphere among the French. The troops from Presque Isle and Frenchman's Creek had not arrived and General Pouchot anxiously ordered his scouts to determine their delay. The French were low on ammunition from daily retaliations and it was taking its toll of men and fighting power.

The trade products of furs and hides had begun to diminish and Pouchot could feel the hot breath of the British general. It was imperative that the fortified castle remain ready and capable to handle the seige, but it was becoming less secure with each attack. Pouchot ordered the powder magazine be kept stocked, and training sessions continued daily in the compound while the rest of his militia, in a failing effort, tried to keep peace along the portage.

Pouchot knew that the raids along the route were instigated by the English. He even suspected his own Indian supporters. Both the French and British knew that Indian loyalties drifted back and forth with the tides; they were as likely to fight for the French today as the English tomorrow. Neither side could be sure, even as they housed, fed and provided arms and trinkets, whether the natives would fight for or against them. But, owing to the lack of troops of their own, both countries depended on the Indian fighter to help win battles.

Mimi continued her work on the wedding gown, putting aside all the worry of the inevitable attacks. She and Paul had decided to marry on the twenty-fourth of July and arrangements were made with Father Virot. Even Madame Gereaud had softened, taking some delight in her duties, stocking up for the feast. It was a challenge, since the Niagara Country lacked many of the ingredients necessary for her culinary attempts. The fires in the kitchen and the bake house were overtaxed with her version of fine French pastries, and deer had been slaughtered and hung, ready for the pit. The soldiers already drooled from the array of food she'd concocted. It would be a feast to remember and Madame Gereaud was seeing to all the details.

## Chapter Twenty-Two

July twenty-fourth finally arrived. General Pouchot had generously turned over his room to Mimi for a dressing room, it being just down the hall from the chapel. Madame Gereaud had appointed herself lady-in-waiting and was fussing about Mimi, fluffing her white silk wedding dress, weaving flower blossoms into her hair.

Mimi had chosen a gown similar to her lavish French dresses, but without the bulky skirts. Mimi was just as happy, however, for if there was anything she was exceedingly grateful to give up it was the bulky petticoats and skirts. They were a nuisance getting in and out of carriages and doorways and although she felt free to express it now, she could also recall her total annoyance with them earlier. She laughed to herself thinking how women had to make themselves four times wider than they actually were for social events back in France. Here in this wild country the doors were even smaller and would surely present awkward situations to the wearer of high French fashion. Aside from finding her beloved Paul Regis again, Mimi was most thankful for the change of style in clothing.

The full-skirted gown hung gently from a tight bodice, with white velvet ribbon flouncing from the hem and sleeves, and Mimi covered her head with a piece of fine, handmade lace she had, surprisingly, found amid the materials at the trading room. Her sleeves, wide and puffed at the shoulders, extended tightly to the wrists. The elegant shoes Chabert Joncaire had given her months ago adorned her feet.

Paul stood in the chapel with Father Virot, awaiting her arrival. Madame Gereaud was to be Mimi's matron of honor, an honor which the large woman did not take lightly. She had taken great pains in her dress, having discarded her large apron and heavy boots in favor of a brightly patterned cotton dress and moccasins.

As Mimi came through the chapel door Paul approached, offering his hand to escort her to the rail where the priest solemnly began. "Dearly beloved, we are gathered here in the presence of God to join this man and this woman in the Holy Sacrament of Matrimony."

Paul couldn't take his eyes from Mimi. She was outrageously beautiful and his heart pounded relentlessly. Thinking only of her, he could barely hear the priest drone through the ceremony, impatient for it to end.

Father Virot continued: "And do you Mimi Pean, take this man to be your lawfully wedded husband?"

The door of the chapel flew open shattering the solemnity of the occasion. "Sir!" A French private snapped to a stiff salute.

Father Virot raised his eyes from the missal and with a resigned sigh dropped his arms to his side.

"What is it?" Paul couldn't hide his annoyance with the soldier.

"Sir, General Pouchot begs forgiveness for the interruption, sir, and requests your presence immediately." He stood rigidly, eyes straight ahead.

"I'll be there in five minutes, Private." Within seconds of the final words joining him and his beloved forever, Paul urged the priest to continue.

Father Virot lifted his prayer missal before him once more.

"Begging your pardon, sir, General Pouchot's orders were 'immediately,' sir," the private insisted as he lowered his eyes in embarrassment.

"Very well." Paul's exasperation was exhibited in his shout. "I'll be there." Turning to the others, "Father, darling Mimi, I must go."

Mimi clung to his hand. "Another minute, Paul." Pleading with the priest, "Father, hurry, please."

"My child, one cannot hurry such important matters. Marriage is a blessed sacrament, not a race." He removed the stole from his neck. The ceremony would have to wait.

"I won't have this!" Mimi shouted as she stamped her foot. "Paul, you can't go." She held his arm. He gently released her hand and followed the private from the chapel.

"Eh!" The cynical Madame Gereaud sauntered to Mimi's side. With a large hand she slapped her hip vigorously. "Well, who knows, my pet, maybe this is your lucky day."

"How can you say that, Madame Gereaud? You're a cruel woman." Mimi's eyes steamed with rage.

"Perhaps, but when the man gets his woman locked up, he finds another to him. It's a fact of life." A smirk crossed her face.

"Oh!" Mimi gave the woman a seething look as she collected her skirt and stormed out.

"Major Regis, forgive the intrusion, but as much as we French respect love, I have a duty for you." Pouchot paced the castle's main entrance. "I know the worst possible time to find a mission is when one has just married and to someone so beautiful as your new wife, but this can not wait another minute."

"Yes, General, I understand." Paul tried to hide his annoyance before his superior officer, but made his point even so. "Mademoiselle Pean is not Madame Regis yet, sir. We had but another five minutes before it would be so."

"I am, indeed, sorry, Major. I had thought surely, by now, the final vows would have been said and you and the young lady would be married. I don't suppose there is anything I can say as an apology, however, I don't feel I owe one. The safety of this castle and grounds are more important to me than a wedding. I'm sure as an officer you can understand that."

Paul wasn't ready to hear any lectures on "duty first." He hurried the general along. "Yes, General. What are my orders?"

"I'm worried about those troops from Presque Isle. They should be here." He pounded his fist into his hand. "I want you and Captain Laloque and your men to get out there and find them. We are being blown right out of our shoes. If they aren't here soon we shall loose everything we have fought for."

"I'll leave immediately, General." Major Regis saluted and backed out.

"Oh, Major, don't worry about Mimi. She'll be safe here."

Paul had no time to return to Mimi and explain. He mounted his horse and galloped out of the compound where Captain Laloque and twenty or so others waited.

Outside the chapel door Mimi slumped to the bench. Her marriage seemed to be slipping away from her. It seemed it was just one more conspiracy to keep her and Paul from being together. However, the girl who once would have had a tantrum at such a disappointment was more resigned to her frustration. She slowly walked from the castle to the cabin she had shared with Paul and, removing her wedding dress, she carefully packed it away to await another day.

Dropping to her knees at the edge of the small bed she folded her hands and bowed her head in prayer that Paul would return to her soon.

## Chapter Twenty-Three

The following day Daniel Joncaire rode into the compound grounds. There was no mistaking his hearty greeting and loud laughter.

Mimi ran from her cabin, delighted to see him, but even more she was desperate for a consoling friend. "Daniel!" she shouted.

Joncaire pulled his horse up and bounced from the saddle. "Oh, my little one, you are married, *oui*?" He laughed as he took her hand.

"No, Daniel, I am not. This Pouchot tore him from the ceremony. I shall never forgive him. Never!"

"Patience, now. You know you can not depend on anything in this country. This is something you refuse to learn it seems, eh? There is nothing normal about these times. However, even Joncaire can see why one would be angry and frustrated. So near and so far, eh, mademoiselle"

Mimi had heard that word "patience" enough. Since leaving France it seemed to her that it was all anyone could say. "Have patience! Have patience!" She cut the air with her hands as she spat out the words. "I do understand, Daniel, but it doesn't make me like it, and I shall never forgive General Pouchot. I want to know—what difference can five minutes make in a war?"

"It could make all the difference in the world, or it

could make none." Daniel had never seen such anger in Mimi, although he could readily understand it. This was no longer childish frustration, and Mimi was no longer that young girl he first knew; he realized there was nothing that could be said to alleviate her anger and he didn't try.

"Do you know of General Pouchot's whereabouts?" Daniel's face took on a most serious expression.

"No, I don't." Mimi still angered, fairly snapped at her friend. "He sent Paul off on some mission or other." She flicked her hand in the air with annoyance.

"Ah, *oui*." Daniel frowned and stuffed his hands deep into his pockets. "The troops from Presque Isle and Frenchman's Creek have not arrived, I know. That is probably what Paul's mission is about. These British dogs are too close mademoiselle."

"Yes, I know and I am worried, Daniel."

"What? About Paul?" he smiled. "Never fear, little one, Regis is tough, he'll make it. I know him well, we settled a few skirmishes together."

"I wasn't aware you even knew Paul until recently, Daniel."

"I, too, was surprised. Paul has been at the castle for a few years now; life is strange, no?"

"It's miraculous," she said trying to smile.

"Forgive me, Mimi." Daniel was abrupt. "I have business with the general, I must find him." Joncaire walked away toward the castle gates. "Oh, mademoiselle, I almost forgot." He pulled a parchment letter from his pocket. "This came for you some days back. It is from France."

"France?" Mimi shrieked. "I wrote to Uncle Nathane months ago. Do you think it could be from him?" Mimi tore at the letter as Joncaire continued toward the castle entrance.

As Joncaire entered the building General Pouchot greeted him. "Daniel, any news?"

"If it weren't for bad news we'd have no news at all, General. Chabert has burned Fort de Portage and will be arriving with the troops and allies soon. The wives and children are coming along also." Daniel sighed. "At least these devils will not seize the post, we have made sure of that. The thing that has me really worried, General, is the troops. They still have not arrived and there is no sign of them. Have they received your orders about crossing the lower river and moving along the far shore toward the English battery?"

"They have. My scouts have given them the message and I have sent Major Regis and Captain Laloque on a search mission along the portage route."

"I'll tell you sincerely, General," Daniel scratched the back of his head, "if they find them coming along the portage, either they did not receive your orders or they are blatantly ignoring them. In either case they will surely lose their scalps. I have just come that route and it's sinister and quiet. I am sorry, General, but should you give me my guess, I would have to say that the English know of our plans and are laying in wait along that route, just waiting for them to walk into their ambush."

"I can't believe that, Daniel. General Aubry and Delignery are good men. I can't believe they would disobey my orders."

"They surely are taking their time then, General. There has been no sign of them, whatsoever. We have been waiting days with batteaux, ready to transport them to the far shore. What could be their delay?"

"I don't know," Pouchot said angrily. "But Aubry and DeLignery had better be ready with their explanations. What could they be thinking of?"

Pouchot became more angry as he spoke. "Tell me, Joncaire, how does one lose an army? Surely, if they'd been attacked someone would have managed to report to the castle."

"It does seem odd, General." Daniel frowned. He could offer no explanation.

The two men walked slowly out of the castle and down the center of the compound. It was almost noon and the heat was beating unmercifully on the dried dirt path. Soldiers were cleaning up the debris from the pounding of the cannons from the other side of the river, which had become routine for several hours each day. The French allies were equipping the bastions with ammunition.

The seasoned Joncaire jumped as General Pouchot hauled him to a quick stop, shouting at the top of his voice. "Joncaire, look . . ." He pointed above the trees where smoke billowed high into the sky and at once gun fire began. Pouchot ran to the bastion on shore, peering up the river.

"*Mon Dieu!*" exclaimed Joncaire. "We are doomed."

Pouchot shouted orders to his men as they ran from their huts, seizing their muskets. Up on the portage route the General could see men running back and forth; colorfully painted Indians were engaged in rapid movements. Volley after volley went off. "Get out there!" he screamed as the soldiers charged up the trail.

Mimi ran from the cabin still clutching the letter, tears flowing down her cheeks. She drew her hand nervously through her hair on seeing the smoke on the trail and the cannons from the shore spewing shrapnel across the river. "General, Paul is out there!" she shouted.

The general ignored the screaming woman, continuing to give his orders. Without a moment of hesitation, Mimi ran back to the cabin and snatched her pistol from the wall. She immediately fell in with the running men, heading for the trail. As she reached the forest the English barrage from the far shore sent heavy hotshot across the trail. Mortar fire exploded on the castle green, leaving gaping holes and where there had been Indian children and squaws, there were shattered piles of rubble and bodies. Cabins blew apart, planks and fragments flying high into the air.

As the men reached the fringes of the battle they flew into hand-to-hand combat. The worst of it was but a few thousand feet from the French compound. Dead men already lay everywhere, with wounds oozing their blood. Bodies lay in the fast-flowing creek which crossed the portage route. Musket balls whizzed past Mimi as she made her way up the rail along side the men, swiveling her head in every direction, looking for Paul.

The haze of black powder smoke blinded her as she ran, stumbling over bloody men, and to her horror, she again saw the appalling sight of French heads impaled on poles. The heavy smoke filled her nostrils but still she ran on, searching each dead man's face for Paul.

Soldiers lay grotesquely across the path and in the stream which ran red with their blood. Mimi charged through the creek to the other side, where others fought with bayonets, tomahawks and sabers.

Seeing Indian fight Indian was very confusing to the young woman. One of them charged toward her flailing a long blade wildly. She raised her pistol, took deliberate aim, and shot him in the face. Then she moved quickly on. A moan reached her ears. She dashed from body to body, searching. Cries of help and last prayers rose from the heaps of dying men. Many still alive, tugged the hem of her skirt, pleading for help, but she ran on. There was nothing she could do for them in the heat of such furious fighting. She could still hear the bombardment going on at the castle. Exhausted, she fell by a fallen log, panting fiercely. Her torn dress was wet; her shoes thick with mud. A body came crashing beside her as she rested and in horror she screamed as she recognized Father Virot. She shuddered uncontrollably, throwing the body from her; drawing clenched fists to her mouth, she simpered as she threw herself back against the base of a tree and turned away from the sight of his open eyes.

Regaining control, she began to rise to her feet when she was swiftly lifted from the spot, dragged along the ground, back through the creek, and down the enbankment to the river's edge. Her feet barely touched the ground the whole trip. Scratched and bleeding, she was almost hysterical from fright when she was suddenly dropped along the banks of the rushing Niagara River. Before she could turn or move someone fell upon her, covering her body with his own.

"Be quiet!" the voice said. "Don't scream."

It was Paul!

For another hour the firing and the torturous screams continued. Mimi and Paul lay there until the final musket went off. Dead silence reigned as the sun set over the battleground. Paul and Mimi sat in the semi-darkness beside the rushing water.

"Those fools!" Paul mumbled. "Those damn fools!"

Mimi pulled close to him. "What happened, Paul? I don't understand this. There are so many Frenchmen lying dead up there. I thought we were so well fortified."

Paul's voice was out of control in his anger. "Those men came marching down the portage route with drums rolling, completely ignoring General Pouchot's orders to cross the river in Lewiston. The British were dug in south of the castle, waiting and, worst of all, our own Indian allies turned on us and fell in with the British in the midst of battle. I don't understand why General Pouchot's orders were not followed."

"How could so much go wrong, Paul?"

"General Pouchot made a grave mistake in military judgment. If he had set up a lake patrol he could have cut off the supplies and brought the English to a desperate state—no food, or ammunition. The castle had enough provisions. *Mon Dieu*! It was no mystery to him that the English had entrenched along the route, and certainly no mystery to the British general of Aubrey and DeLignery's troops coming in." Paul covered his face with his hands. "Worst of all, when our Indians saw our French losing ground they fell upon us like butchers. Oh, Mimi, there have been some grave errors here and they have cost the French nation this rich territory."

Mimi was still too horrified by the sights and the stench of death to be of any comfort to Paul. She remained on the fringe of her nerves, incapable of finding the words of solace.

## Chapter Twenty-Four

Paul drew himself to a hunched position beside Mimi. "You've got to stay here by yourself. Do you think you can do that?"

"What are you going to do?" she seized his arm.

"I've got to be sure whether the British have occupied the castle. I haven't much doubt, but I must be sure. We can't go back if they have . . . and we can't return to the portage route. I've got to find a way out. You must wait till I return and it is imperative that you remain absolutely quiet. Not a sound! The English will, no doubt, search the whole area." His voice was as stern as it had ever been.

Mimi was too exhausted to consider the danger. Paul loaded his musket and stealthily began to work his way along the river's edge toward the castle.

The sun had set and the darkness at the bank of the river was impenetrable. The aroma of black powder from the battle still hung in the air. Now and then moans drifted down the embankment. Mimi's heart still pounded; thinking of Paul out there did little to lessen her anxiety. If she could just see, she could move from the brambly bushes to a rock by the water, she thought. She was hot and thirsty and the humidity of the July day hadn't diminished at all since the sun had set behind the trees.

Mimi remained at that uncomfortable post as long as possible; her entire body ached, and she had to move. She could no longer tolerate the awkward position in spite of Paul's orders. Stretching her legs toward the water, her foot hit a boulder. She reached out with her hands to determine the size of it, then slowly inched her way, pulling herself on top. Stones rattled as she moved from the bush, and, in the exaggerated quiet of the night, it sounded like a small avalanche. She knew the slightest sound would give her position away and breathing excitedly, she stopped to listen. When she was satisfied she was still alone she reached the boulder, stretching out on it. The rushing water against her hand felt cool and inviting. Tearing a swatch from her dress she dipped it into the water, soothing her face and dabbing at the cuts on her arms and legs.

As she bathed herself she suddenly stiffened. Detecting a slight rustle of sound she lay there, in a frozen position, not daring to breath. From out of the darkness appeared a tall form, approaching her. If this is not Paul, it is my end, she thought as her breast heaved with fear. At the touch of his hands she jerked away and tumbled into the river. Two hands hauled her back to the narrow shore, pulling her to her feet. She came face to face with a British redcoat.

"What have we here?"

"Please, monsieur . . ."

"A Frenchman, huh? Well, now a pretty plight you've gotten yourself into ain't it? What are you doing down here?" He held her arm tightly. Mimi didn't answer.

"Hiding, eh? Well, come along. The general wants all you survivors at the castle.

Mimi drew her breath. Paul was right, they had captured the castle. But where was he? What would he do when he found her gone? Mimi didn't have time to fathom these questions as she was abruptly shoved along the river's edge.

"Get up the hill," he shouted.

"But, there is no way up, monsieur," she said.

"You'll get up if I have to push you by your behind," he said. "Ya got down here, didn't ya?"

He pulled her along, grabbing one tree limb after the other. Her arm ached so that Mimi decided to cooperate and began pulling herself up. When they reached the top the soldier pushed her onto the portage road toward the castle, all the while holding his musket at her back.

"Move along, now. We ain't got all night to follect you frogs."

Mimi stumbled and fell in the darkness, while he shouted orders for her to get back to her feet. Dead men still lay along the route, some scalped, others torn apart by bullets and bayonets. They waded through the creek where more bodies lay and up ahead she saw the flicker of campfires at the compound. Reaching the entrance, they were halted by a British guard. The sharp blade of his bayonet glimmered in the campfire light.

It all seemed so strange. Just hours before, French guards challenged all comers at the castle compound. The wooden huts which housed the soldiers and Indians were now piles of shattered rubble, and she found herself being pushed through narrow paths between rows of wounded men. Soldiers held lanterns while others bound their wounds.

All around the edges of the castle grounds stood British guards. Mimi slowly passed the place where once Paul's cabin stood. Now it was shattered, the planks blown asunder. A fleeting thought of her wedding gown crossed her mind. Ahead of them lights flickered in the windows of the great castle. With its huge doors braced wide open, guards on either side, it bore scars from the battering of hotshot and cannon balls from the far shore of the Niagara River. Still the great fortress had withstood the attack and loomed majestically amidst the wreckage everywhere.

Mimi was unceremoniously thrust through the entranceway. Inside soldiers ran with a sense of urgency—in and out of rooms, up and down the stairs. In one corner, two French soldiers huddled on the floor with guards standing over them. Then Mimi was shoved into one of the smaller rooms; there on a bench sat the dejected Madame Gereaud.

The disheveled Mimi wearily pulled herself to the bench. "Madame Gereaud! I'm so glad to see someone I know. What are they going to do with us?"

"Heh! What can they do with us?" she snapped in her usual fashion. "Rape us and toss us into the river, what else? These men . . ." she flourished her hand wildly. "They are all alike, French or British; that's all they think we're good for," she said with a disgusted twist to her mouth.

"Have you seen anyone else, anyone we know?" Mimi asked hopefully disregarding the woman's predictions.

"No one. I've seen no one but these British dogs. They haul me from my kitchen and throw me in here. I expect, by now, they have cleaned out my kitchen, like the vultures they are. These bastards want to own the whole world," she hissed.

"Somehow we've got to get out of here. Paul will be searching for me."

"And what makes you think that?" Gereaud growled.

"He left me waiting by the river while he went to see if the British had occupied the castle. He will find us, I know he will."

"Don't count on it, my little miss. These ruffians have covered that. If you see him at all it will be in death. What do they want with captives? We are just in their way. Mark my words, they will rape us and kill us."

Mimi pulled herself back on the bench, sighing dejectedly, since Madame Gereaud had said nothing which would lift her spirits, she vacantly looked around the room. "He will find us," she said quietly but determinedly.

It was hours before the door opened and a British soldier ordered them to follow. Mimi had fallen asleep, then awakened and paced the room while Madame Gereaud continued to puff at the air with venomous words as to their destiny at the hands of the Englishmen. Mimi, lost in her own thoughts and worry for Paul, had given up listening long ago, but Madame Gereaud remained strong in her convictions of their fate. It seemed to Mimi that while death did not appeal to Gereaud it didn't seem quite so atrocious to the large woman that she might also be raped. Mimi detected somewhat of a hope in the woman's predictions.

Passing the soldier, the undaunted Madame spat on him, making an obscene gesture.

The infuriated soldier threw her into the hallway. "Get up, you wench!" he brought his musket stock in position to ram her head.

"Sergeant!" A loud voice boomed from the door on the other side of the vestibule. "That's enough! Get on about your bloody business," he shouted. Then he gallantly aided Madame Gereaud to her feet. "Ladies, if you don't mind." He gestured toward the long council room. "Please go inside. We shall chat." He smiled pleasantly.

Once inside he assisted them to a chair at a long table, giving the hulking Madame Gereaud the same kind courtesy as he did Mimi. "I am General Johnson, Sir William Johnson." Looking at both women seriously he said, "We had not expected this problem. It *is* a very serious problem, too, you know." He leaned on the table toward them. "We have no place for ladies in captivity as I am sure you are both well aware. What are we to do? The cabins on the grounds have been blown to bits and there isn't enough room in the castle for the officers. Yes, indeed, we have a very serious problem confronting us." He slapped his hands behind his back and strode about the room, thinking. "What are we to do?" he asked with a polished, polite lilt.

"Heh!" said Madame Gereaud. She sat in an unladylike position in the chair across from the general, one arm over the back, an act of total disrespect for her captors.

"Yes, madame, you have something to say?" He leaned toward her questioningly, a look of hopefulness on his face.

"I've got a lot I could say about the British blackhearts. I know what you will do with us." She waggled a finger in his direction.

"And, what is that, madame?" he sat back in his chair spreading his hands to indicate he was open to any suggestios she might have.

It was more than the woman expected and she was taken aback. She was at a loss of words momentarily. "Well, let us go, what else?" she replied as she leaned her arm on one knee bringing herself quite close to the general. "We can take care of ourselves. We don't need the likes of you and your soldiers." Her scorn for the English was undeniable.

Mimi sat quietly hoping the general would take none

of Madame Gereaud's attitude as her own, since she and the woman were worlds apart in every respect. Mimi's attitude was less one of valor than hope that they would be respectfully treated as women.

Johnson, who had begun to pace the stone floor, swung around to answer Madame Gereaud's reply. "I'm afraid I can't do that, madame." He resumed his pacing then stopped and turned to Mimi. "You have been very quiet, madame. Have you no suggestions?"

"Release us, General. We will find a way."

"A way for what, madame? Surely you don't believe you can find a way to France?"

"Would you stop us if we could?" Mimi found a certain comfort in the general's friendly attitude toward her.

"No I would not. My soldiers will not stop you either, but these Indians, well, I am not so sure that I can vouch for them. We have difficulty getting them to respond to our orders at all."

"But you command them, General. Surely they will listen to you?"

He shoved two fingers into the pockets of his uniform. "They are not that reliable, I'm afraid. They will fight alongside us, and trade with us, but beyond that I have little control. The only hope we have over the Indians is our trading power. As long as we can furnish them with whiskey and trinkets, and they ply us with furs and pelts, we have a contract. You see, ladies, that is really our only bond. Without that they would be slicing our throats too, I fear. No, I do not think I can let you leave. We must find another answer."

"Just as I thought," said Madame Gereaud gruffly. "We are women, no? You will find a use for us, don't worry." She wagged her head knowingly and turned away in her chair.

The general's good nature faded. "My dear lady," he

said placing his hands on the table, leaning close. "Rest assured that my men are not *that* desperate." He recognized her reasoning all too well.

Returning to his floor pacing, fingers in his pockets, he stood looking at the lake through the barred window. "No, I think we shall keep you in the kitchen, both of you. That will have to do till something better comes along. And now, ladies . . ." He strode to the door. "Escort these ladies to the kitchen, Corporal." Then, turning to the two women, "I'm sure you can find something for us to eat." Watching them exit he quickly closed the door after them.

The guard took Madame Gereaud's arm, ushering her toward the kitchen. She shrugged from him belligerently. "Don't you think I know where the kitchen is, you fool? All my life I've been in a kitchen and now you have to show me the way?" She glared at him, totally unafraid as to what he might do.

"Get in there!" he shouted.

Madame Gereaud sauntered in defiantly, both hands on her hips. With a sneer slanting her large mouth she flung her arm in the air slapping it on her hip. "Look at this place!" she shrieked. "They think I will clean this mess? Never!" Her generous bulk thudded on the bench where she leaned back with her elbows on the table.

"I don't think we'd better test them," Mimi said strongly. "We must do what they say and bide our time. I know something will happen and we will escape."

"Nonsense! You are too stupid to know. I know!" She jabbed a finger at her chest. "Haven't I been an army cook for all these years? They will use us, you watch." Walking lazily to the fireplace she suddenly seized the poker and slammed it hard on the table top shaking Mimi from her seat. "I will kill them first," she said with fervor.

## Chapter Twenty-Five

It took Madame Gereaud many days to realize the futility of her firm stand against the British, but even her strength was slightly weakened and she was again back to the duties of cooking and baking for soldiers. Her heart was definitely not in the task, a fact that she made increasing clear with her every move and her every meal. She displayed her great displeasure openly, slamming the soldier's food on their plates and taking a particular delight in making a big production when she served General Johnson. Her decorative flair was gone entirely, and a thumb in their dish was her gesture of displeasure and hatred for her captors. "They can eat what they get as long as I am cook," she had said to Mimi more than once.

In the meantime, Mimi was assigned new chores sweeping up the rooms and tending to officer's quarters. General Johnson realized Mimi was totally under the huge woman's control and sympathized. It was not only for Mimi's benefit and safety, but there was less chance for them to conspire—and things in the kitchen, including the preparation of the food, were in a bad enough state as it was. It was while working on her new assignment that Mimi discovered General Pouchot and sixteen others being held captive on the third floor of the castle. One of her duties was to carry them their meals and sweep the floor of the huge room.

When first she saw Pouchot he was a broken and dispirited man. "When I heard the guns fire on the portage I had no idea of the seriousness, until one of my Onondaga scouts finally returned with the news of the horror taking place. I couldn't believe my ears. I had relied on the troops from Presque Isle and Frenchman's Creek, but certainly I never dreamed they would disregard my orders and take the portage route as they did. And to think that Generals DeLignery, Aubrey and the others were already wounded and dying . . . I just couldn't believe it. We tried our best to defend the post, but with less than a hundred muskets, we could not beat them back. The indignity of it . . . I cannot face my nation again."

"There was nothing else to do." Mimi tried to restore his confidence.

"Ah, my child, that may be true, but it still remains that the French dreams of an empire in Niagara Country, and the west, have been blasted for all time. When I gaze from these windows and survey the ruins of this post, when I think of the dead French soldiers and our Indian allies, my heart is sore. The most one can say for the infallibility of the French, is that the stone fortress can withstand any bombardment. At least, this we did right."

Pouchot was implacable and nothing Mimi could say was he willing to accept. He would rather see himself hanged by the enemy than returned to his own country a disgraced man.

Mimi's duties took her in and out of the castle, hauling staples for the kitchen. The British-allied Indians were camped, to the right of the castle, along the lake's shore and frequently she was sent to their camp to bring food and other necessities. It was not a duty she liked but it did get her outside and away from the enemy soldiers.

As the days wore on her thoughts were with Paul more and more. She lay upon her hard bed set up in the unused chapel of the castle, thinking of him and entertaining thoughts of escape. She talked to Madame Gereaud about it, lying there after the hard days of work.

"What are your thoughts, tonight?" the woman asked, knowing Mimi's quiet mood could mean only that she was attempting to devise another plan, having failed the night before and the night before that.

"I still think it can be done. You know, there are canoes along the shore. If we could sneak out one night and take a canoe we could make it to Mont Real."

"Get past the guards and those savages—never!" Madame Gereaud waved off the whole scheme as insane.

"There is a prisoner in that small room just on the other side of these walls. I wonder who it can be?"

"That's true, they have a guard take him his food," Madame Gereaud explained. "I know, I must fix it for him. I, too, wonder who it can be," she mused. "But, of what possible good will it do for us to know who is captive in that room. That doesn't get us out of here?"

"I've got to know if it is Paul."

"That's true. He hasn't shown up yet and you were so sure he would. It may well be that he is a prisoner also. If so, he can do us no good and we are still left to our own devices, no?" The cook looked at Mimi strangely. There was more to her remark than Mimi was able to discern. Still she was quite sure it was clear in one respect; Mimi would never surrender herself to be used, even if it meant she would never be free to return home. She held out little hope for Madame Gereaud as well.

Had the woman branded her intentions and propositions on her forehead there would still be no takers.

Madame Gereaud rose to the idea. "Tomorrow I will make some excuse to the guard. I shall think of a good reason why I must take the meal instead. These stupid English will believe anything. That way we will know who it is. Although what good it will do you is beyond me."

"At least I will know whether it is Paul or not. If it is, I shall make no attempt to escape. I shall stay."

"And if it is not?"

"I will think of something," Mimi stated firmly.

The following day Madame Gereaud was set with her plan. As the guard came in for the prisoner's noontime meal she made ready. "Monsieur, this prisoner of yours, he is not well, *oui*?"

"He's not doing too good, I can tell ya that," the soldier replied, picking at a pastry on the table. Madame Gereaud slapped his hand, then, reconsidering, she smiled and handed it to him politely. It wasn't the time for such attitudes if the plan was to work.

"Maybe I should see him. Perhaps I can do something. You know . . . a woman's touch? What can it hurt? You will be right outside, no?" She turned on all the charm she possessed, which was little. Still, it seemed to be making some sort of impact on the Englishman.

"Not much can be done for him," the soldier replied carelessly. "But if you think you can do better there ain't no harm in seeing 'im. Ya can't get away anyhow."

"*Oui*, monsieur. I know that." Madame Gereaud smiled and plucked playfully at one of his coat buttons. "You strong soldiers would not let us escape. it is far from our minds," she lied. A cynical smile crossed her hard face as she turned from his view.

Madame Gereaud walked from the kitchen carrying a bowl, the guard right behind her. Inside the dungeon it was pitch black. There wasn't so much as a window for light or air. "Monsieur," she whispered. 'It is Madame Gereaud. Where are you?"

"Gereaud?" a thin weak voice said.

"*Oui*, I cannot see you. Where are you?" She extended one hand, feeling the stone wall.

"To the left of the door," the voice whispered.

Gereaud bent to the floor, feeling around. "Ah! There you are, monsieur. I have brought your food. Are you wounded? How badly?" She searched for his hand to place the bowl in it. "How badly are you hurt?" she repeated.

"Mortally. I shall not live much longer." The voice was weak and labored.

"Who are you, monsieur? Tell me, I must know. Hurry before the guard opens the door."

"Captain Laloque."

"*Mon Dieu*!" Gereaud drew in her breath. "Why are you not upstairs with the rest of the captive officers?"

"They say I killed one of their generals. I am to be executed, but I shall not live to see it." He struggled to talk.

"Eat. Keep up your strength. Mimi is here also. We devise an escape plan. Somehow we will release you." Her words spilled out before the guard returned. "I must go now or they will be suspicious, Captain."

"Do not wait for me, madame. I am too weak. I shall never see France or Mimi again." His voice grew weaker. "Madame, please mention nothing of this to Mimi. I should not want her to know that I was executed."

"But not even that you are the captive?" Gereaud asked.

"Nothing, please, madame."

"Monsieur Captain, Monsieur Captain." Madame Gereaud shook him, but he no longer responded. Standing, she felt for the door and beat on it. "Are you going to leave me in this dark hole forever?" she queried as the guard opened it. "It is not my intent to go blind in this pit," she bellowed at the guard as she headed for the kitchen. "What do you British use for brains?" She continued mumbling expletives to the guard and the British, in general, as she lumbered into the kitchen. "Poor Captain Laloque, he is not long for this world," she whispered to herself, leaning against the closed door.

Mimi rushed into the kitchen, slamming the heavy door behind her. She leaned against the table, panting.

"What is it, girl? Have you see a ghost?"

"Not a ghost, Madame Gereaud. I have seen Paul." She slipped onto the bench.

"You must be mad. How could he be here among all these soldiers?"

"He is! I know it was he, in a British uniform," Mimi insisted.

"Pshaw! This hard work has gone to your brain. This is impossible." She waved off the thought and went back to her pot of stew.

"I tell you it was Paul," Mimi's voice rose.

"Shhh! That dumb jackal in the hall will hear you."

"I've got to find out for sure. If it is Paul we must let him know our plans."

"Where was he?" Madame Gereaud sat beside Mimi wiping her hands on her apron. She was ready to believe that it was Paul and a plan was taking form.

"Standing guard on the edge of the compound."

"Ah!" said Gereaud. "That is very smart. He doesn't have to mingle among the others and their shift changes in the dead of night. I wonder how he has accomplished this? But, that's of no matter now. We must move before he is detected." She placed her chin in her hand.

"What is it? Have you an idea?"

"I was just thinking," Madame Gereaud hummed. "The Indians are bringing their families to join them, are they not?"

"Yes, but . . ."

"My dear Mimi, I think I know what we will do." Her face lit up as she contemplated the brilliance of her plan.

"Tell me, Gereaud."

"There is no time to waste, so it must be done tonight."

"What? What is your plan?" Mimi's excitement rose.

"Tonight just as dark is falling you must go to the trading room and make some excuse to get these English blankets. Tell them it's for the squaws and children. I don't think they will question that, you have done it many times. You will head toward the Indian camp. Go toward the lake shore where you saw the major on guard."

"Where will you be?"

"Don't worry. They are accustomed to my coming and going to the bake kiln."

Mimi began to understand. The ovens were just ahead of the guard ridge. "*Oui*, that is perfect!" She beamed. "Paul will be sure to see us. He will know what to do."

"We will have to be very careful," Madame Gereaud went on. "I will watch for you. When you reach the ridge near Paul I will slip past the bakery house. It is to be hoped that your major is smart enough to fall in with us. Without him it would alert those savages, but with him, it would merely look as though we were under guard. Delay your step, Mimi, the darker the sky the better. Only then we can slip away in those canoes."

"Oh, it's perfect," Mimi almost shouted.

"Shhh!" Madame Gereaud waved her hands before Mimi. "You idiot, they will hear us. The British are stupid but not *that* stupid. Be careful from now on or our plan will go bust!" Gereaud filled her cheeks with air, popping her mouth.

Mimi quickly took a bowl of cornbatter and began to beat it as a soldier walked into the kitchen.

"What are you doing in my kitchen?" Madame Gereaud screamed at him with indignation. Seizing the broom from the corner she heaved the bristles into his face and the intimidated man quickly left. "Get on about your business, girl. We meet as planned and may the good Lord see fit to help us." She raised her eyes to the ceiling.

Mimi took the broom and headed upstairs to clean the officers' quarters.

The sun was beginning to set. It would still be another hour before darkness settled. Mimi was in the chapel pacing the floor. The English general had seen to it that her gown had been replaced and she donned the cotton replacement, casting aside the other. There would be no room for excess baggage in this plan. Madame Gereaud continued with making bread. It was her reason for being in the compound and she made sure there was plenty of dough.

As the night settled over the camp, Mimi cautiously left the chapel. She walked across the hall toward the trading room, passing the guards who sat talking on the long bench. She hid her surprise as the man in the post stacked her up with blankets without question. Leaving through the front door she headed down the green toward the lake. Her body shook with excitement as the moment came closer. Rounding the bake house she gave a quick glance toward Paul. He continued to stand so rigid Mimi wondered if he saw her.

Swiftly, Paul raised his musket and ran toward her where he pulled her to a halt. "If I shout a command, they will know I am French. Keep talking to me. Act as though I am questioning you," he said.

Mimi pulled herself sharply from his grip. "Where do you think I'm going?" she shouted. Then, quietly she said, "Madame Gereaud is right behind you. We are going to try for the canoes."

"It's useless, Mimi. The Indians will be suspicious. There's no way it will work. Talk louder, say something sharp to me," he urged. The other guards were throwing questioning looks in their direction.

"Will you leave me alone? I don't take kindly to your proposition, monsieur!"

The other soldiers shot knowing winks at each other, smiles spread across their faces. "These French maids are good," one said as the others laughed loudly.

"Perfect!" Paul said. "They think I want to take you into the woods. That's exactly how we shall play it. Now! Act as though you are melting to my request." Paul took her by the arm as they walked toward the trees.

At that moment, Madame Gereaud showed up. She was puzzled to see Mimi and Paul heading away from the canoes, but her mind worked quickly. "You blackheart!" she bellowed as she ran toward the two.

The guards thought it humorous and loud laughter resulted. When she reached them, Paul put his arms around both women. "They think Mimi has accepted my proposition. We will stop but a moment while I try to convince you to join us," Paul said.

"Ah! I see!" said Gereaud. "That is even more clever than my plan. But, monsieur—two women!"

"These Englishmen will think I am a lucky fellow, but make it look good."

Gereaud began to laugh liltingly and the three of them threw their arms around each other and entered the woods while all the guards laughed uproariously and the Indians smiled knowingly.

Once out of sight, Paul made haste moving the two women down the embankment along the river's edge. "I took one of their batteaux several nights ago. It's hidden in the woods down river."

"But, monsieur, there are three of us," Gereaud protested. "My size alone needs one."

"We'll have to try it. There's no other way," Paul said. "The canoe is hidden in these bushes. I think it would be best to leave now, before the soldiers decide we have escaped and come after us." Paul began to uncover the hidden canoe, moving it effortlessly into the water.

"This small boat!" Madame Gereaud said sharply. "It will sink with my weight. No, monsieur, this is not for me." She backed off.

"Come, madame, we don't have time for this. If we don't leave now it will be too late," Paul urged.

"Not for me," she insisted. "You and Mimi go, I shall take my chances."

Mimi jumped into the canoe. "Hurry, Gereaud!"

"No! Go quickly! Do not worry about me." She backed into the woods.

"Madame!" Paul called after her trying to keep his voice down.

Madame Gereaud had gone. There was no going back for her, so Paul shoved the canoe from shore and jumped in. The current immediately took the small boat away from the shore and before they could get the paddles into the water, it began to spin in the strong movement. Paul regained control, directing it down the river toward the mouth of the lake. He dipped his paddles silently, pulling with long, sweeping strokes as the current took hold of the small boat and carried it down river.

Now, opposite the British encampments, on both sides of the river, they could see the campfires. Silently, they drifted by the shores, shrouded in the black of the night. Back on land, they could hear Madame Gereaud's booming voice carry over the water. "These British think they can handle two women. Bah! They aren't men enough!" she bellowed at the top of her voice. "Hah," she went on, "you all make me laugh. You think you are world conquerers. Well, we French will show you. Just you wait. You will regret this whole thing when we get through with you." It was her unique way of explaining her reappearance and drawing attention from the canoe. Mimi and Paul could hear her continue to deride the English soldiers' prowess as men, and the guard's laughter rose from the camp as they took delight in her obvious frustration.

"Good old Gereaud, she has kept them guessing," said Paul. "I shall miss that big, loud woman," he added, looking ruefully toward the shore fires.

## Chapter Twenty-Six

When the first light of dawn arose Paul and Mimi were well into the lake, miles from shore. Nothing could be seen in any direction. The sun rose to another brilliantly warm day. Mimi, who had fallen asleep, sat up rubbing her eyes. "Where are we, Paul?"

"We're heading north. I think it's best to stay close to the north shore, through the lake and then up the St. Lawrence River. When we reach Mont Real we will be safe," he said.

Paul pulled the paddle into the canoe and removing his bright red British coat he dropped it into the water. As they both watched it drift out of sight behind them Mimi pulled an ore from the boat floor and began to paddle.

For hours they pulled through the choppy water. Seagulls dipped and swooped close to their craft, trailing behind them in anticipation of dropped tidbits. They glided in, landing beside the canoe, and drifted beside them. Their antics amused the two, but Mimi began to feel extremely hungry and soon their play began to pall. She could think of nothing but her hunger. "I'm thankful for our escape, Paul, but I am so hungry I could gladly consume one of these birds."

"It's only a matter of another hour or so before we reach the north shore. We will find something there to eat. I'm sure." He drew a hard biscuit from the pocket of his breeches and tossed it to her.

"Leave it to you, my darling. You thought of everything."

"Don't thank me. It belongs to the dead soldier who owned this uniform." He pointed to the sky behind Mimi as he talked. Dark clouds were beginning to form. "I hope it holds off till we reach shore."

Mimi's arms began to ache from the strain, but she refused to quit. Lightning forked to the ground, followed by distant rumbles of thunder. Paul again directed her to the thin streak of shoreline on the horizon.

The canoe bottom scraped on the shale as they hauled it in to shore. Pulling it back among the trees, they flopped on the ground to rest. Suddenly, huge drops of rain began to pelt the leaves overhead. They rose, dashing to a cluster of large boulders for protection. It was a quick summer shower, lasting only minutes, but Mimi and Paul were thoroughly drenched. As they stood they looked at each other and began to laugh uncontrollably. Mimi's hair hung in long wet strands and her dress was molded to her body.

Their relief at reaching the shore manifested itself as they laughed all the louder, completely releasing their emotions. Paul looked at Mimi lovingly and taking her face in his hands he softly kissed her. "Darling, I never thought this would happen. When I knew the British had taken you I thought it was all over for us."

"I, too, thought it would be the end." She wrapped her arms around him pulling herself close. "We are safe and together, now," she said, putting her head on his chest.

"I pray it will be that easy, my love." Paul reclined on the ground placing his hands beneath his head.

"Aren't we safe, Paul?" Mimi looked at him quizzically.

"Certainly more than before," he assured her. "But, we still must reach Mont Real, and then France, before we shall be completely safe."

"There is that . . . and we have no money for our passage." A thought which had only now occurred to Mimi.

"Oh, but we do." Paul sat up and thrust his hand into his pocket, withdrawing a packet of French money.

"Where did you get it, Paul?" Mimi was perplexed.

"From your Uncle Nathane," he laughed.

"You mean you have the money from my passage to Niagara?"

"I do. It has traveled in my breeches. Our passage is paid. All we need is to get to Mont Real. And, my love, did you not plead with your uncle to pay for your passage with your dowry? What better use for a dowry than to pay for passage home to our beloved country?"

Mimi turned serious. "Did you hear anything of a war in France?"

"Yes, the British are trying to take our home also."

"What will we do? I hate the thoughts of another war. I don't think I could live through it." She slumped on the ground. "Poor Uncle Nathane." Mimi remained quiet and thoughtful. "Paul, I received a letter from Uncle Nathane. It came just as the attack on the castle began. It was written by uncle's servant." Mimi's eyes began to mist. "Paul, he was dying when he wrote it and that was months ago. I have no hope of seeing him alive again. It is only now that I understand what Uncle Nathane was trying to say to me before I insisted upon sailing for Niagara. He said he would never again see me and I shrugged him off, laughing at the idea. Oh, how hard and cruel I used to be. I can't believe that I could have been so unthinking, unfeeling—so spoiled that I would have treated such a dear, dear man as I did him." Mimi remained quiet, again thinking of things past. She fairly whispered as she thought. "It breaks my heart now, Paul, to think that I shall never be able to thank him for my most beautiful life and his most unquestioning love for me after my parents' death. I was so horribly pampered, taking everything for granted. It seems that I needed these past years to awaken me. Uncle Nathane surely deserved better than I gave him. Now I shall never be able to tell him."

Paul let Mimi ramble on. He was aware that she needed to say what she was saying—to let it all out. And he was gratified that she had finally seen herself as she was in the past. He knew now that Mimi would never expect things that she didn't deserve, nor take things she did receive for granted. Mimi had grown up and was now ready to live.

"Darling, you can't concern yourself with things you can do nothing about. I'm sure your Uncle Nathane is safe." He stood, dusting the dirt from his damp clothes. "Now, I have to see about finding us some food. You'd better come along with me this time. I can't take the chance of having you captured again."

They walked through the woods, Paul's musket thrown over his shoulder. He drew a pistol from his belt and gave it to Mimi. She no longer needed instructions as to how to use it since she was now a veteran of war.

Deep in the forest a rustling sound stopped them in their tracks. Paul pulled her down beside him, his eyes darting from tree to boulder and back again. He raised his gun, throwing the firing pin as quickly as he raised it and fired. Then, with crackling of tree limbs, a large wild turkey fell to the ground.

Back at their canoe Paul playfully tossed the bird to

Mimi. "While you pluck I'll make a fire."

"Do you think we should? It will be seen."

"You're becoming a regular frontiersman," Paul laughed. "There's not much else we can do if we're going to eat it, but this bright sunlight should cover it." He began collecting twigs into a pile.

The two had just fiished cleaning the carcass when Paul seized Mimi and pushed her flat on the ground.

"What is it?" she said quietly.

He clapped his hand over her mouth. She pushed it away and reached for the pistol. Slowly, deftly, quiet moccasined feet came nearer. From behind the boulders they saw the painted face of a native standing close by. He had not yet seen them, but his eyes were on the dying fire. As the Indian took another step toward them Paul raised his gun and blasted. The savage went down. Paul cautioned Mimi to remain still.

To Mimi, it seemed like hours before Paul whispered, "He must be a scout for the tribe. There doesn't seem to be any more of them. We must leave at once, though. They can't be far behind."

As they stood to run for their canoe an arrow whizzed past, then another. A warrior dove from the top of a nearby boulder landing on Paul, dragging him to the ground. Mimi pulled herself back, her pistol ready, waiting for a chance of a clear shot. Paul came up on his feet, heaving the savage from him. The Indian rolled away, and as he hunched to spring again, Mimi shot. The savage fell at Paul's feet.

"Come!" Paul shouted as he charged for the canoe. He dragged it to the water and shoved Mimi into it. He pushed it from shore jumping in as it slipped away. Arrows sped past them, slicing the water as they paddled from shore.

Finally, out of reach of the savages, they could see

splashes of bright color along the shore as the natives followed their canoe up river.

"I shall never get used to this." Mimi's anxiety turned to anger. "I'm tired of running for my life. It will take me years to settle down when we reach France." She was still puffing from the run.

"It's best we continue right on till we reach Mont Real. These natives will be all along the shore and won't give up. It will be a long pull, but at least it will be safer."

The lake narrowed into the St. Lawrence River, the current pulling them easily along, allowing Paul to rest. Mimi had only to rudder the light craft, directing it along its path. The sun was beginning to hide behind the tops of the trees. And, now on their second day they were miles up the river and Paul was sure that Mont Real was not far.

When he awoke from a much needed sleep they were just entering the waters surrounding thousands of small islands. He maneuvered their boat in and out of the clustered, green peaks where the shore on either side of them was only a few hundred feet apart. Now, staying as close to the north shore as they dared, they were almost at their destination.

## Chapter Twenty-Seven

To Mimi's surprise, the inland port of Mont Real was bustling with activity. It was not at all what she had imagined and, certainly, a far cry from Lewiston, which was the largest village she had seen in Niagara Country.

Large-masted sailing ships crowded the dock where streams of soldiers and sailors hauled large crates up and down the gangplanks, stacking them on the dock or onboard. The faces of the dock workers dripped with perspiration in the heat of the July day.

Paul had sailed the *Premier* many times to this port and he had the feeling of having arrived at home, a feeling that delighted him until he thought of the new hardship of finding passage to France.

"So many Frenchmen and so many ships—we should have no trouble getting passage." Mimi was astounded at the scene she was observing.

"Some of these ships remain at port for weeks, Mimi. They must wait for full loads, so don't get your hopes up. If passage is possible at all, we may have quite a long wait. Besides, it will give us time to think about proper clothing. It wouldn't do to arrive in France like this. And you, my lady, require a dress befitting the occasion."

Mimi laughed. She was a shoddy mess, to say the least. And the thrill of a new dress raised her spirits.

"Yes, can you imagine Uncle Nathane's face if I arrive like this?" She spread her arms and twirled.

Seeking her hand Paul lead her from the beach into the heart of the throng. They wandered through the village craning their necks to keep abreast of the constantly moving inhabitants.

"Where are we going?" Mimi finally asked trying to keep up with his steps.

"There is a wonderful priest who runs a settlement. I'm sure he can advise us about rooms."

"I do hope we won't have to stay too long. I want to get home as fast as possible." Mimi wasn't ready to stay in Mont Real even with the excitement of it and she couldn't forget Uncle Nathane. Her hope was to see him alive and well.

"My love, will you ever learn patience?" Paul smiled as she turned to watch the passing villagers, taking particular notice of women in their dresses.

"Patience!" Mimi dropped Paul's hand abruptly. "You, of all people, should know the patience I've had to learn, not to mention living with death around every corner and hunger and killing—the killing I've had to do!"

Paul instantly realized his insensitivity. The two years of horror Mimi had endured, much beyond the tolerance expected of someone raised to enjoy the finer things of life, had reached its peak. She had been living on the edge of her nerves too long and now, having reached the haven Mimi had conjured in her mind these years as the one last step to her home in France, her last ounce of strength had been tried.

He drew her to him and threw his arms around her tightly, holding her close. Paul knew it would take more time than he cared to think to find a ship that would willingly take on passengers. And now, with the air of urgency all too apparent at the seaport, Paul knew it was just a matter of time before the British would make their assault here too, as they had in Niagara.

There in the midst of the milling throng Paul tried to assure her. "As quickly as possible, I promise, my darling, I promise."

"It's just that I feel so close to France being here."

"I know, I know and just as quickly as arrangements can be made we'll leave. I promise." Paul hoped he could fulfill his promise.

Again they pushed their way through the workers loaded with bundles, some coming, others going, making their way toward the wooden trading posts for food staples and clothing.

Mimi was pushing her way ahead of Paul and hauling him along, sometimes going against the waves of people, then moving steadily ahead with the stream, inching across the dirt road.

At the edge of the hubbub she eased her stride. The trading post was but a few steps away. Passing closely to the buildings, a hand swiftly darted from between, grasping Paul by the neck. The strong pull forced him between the buildings and Mimi was dragged along by Paul's tightened grip on her arm. A grimy man forced him against the wall, holding a blade to his throat. He yanked the pistol from Paul's belt and shoved it into his own, while his equally grimy friend twisted Mimi's arm behind her back.

"Ya dares to strut in the open, do you?" the man said to Paul who was still stunned by the surprise attack.

"What is this?" Paul asked.

"Don't play games with me," the man hissed, tightening his grip.

"What do you want of us?"

"Don't give me none of that. You British think

you're so smart."

"British!" exclaimed Paul.

"Aye! British."

Paul could see the dirty uniform of a French sailor on his attacker. His partner, too, was a seaman. "I'm afraid you're mistaken, gentlemen. As you can see I speak French as you do."

"Ha! That means nothing." He slammed Paul against the wall. "You British can speak French like a dyed-in-the-wool patriot. That's part of your plan. You don't fool us."

Mimi, who had been forced to the ground by the pain in her arm, shuddered in fear. The man holding her stood straddling her hunched body.

"You British are fools! Did you think you could strut openly in that uniform and not be found out?" he snarled.

"But, I wear no uniform. Merely pieces of clothing collected here and there to make do. We've lost everything in the battle at Niagara. Perhaps, you've heard of me. I am Captain Paul Regis, commanding officer of the ship, *Premier*." Paul was stalling, trying to devise a way out of the situation.

"Ya don't say," mocked the sailor. He looked at his partner and they both laughed.

Down through the narrow passageway, where they were being held, Paul could see the people continuing past in their duties, paying no attention to their plight. "This is getting us nowhere," he finally said. "If I can't convince you, talk to Father DeVeaux at Village Maria. You trust him, don't you?"

The sailor tightened the knife against Paul's flesh, almost drawing blood. His face muscles slackened slightly. "You know Father De Veaux?" he asked, a little surprised.

"*Oui*, we are good friends. I visit him every time I come to port."

Paul was unable to see Mimi from his position against the wall and when he moved to try, his head was slammed against the wooden building behind him, the knife digging deeper into his flesh.

"Never mind your ladyfriend, mate. Tell me about Father DeVeaux."

"If you will just take us to the Villa, he will vouch for us."

"Ya say you sail to this port from France often?" the gruff sailor asked.

"*Oui*."

"You lie! Father Deveaux has been dead a full year now. What do you say to that?" he growled.

"I have been fighting with the French militia in Niagara Country for two years. My fiancee and I barely escaped with our lives from the British attackers," Paul explained.

The man released his grip slightly. "You was in the fight when the British attacked?"

"*Oui*, both of us fought before they took over."

Paul could see the man beginning to put stock in his words. The knife relaxed somewhat from his throat. As the man looked at his partner, Paul seized the opportunity. He gripped the arm holding the knife and quickly forced it back against the wall, pounding it until it fell to the ground. Bringing up his knee he caught the sailor in the stomach, crumpling his assailant in pain. Paul banged his fists on the back of his head and the man passed into unconsciousness.

His slightly built partner began to run, dragging Mimi through the passageway. Paul lunged, sprawling full-length, catching him around the legs. Scrambling atop the sailor he pounded his fist into his face until he too was unconscious. Mimi pressed against the building, dodging Paul's flailing fists.

With both men out of the way, Paul took Mimi by the arm to move out when the leader regained consciousness. "Cap'n." He struggled to his feet, staggering toward them. Paul pushed Mimi behind him.

"I've had enough, Cap'n." He held up both hands in a gesture of surrender. "That British tricorn is dangerous. I'll take you to the Villa if ya want, but how do you happen to be wearing a British uniform if you fought with the French in Niagara?"

"It was our only means of escape after the English captured our fortification." Paul could see his opponent was finally beginning to believe his story.

"Well, I'll tell ya, yer making a mistake wearing it here in Mont Real. We are all familiar with that regimental black-trimmed hat. The English have been giving us trouble too. They plan to attack Mont Real the same as they did Niagara."

Mimi drew in her breath. "Paul, we must get back to France immediately. This is too much."

"Aye, madame, the English are encamped all around. We expect it any time. A Frenchman by the name of Joncaire has told us of your British takeover in Niagara."

"Joncaire!" Both Paul and Mimi exclaimed in unison.

"He and his wife managed to get here."

"*Mon Dieu*!" Mimi exclaimed with glee. "Daniel is here!" She turned to the seaman. "Where? Where is Daniel, do you know? Can you take us to him?" The name Joncaire was almost as assuring as a sacred medallion to Mimi. She associated everything that had anything to do with her well being in Niagara with the Joncaires. It had seemed to her that everything that moved her closer to her goal was at the hands of one of them.

The sailor's unconscious friend revived and was struggling to his feet. He made a move toward Paul to continue their melee but was stopped by his partner. "They are French, Jean," he said. "Friends of Daniel Joncaire." Then turning to Regis, "I'll tell you, Cap, you'd better ditch that uniform or you'll get yer head blown off, fer sure."

"That was exactly our intention, monsieur, when you interrupted us."

"Well, ya can't be too careful. You'd better dash in here, then." He motioned over his shoulder toward the trading post. "I'll go along—to vouch fer ya." He looked at Paul with a sly twinkle in his eye.

Paul glanced at Mimi and back at the sailor. Suddenly the three of them broke into loud laughter.

## Chapter Twenty-Eight

Mimi was unable to find a French gown like the dresses she used to own, in a fact that didn't surprise her—not anymore. Anyway, these days it was always a case of replacing one dress for another. She had lost many articles of clothing during her trials in the New World. Paul urged her to get a heavy cape since their trip aboard ship would certainly not come about until the fall or winter. Actually, she had seen her share of pelts, but to please Paul she selected a beautiful beaver, lush and thick.

The selection of attire for Paul was just as meager. He settled for blue breeches and a black waistcoat and boots. Anything, he thought, that didn't resemble a British uniform, although even that was a challenge since the military of both sides had reached the "make do" point and pilfered what they needed from the dead and captives.

With the clothing situation settled their new-found guide urged them across the dirt road, through the streams of porters to the second floor of a wooden building.

The man pounded on the door. "Joncaire, it's Martin."

The door opened a crack with one cautious eye scanning the three of them. "*Mon Dieu!*" Daniel exclaimed, throwing his arms around the pair. "My friends, come in, come in. Prisella!" he shouted.

She entered from a small room, stoic as usual, but in her own way she welcomed Paul and Mimi and rushed to a small kitchen to prepare food.

"Tell me," Joncaire said excitedly, "how have you made it to Mont Real?"

"By canoe," said Paul as he sat in a wooden chair. "We managed to escape from the castle in one of their Indian canoes."

Joncaire slapped his knee. "The same as me." He exploded with laughter. Then turning serious he said, "My friends, I knew that day I rode into the castle grounds, when Aubrey and the others had not yet arrived, that something was about to happen. In fact, I went to Pouchot to tell him. We waited for days at Lewiston, but no troops arrived. Chabert had already set fire to Fort de Portage and fled. Alas, I have heard nothing from him since. I told Prisella to take a canoe and drift slowly downriver. I planned to meet her at the lake shore by the castle. Well, I had no sooner arrived when the barrage began. Pouchot tried to round up his men and send them into battle but I, Joncaire, was prepared. I dashed to the shore. The English were already bombarding the grounds from the far shore and Four Mile Creek. I could see Prisella drifting just passed the powder magazine. I ran to the river and waded out. I'll tell you, my friends, it was quite a feat—maneuvering that canoe past those English guns. But, as you can see, we made it." He spread his hands wide. Daniel Joncaire lowered his eyes and for a moment said nothing. Then he raised his head and looked at them directly. "I know, my friends, it looks to you as if Joncaire turned tail on his country. But I don't think so. You see, we were doomed. The only one who could not realize it was General Pouchot. His capture was imminent, as was the capture of the fortress. I know not what will become of them, but I can tell you one thing." Daniel waved a finger at his friends as they listened intently. "Joncaire, shall remain. I am going back to Niagara to finish my father's work. They have defeated the French only for a short while. The Joncaires shall resurrect the French claim to the Niagara Country. That is my aim; that is my life."

Prisella entered with cornbread, fresh vegetables and tea, at which time Paul and Mimi had to apologize for their manners as they began to eat, earnestly enjoying it.

"How is it you know my friend Martin?" asked Daniel, gesturing toward the sailor.

Paul began to laugh. "It is a long story. I shall carry the scar forever." He indicated the cut on his neck.

"I thought he was an English dog, Daniel. He wore the British regimental tricorn," Martin explained.

"A British uniform?" Daniel questioned.

"That too, is a long story," laughed Paul. "After the battle along the portage, Mimi was taken captive. One night I crept into the camp and picked off the nearest guard with a bayonet. Everyone was too busy with the wounded to notice. At any rate, I managed to kill him and, thankfully, he didn't make a sound. I dragged him to the woods and switched uniforms, quietly taking his post along the lake. If Mimi hadn't noticed me we might never be here at this moment."

"*Oui*, this Mimi is a fighter. I know, monsieur. She is a lady to be proud of." He patted her hand. "And now? What are your plans?"

"To board a ship and go back to France," Paul replied firmly.

Mimi squeezed his hand smiling at him. It was the first time Paul had said that he was ready to leave, without any qualifications.

"*Oui*, and you should," Daniel agreed.

"All we must do is find a captain who will take us," said Paul.

"Well," hummed Daniel, "Martin here is the man for this job, no?" he said looking at the sailor. "He knows all the captains, having sailed with most of them. Can you do this, Martin?"

"Mmm, I don't know, Daniel, these ships are for cargo."

Mimi and Paul looked at each other and broke into loud laughter.

"*Deja vu*," said Paul, taking her hand. "Exactly my words two years ago when this young woman first presented me with the dilemma of her trip to Niagara."

"It won't be too easy, Monsieur Captain. There are many others who wish to get out of Mont Real. The captains want seamen, not passengers."

"Then, you would say it is impossible?" Paul inquired.

"No, not impossible, but not easy. I will see what I can do."

"You may tell the captain I can pay a reasonable fare, Martin. That might entice him."

"It should help. French money has gone the way of everything else. Now, I will go see what I can do." Martin left.

"In the meantime, my friends, you are welcome to stay here with Prisella and me. Our accomodations are modest, but at least you will be safe."

"We're grateful to you, Daniel. I shall miss you when we leave," said Paul.

Joncaire laughed, leaning his chair against the wall. "I would join you, but France . . . well, France was never my home. I am American born, as you know. I have promised my father to go to his country and perhaps one day I will, but today I stay and fight for my own land."

"I tend to forget that," Mimi said. "Speaking French as you do."

Joncaire looked thoughtfully. "The apple falls closely to the tree. If I had a son, he would live to see this new country become a part of France, as I know it will. And I shall fight to see that it is so. Ah, but I get too serious." His jovial laugh broke the mood. "Paul, you and the lovely Mimi—when shall you marry? *Mon Dieu*, I have never seen such trouble getting married. It is usually the other way around," he laughed.

"We almost made it," laughed Mimi. Now in this safe, small haven even she could find the humor in it.

"And we shall, my darling." Paul looked at her tenderly. "We shall."


With Indian fighters sneaking into Mont Real daily, the villagers had a constant battle on their hands, burying the dead. The French organized into groups, patroling the seaport and outlying areas. Word filtered through that the British, along with the Iroquois, were armed and ready for an all-out attack.

Martin, good to his word, had talked to the ship captains in an effort to find passage for Paul and Mimi. While he found many willing it depended on when their sailors, now beseiged with war with the Indians, were able to man the ships safely out of port.

The French seamen were diminishing in the fierce battles and ships were being waylaid at the mouth of the St. Lawrence before they reached the port of Mont Real. It would be a battle sailing past the English into the Atlantic.

Paul had followed through on Martin's initial attempts to book their passage and he and Mimi decided it would be worth the effort to leave Mont Real if they could convince a captain to sign Paul on as a sailor.

Months went by. It was now October and Paul had finally completed arrangements for their departure. He had been able to sign on as a captain's mate with the *Boussole* which had been sitting in port for months, awaiting a full crew. And now the captain was willing to try the voyage with a minimal crew.

The summer sky had, long ago, turned to the lavender hue of autumn. Leaves were brilliant reds, oranges and yellows and were already covering the ground. The fall air was cool and brisk as they ascended the gangplank. Mimi wrapped her cape around her shoulders against the wind. Paul followed, carrying the small leather pouch containing their meager possessions. Mimi solemnly stood at the rail as Paul and a handful of regulars hauled in the ropes, releasing the ship from dock. It shifted and creaked as it moved from its mooring into the St. Lawrence.

As much as Mimi wanted to be in France, she felt a sadness as this last part of the journey began. She hated the wild land of America but she had also found good friends and, now, she thought of each one—Sergeant Mileaux, Liliyana, Chabert, Daniel and Prisella, and even Madame Gereaud. She would never forget any of them. Had it only been two years since she left France? Mimi thought as they drifted out of the port. She had mixed emotions, knowing that little better awaited them in their own country.

Once again in the small cabin of the ship's mate she placed their belongings into the wardrobe, reminding her again of the day she began her voyage to Niagara Country and all that had happened in those few years.

She had grown from a child into a woman.

Paul was busy on deck as the captain plotted their course. "Our foremost danger is getting into the Atlantic. We surely will be met by British ships, if I know my seas," said Captain DuGoyne. "It is a great risk we have taken, Regis, leaving with half a crew."

"I'm most grateful for what you have done for us."

"Well, monsieur, it is not only for you that we leave this shore. I too, have a duty to return to France, and I fear that if we don't leave now we may never have the chance again."

Paul scanned the horizon and shore. "If I may make a suggestion, Captain?"

"What is that, Regis?"

"If we are not met by British ships at the mouth of the river do you think it would be wiser to steer a course south along the shore, then veer easterly? The British ships, if there are any, will no doubt take a more direct route across the sea."

"You may be right, Regis, however it will depend on what we encounter." DuGoyne turned to shout his orders to the men on deck.

"Aye, Captain." Paul left the deck realizing that, as a junior officer, it wasn't his place to make suggestions to his captain, a thought he would have to keep in mind.

Sailing up the St. Lawrence they were entirely alone. No other ships had left Mont.Real that day. The shores were eerily silent and foreboding.

Mimi, now on deck, watched as the ship turned in the bend of the river and the tree-lined shore obliterated the last view of the port. As she watched she saw pillars of black smoke rise high into the air. It has begun, she thought. She ran to be near Paul, at the helm. "It has begun hasn't it, Paul?"

"We made it out on time. Now, all we can hope for is

that no British ships await us. They will be armed with cannons this time. Our cargo vessel is no match for them." Paul thought, as he spoke, that there was a time when he would not have been able to speak so frankly to Mimi about these things, and now she stood stiffly beside him, no longer shattered as she once was. It had been her wish to sail home and she was willing to face the consequences along with the rest of them.

Captain DuGoyne moved beside them. "I fear it will be the worst for the people of Mont Real. They don't have the equipment to hold the village in such a battle as this will be. The English are intent upon taking the land and for the moment it looks as though they will have their wish. But," he said resignedly, "there is nothing we can do to help them."

Paul and Mimi stood at the rail full of reminiscences of their friends, especially the Joncaires. "I shall never forget them." Mimi said quietly.

"Nor I." Paul slid his arm around Mimi.

A shout from the helmsman turned their attention to the horizon. Captain DuGoyne seized his glass and extending it full length he searched the water where another ship was looming toward them. "French ship," he said matter-of-factly.

"French? That means they are still getting through."

"Make ready to heave to," DuGoyne shouted to the helmsman. Turning to Paul he said, "I want to question this captain as to the conditions. Best we know what to prepare for."

"They seem intact," Paul replied, moving his glass from his eye.

The wind on the river was sufficient to move them along at a steady pace. The two ships moved cautiously, now side by side.

DuGoyne shouted: "We're heading for France. Did

you encounter the British?"

"Clear sailing," came the reply. "How did you leave Mont Real?"

"Planning for an attack, we left with half crew. Your ship is unarmed. Best not to try to port there."

"Aye, Captain, I understand your message. Sighted only one Dutch ship, heading home."

"Excellent!" DuGoyne said to Paul. "When we get into the Atlantic we'll head south, then east. No point in looking for trouble. If the British are on their way we will avoid them if possible. However, I expect it will be six of one and half dozen of the other. The British are sure to be up and down the coast as well. It will be a good trick to find a lane where we pass undetected."

Mimi stood listening as they plotted and conjectured. She knew there was a strong possibility they would never make it through. But she had understood that when she boarded. It was a calculated risk for them all. Captain DuGoyne was grateful to have a seaman such as Paul aboard. Throwing in their lot and filling in on duties was the only way. Both were prepared, and Mimi was willing and ready to help where she could. She had again forsaken her dress for seaman's attire. Now nothing but practical measures were to be taken.

"That French cargo ship has decided to throw in with us," Paul observed.

"*Oui*, I see they have turned. I hope they follow us. I think we may need them," DuGoyne said. "Although without cannons I don't know what good we can be to each other."

The river widened before them, the sea mixing with the fresh river water. The tree-lined shores of the New World were out of sight and the great ocean spread ahead.

Captain DuGoyne scanned with his glass. He shouted

to his men to raise more sail and Paul jumped to action at his command. The stronger wind on the ocean flopped the heavy canvas. Mimi joined in and was pulling the ropes, putting all her strength into it. The force of the wind whipped it from her and she dove to grab it. Paul secured his ropes running to her side to help. Mimi rubbed her burned hands together, but took little time about it as she dashed for another loose-hanging rope.

The ship that had joined them was staying well behind. DuGoyne thought it was a good decision as it afforded less of a target than the two ships together. As they moved south the ocean gale picked up and they were now under full sail.

There would be no sleep for anyone as the night lowered. Each would have to remain at his post. Mimi, however, had slipped to the galley to try to prepare supper. It would be a strange trip; there was no time and the lack of sufficient crew hands wouldn't allow for regular meals. Mimi knew they would have to catch their meals on the jump and then only when things were quiet enough. Most of their meals would consist of dried meat and dark bread. The fruit brought aboard would be their only fresh food and she knew that spoilage would probably take most of that. Still she was prepared to do the best she could under the circumstances. No longer would she moan and worry about her welfare.

After passing out meals to the men on deck she and Paul sat against the ship's side. The importance of their danger prevented conversation and Paul hurried his meal to relieve the captain. Mimi, totally exhausted, went to their cabin and, fully clothed, succumbed to sleep.

## Chapter Twenty-Nine

Paul stood looking at Mimi before he bent to kiss her. "Wake up, my darling." he stroked her hair softly.

Mimi squirmed and stretched in the bunk. "What time is it?" She brushed her hair from her face and looked at him.

"It's past noon, my love." He gently helped her to her feet.

"You must be jesting."

"No, I do not jest, my sweet, see." He opened the door where the sun shafted through. He was showing a good deal of vigor for one who had been up all night.

"Why didn't you wake me sooner? I feel so foolish."

Paul laughed. "You're really getting into it aren't you, my darling?"

"About time wouldn't you say?" She threw her arms around his neck and kissed him tenderly.

"I like your spirit, Mimi, and may I say I'm very proud of you."

She smiled at him as she moved from the bunk. "Did you get any sleep?" she asked with concern.

"Not yet, but I am about to do just that." He flopped on the bunk. "DuGoyne slept awhile and he's back on deck now. Mimi, awaken me in a few hours."

"Darling, I don't know how you've managed to stay on your feet this long." She threw the cover over him and bent to kiss his forehead. She could hear him breathing heavily, already sound asleep.

Mimi left the cabin, closing the door quietly. As she ascended the stairs she covered her eyes, shielding them from the bright sun. It was brighter and warmer, now, as they sailed farther south.

"Good morning, madame." Captain DuGoyne stood at the helm.

"Good morning, Captain. I want to apologize for sleeping so late. It's inexcusable."

"No need. It was a quiet night and we've made good time. You put in a hard day yesterday."

"I was exhausted, but no more than the rest. I should have been more considerate. Have you eaten, Captain? May I get you something?"

"We have all had something, madame, however I would consider it a favor if you would be so kind as to deliver me the flask from my cabin. I feel the need of a strong jolt."

At first Mimi thought nothing of it, but as she watched the captain drain the flask she became apprehensive. She had stood silently against the rail watching him gulp the amber liquid, and now he prattled on senselessly.

"Aloo, aloo, aloo," he chanted as he swayed.

The wheel spun aimlessly from his hand. Reeling, he began to chant:

"Aloo, aloo, aloo,
We men of navy school
We sail by day, we sail by night,
Aloo, aloo, aloo."

He staggered against the rail with a stupid smile on his face, reeling back to the wheel.

"I think I'll go to the galley, Captain." Her thought was to warn Paul. She picked up speed as she jumped the steps to the lower deck.

"You do that, my lady. Cook us up a rare and exotic feast," he slurred.

She dashed across the deck and down to the cabin. "Paul, Paul." She shook him awake.

"Yes, what . . . what . . . is it time?" he asked languidly.

"No! DuGoyne is drunk! He can't handle the ship."

"Drunk! Where did he get the liquor?" He snapped to his feet.

"He asked me to bring it from his cabin. I had no idea he'd drink the whole flask."

"I've got to get up there." Paul, still sapped of his strength, struggled up the stair with Mimi behind.

As they reached the deck they saw DuGoyne trying to get to his feet. "Ah! Monsieur Regis, come join me in a freedom toast." He raised the empty bottle in the air, weaving unsteadily.

"Not today, Captain. Let's get you to your cabin. You need to sleep this off."

"I'm perfectly capable of walking under my own steam, monsieur." He shoved Paul's hand from his arm. The wheel spun aimlessly when he released his hold. Below, the sailors had wandered from their posts and stood watching the drunken captain become more abusive as Paul tried to ease him from the helmsdeck.

"This wench of yours carries tales," DuGoyne said scurrilously, pointing a limp finger at Mimi. "Bad enough to have a woman aboard, but a lying wench . . ." He slumped to the deck still clinging to the wheel. Paul lifted the inebriated captain hurling him over his shoulder. DuGoyne continued his chant as he was rushed past the gathered seamen.

Quickly dumping the limp body on the bunk, Paul wheeled out of the cabin. He could hear DuGoyne's threats follow him. "I can't abide a drunken captain," he stormed to no one in particular, but Mimi had remained where she stood. "You men get back to your posts," he shouted at the staring sailors below.

"We don't take orders from you," the apparent leader snarled.

"You'll take orders from me now," Paul steamed. "Your drunken captain isn't fit for this post."

"Are ya surprised at his condition, Regis? DuGoyne can't set foot on ship less'n he has his liquor. Now, didn't ya know that, mate?" The men laughed in unison.

The leader suddenly became more invective and propelled himself threateningly toward Paul. "I'm gonna cut yer heart out and feed it to ya, mate. Our plans are made." He grit his teeth as he moved closer and closer to the wheel. "The likes of you ain't gonna change our taking of this ship," he said menacingly.

"You'll be taking orders from me from now on. I'll see to it that DuGoyne never reaches the helm again. You might look to your own safety; you sink or sail, just as I. If that means anything to you you'll get back to your posts and help bring this ship in."

Mimi watched as the sailors moved closer to the stairs. Paul whipped his pistol from his belt. "I suggest you men rethink your plans," he said firmly. "Mutinous or dead—either way I shall have no crew, but *mutinous* you shall be *dead*!" His pistol remained firmly pointed at the approaching men.

The leader raised his hand to halt them. "Aye, Cap'n." As they sauntered back to their posts he sneered, "For now, Cap'n, but only for now." His tone was defiantly derisive.

"I can't imagine how DuGoyne has remained in command. This isn't the first. Captains have firm reputations long before a sailor sets foot aboard his ship. How did he get all the way from France?" Paul ranted for some time. He was exhausted with half a crew, and those few ready for mutiny, he had the added problem of keeping a watchful eye on DuGoyne. "I shall have to see to it that he doesn't get his hands on more whiskey. This crew would take over in a minute. They're not anxious to get back to France and war. It's been their intent all along to mutiny." Paul now knew why the *Boussole* was one of the few ships to sign on sailors at Mont Real.

The wind continued to hold constantly; they were steadily on course. Paul lashed the wheel, leaning against it, his fatigue showing in his every move. Mimi worried whether he would be able to cope with all the problems he confronted. For a brief moment she despaired that they would ever see any peace again, but now she no longer worried about herself.

Paul could still see the ship behind them. He hadn't agreed with DuGoyne that they should remain so far apart but with new responsibilities he considered it a good job if he managed to bring his own ship home safely. Certainly there would be no way to assist another ship without a willing crew of his own.

The sails slackened as the warmer air hovered over them. Issuing orders to tighten the ropes Paul took the glass and scanned the sea. Pivoting, the ship behind came into full view. He was startled to discover that it wasn't the same ship that had been following the day before. Glancing up at the sails Paul could see the wind beginning to die. Drier air of the southern sea was stilling their progress. Paul altered the course easterly, hoping the wind would pick up as they headed away from the continent. The ship slashed through the rolling sea, sails filling once more. He could feel the ship pull ahead as the sails again caught the air flow.

The heat of the southern ocean became more intense, causing Mimi to remove her jacket. Glancing at Paul she saw perspiration staining his shirt and beading on his forehead. The sailors also had removed their shirts and, bare-chested, they adjusted their lines, still keeping their eyes on Paul at the helm.

"It's so much warmer," Mimi remarked more to break the silence than anything else.

"We're getting closer to the equator. We're reaching the tip of the continent. Soon we'll be in the Carribean Sea." As he spoke, Paul could see DuGoyne wander back on deck, still unsteady on his feet. He suspected he had found a new supply of liquor and was sure there would be no reliance on Captain DuGoyne for the rest of the voyage. It was more than Paul had bargained for when he signed on.

"I'll take over now," DuGoyne shouted from the deck.

"You'll not take over this ship," snapped Paul, resting a hand on his pistol. "I'll not sail under a drunken captain."

DuGoyne staggered up the stairs toward the helm and Paul. "That is mutinous talk, Regis. I'm captain of this ship. I demand you release that wheel."

Mimi sensed the beginnings of an all-out confrontation between the two men. She knew Paul would never turn the ship over to DuGoyne and she pressed herself against the rail in an effort to stay out of their way.

The captain wouldn't be put off. He stumbled toward Paul, feebly trying to wrench the wheel from him.

Unwilling to put time into the nonsense, Paul repeatedly warned DuGoyne. He knew that only force would finish it. As DuGoyne reached for the wheel, Paul seized him by the back of the coat and spun him, sending him against the rail. The sailors below headed toward the helm as soon as the fracus began; their intention was to finish off both men.

Mimi rested her hand on the pistol beneath her breeches and waited. DuGoyne, maddened that his authority had been ursurped, drew a blade from its sheath and stumbled toward Paul, catching his bulky sleeve and just missing the flesh beneath. The wheel spun in all directions as the two men scuffled. Drunk as he was, DuGoyne was strong and Paul had his hands full.

The sailors slithered up the stairs, inching toward the fighting men. Just as Paul released DuGoyne's grip sending him smashing to the floor, the leader of the men jumped him from behind. They crashed to the deck, rolling over and over, while the others poised, ready to jump into the fight to finish off Regis.

Mimi backed against the rail behind the men, presenting such a picture of terror they ignored her. Had they entertained thoughts of taking their pleasure with her, it would surely be after Paul had been done in and Mimi knew it. She could see Paul's strength ebbing as the knife came closer to his throat. Quietly but calmly, Mimi maneuvered the pistol beneath her breeches and pointed it at the man's head. The shot went off meeting its mark between the eyes of Paul's opponent.

The startled men stopped in their tracks, then began shuffling toward Mimi who steadfastly held her aim on them.

One of the men jumped for Paul. With barely a move Mimi shot him in the back and with a piercing scream he fell backwards, overboard. Another lunged and she shot again. As one of the remaining heaved a belaying pin at Paul, Mimi's bullet caught him in the neck. Seeing their defeat the last two sailors backed off, raising their hands in a surrendering gesture. They slowly returned to their posts keeping a steady gaze on the girl behind the gun and Mimi's eyes never wavered as she stood there, both feet firmly planted.

DuGoyne had remained unconscious throughout the melee and lay quietly on deck. Paul checked the fallen seamen and, finding them all dead, picked up their bodies and hurled them over the side.

"Take the captain to his quarters," ordered Paul.

The two remaining sailors ascended the stairs, cautiously keeping an eye on Mimi. One on each side, they dragged the captain to his cabin below.

"It's two against two, now," Paul said firmly. "But, I don't believe I can sail this ship alone."

"But, you are not alone, my darling."

Paul slid his hand into Mimi's. "That is the pure truth." He looked at her with prideful eyes. "Yes, my love, I have never been less alone in my entire life." He pulled her close and kissed her tenderly.

"Paul!" Mimi pulled from his embrace. "That ship behind—it's closer. Isn't that a British flag?"

"*Mon Dieu*! I was afraid of that. They have put a good deal less sea between us too."

"You mean it's been a British ship all this time?"

"It's my guess they rammed the other during the night. We've got to make some headway or they'll be on top of us." Paul seized the wheel, again changing course.

"What can we do?" Mimi asked.

"They don't have any more wind than we do. Unfortunately I have wasted time dealing with these sailors. The best we can do is keep heading south. We'll never make it to France now, Mimi."

Paul unrolled his maps to study them, then tapping a spot with his finger said, "There. This is our only chance." He carefully measured with his sexton, then headed the ship toward the small French island of Martinique.

## Chapter Thirty

The wind had completely died and for hours they drifted, the ocean current slowly moving them along. With a strong hand on the wheel Paul managed to keep it heading in the direction he'd set.

"Isn't there anything we can do?" Mimi was now totally frustrated. It seemed that everything was against them.

"Nothing! We're at the mercy of the wind and right now there just isn't any."

The two of them sat on deck near the helm. The possibility of either of them getting to the galley alive was remote and their hunger pangs were wrenching their stomachs unmercifully. The sailors had calmly walked past them to the galley for their food and both Mimi and Paul were fully aware that their strength was slipping past the point of no return, and the remaining crew men were waiting and ready.

Suddenly, Paul realized the ship following was no longer in sight. "This doesn't make sense," he said with some concern. "Why should they suddenly leave? Unless . . ."

"Unless what?"

"Unless they know there are other ships ahead—their own or French ships," Paul said thoughtfully. "Yes, Mimi, that's it!" His spirits rose.

"There are French ships ahead; we are safe now." He seized her and pulled her close to him. "Mimi, I don't know what is ahead or what is going to happen, but we have no choice except to continue as we are. It's impossible to do otherwise. If we head east the ocean will gobble us up without a crew to man the sails."

Mimi pressed a finger to his lips to silence him. "Do what has to be done, Paul."

As the sky darkened the only sound was the slapping water against the becalmed vessel. Mimi had settled in a hunched position beside Paul, her pistol loaded and ready.

Captain DuGoyne staggered on deck, trying to speak. He reeled slowly and slumping to his knees he reached his hand toward the two of them, as if trying to tell them something he couldn't say. Paul lashed the wheel and jumped to the deck below reaching the captain as he fell flat out. As Paul bent to lift him he saw the blade protruding from the captain's back. In a dying gesture DuGoyne pointed a shaking finger at the two sailors then slipped limply from Paul's arms to the deck.

Now everyting tore loose in Paul—fury, fatigue and frustration. With an ear-piercing scream he lunged toward the two men, pulling them to their feet so savagely they had no chance to react. He slammed his fist into one then the other. Seizing a pin from the rail he pummeled them again and again. Mimi bit her hand, almost drawing blood, as she watched Paul give vent to his fierce anger. Neither man had a chance to defend himself, Paul so furiously set upon them. Still enraged beyond anything Mimi had ever seen, he tossed the men into the sea, one by one. He swayed against the rail then staggered back toward the prone body of the captain. It seemed to take all his strength to lift it from the deck and heave it into the sea. Then Paul fell against the rail where he hung, absolutely drained. Mimi rushed to his side.

"We are alone, Mimi," he panted. He could find no strength to say more.

As the night pressed in on them, once more Paul and Mimi sat where they had fallen. He fell into a deep sleep, his head on Mimi's lap. She had no idea what would become of them, but she was prepared for whatever it would be. At least, she thought, she would leave this world with her beloved Paul.

Mimi awoke with a start. The ship had stopped and it listed on its side. "Paul." She shook him awake. "We're not moving."

He jumped to his feet and turning full circle, he gazed in every direction. His laugh broke the intense quiet. "Look, Mimi, land!"

They both stood at the rail. Paul's elation coupled with his fierce exhaustion vented itself in his laughter. He slowly slid to the deck floor. Still smiling he pulled his beloved Mimi to his side. "My darling, with any luck at all, this is the island of Martinique. We don't have a prayer of reaching France now." He touched her cheek softly. "Darling, we can make our home here. They have already finished off the British. At least here we won't suffer through another war as we would in France."

Mimi could see his concern as he tried to explain. She ran her fingers through his hair and pulled him to her, pressing her lips on his, holding them there passionately. "My darling, you needn't worry about me anymore. I can make a life with you anywhere."

"I believe you can, now, my love."

He rose and took her hand, slowly leading her to the prow of the listing ship. "Can you swim, my dear?" he said joyously.

"Of course." Mimi smiled.

"Then, hold my hand, Mimi. We're going home!"

They dove into the crystal blue water.